THE LEAF BOATS

THE LEAF BOATS

JOHN FINK

A THOMAS DUNNE BOOK

St. Martin's Press
NEW YORK

 For information, address St. Martin's Press, 175 Fifth Avenue, New York, N.Y. 10010.

Design by Judy Dannecker

Library of Congress Cataloging-in-Publication Data

Fink, John.
The leaf boats / John Fink.
p. cm.
"A Thomas Dunne book."
ISBN 0-312-04977-3
I. Title.
PS3556.I475L4 1991
813'.54—dc20 90-15535
CIP

First Edition: April 1991

10 9 8 7 6 5 4 3 2 1

To Sara, Joel, and Alison, whose sails are set, and to Megan, who was launched not long after this story was.

THE LEAF BOATS

1

Driving north out of Chicago along the lake, the first town you encounter is gardenlike in the spring, full of green lawns, shrubbery, towering trees just breaking into leaf and tall, handsome houses. It is called Evanston. In the evening rush hour, two unbroken ribbons of cars wind along Sheridan Road, one into the city, the other leaving it for suburbia. Now, in the heavy downpour, the cars were barely moving. It had been raining all day, nine inches so far, possibly a record. High winds wrapped each driver in a tight little hurricane of his own, leaving the pavement awash. In these slick and risky conditions, brains were frazzled, nerves were frayed.

For a few blocks in front of the university, where Sheridan becomes four-lanes, the cars maneuvered for position. One in particular, a powerful black Porsche, wove its way stubbornly through traffic, darting from lane to lane and intimidating the other motorists. The driver of the Porsche seemed not to be driving it so much as wearing it, as if he might be an agitated Mafia don in an expensively tailored black cashmere overcoat.

In the pounding rain, the street was like a gang war waiting to begin. The sleek black car crouched at a stoplight, its engine throbbing, its left-turn signal pulsating feverishly like the pounding heart of the hoodlum chieftain, compact body tensed, eyes hooded, waiting to strike. Across the intersection, the oncoming traffic was poised like a rival battalion. Fumes rose, pistons churned, engines seemed about to explode. Everybody was going a little crazy from the dreadful urgency of the coming combat.

Without warning, a lone yellow Toyota emerged from the side street, split the opposing armies and splashed off, trailing a wide wake. Then, an instant before the light turned green, the black Porsche leaped, nosed sharply into the side street and was gone. Engines roared, furious at having been outwitted. As the light changed, enemy forces blindly advanced, missing each other completely in the heavy downpour.

In fact nobody looked less like a gangster than the man bent over the wheel of the Porsche, and he never would have pictured himself that way, any more than he would have thought of himself in traffic as a well-muscled dancer in a black body stocking, skipping from lane to lane and pausing at the stoplight, his balletic muscles ready, waiting for the next bit of choreography to unfold. Nor, as the Porsche continued up the side street in the gusting rain, would he have imagined himself as a wounded soldier coming home from the war. He would have been more likely to see himself, as he turned into a narrow alleyway, as a weary, forty-year-old prince whose kingdom was in danger. For he was tall and handsome enough, and only ten or fifteen pounds overweight, and he had driven through a deluge after a day in the city that had left him riven with anger, feeling closer to death than to life, and now he was in all probability coming home to an empty house.

He pulled up to a two-car garage built parallel to the alley. Its door rose at the touch of a button and the drowned black Porsche disappeared inside. The door descended. In the crashing downpour, the rear lawn was a rippled lake of muddy rainwater. Beyond it rose a three-story brick house many decades old. Clinging to its back, and almost as large, were a half-completed addition and the timbered framework of an unfinished deck. The entire structure was shuttered and still, like a stage set for an Elizabethan tragedy, although if Macbeth's hellish witches had been rioting inside, in the storm they would not have been heard. Rain battered the garage roof. Thunder crackled and rumbled. Wind blew.

Inside the garage, the driver reached for his briefcase and raincoat and got out of the Porsche, losing his balance and nearly shutting the car door on his hand. He was like that, the owner of the Porsche, both fussy and clumsy, orderly and inefficient. People liked him and didn't like him by turns. They listened to him enthralled and then found an excuse to get away. They were of two minds about him because he was of two minds about himself and the life he led. He would have preferred to be in some quiet, studious occupation, a professor or a director of educational films, and here he was, screwing around in a public relations job that required high-level decision making and political maneuvering. Oh, he could handle it all right, and he liked a certain amount of action. But there were too many blackbirds in this particular pie, too many executives jockeying for authority, and he wasn't among the chosen. How in God's name had he gotten into a job he hated?

By means of a fluke, he told himself. By having gone to the same school as the head of the firm. And how could he get out of it without risk? He couldn't. He had a family and a house that were both growing organically, like a jungle plant. He felt trapped and in need of sympathy and help. He was in the middle of his life, he was taking on more responsibility daily and he was no longer who he was supposed to be.

Who was he, anyway? Well, he didn't look very much like anyone else, but he was far from being one of a kind. If he had played Clarke Gable's roles in the movies he would have gone almost unnoticed, a Rhett Butler who had passed by virtually without a trace, yet he would be remembered by a wistful few, for like Gable and a certain number of other men across the world he was in his way unforgettable. He had a carefully trimmed mustache that seemed oddly unattended, small only because it was not very large, but it might have been much smaller. He had a tidy, straight nose that turned red when he was excited, and fine gray eyes set in soft, vaguely discolored pouches. His jaw was a leader's jaw, wide and hard, but his pink cheeks were careworn. His chin was firm, but in a crisis in which he felt himself under attack it bobbled helplessly. His dark gray business suit, almost imperceptibly striped, was expensive but tight, as if he had recently gained the extra weight he carried. He was obviously tired, yet he had the look of a much younger man who regarded himself as still lean and active. Overall, he was like a large infant, but as he opened the side door of the garage against the driving wind and rain he struck a pose that was assertive and resolute. It was a look he could maintain only briefly, and then he would be overcome by a sense of his relative unimportance in the world, or simply by a really very endearing playfulness. He liked having fun, telling a joke, seeing everyone about him in good spirits. He was a good family man, and good in a social crowd. These qualities indeed made him a prince, at least within a narrow circle.

Have I said it was raining? Cats and dogs, though not necessarily in that order? The man standing in the doorway of the garage glanced upward warily, as if the downpour overhead might come crashing through the roof and engulf him. It pelted into the doorway, spattering his clothing and his face. Outside it sluiced down by the bucketful, threatening to make the yard a sea. It fell in arrow-sharp javelins, swept this way and that by gusts of wind coming from all directions. The man holding the briefcase stared out at the rain as if he felt it might change his life forever.

The truth is that he was barely aware of the rain, and in forty years his life had been changed forever a number of times without his noticing it. Things happened, decisions were made, a new course was taken, that was all. Nevertheless concern showed in the lines around his eyes as he grimaced at the potshots of rain in his face. Buffeted by the soaking wind, he seemed unwilling to leave the shelter of the garage. He seemed, in fact, confused yet alert, missing nothing, dreading everything but determined to persevere.

What he did finally was put his briefcase and his raincoat back into the Porsche and move over to a garage window that gave him a mottled, waterswept view of the yard. He tended to think in outline form, and he did so now. Several things were making him uneasy. Point A was the office, where a number of matters were unresolved because (1) he did not have the power he deserved and (2) he was the victim of several bureaucracies otherwise known as empires. He decided to deal with Point A later, when he had opened his briefcase after ducking through the downpour into the house. Point B was the drive home: (1) the weather, (2) the traffic, (3) his aching back, (4) his swimming eyes, (5) his distaste for combat. He (a) loved driving the low-slung Porsche, feeling the powerful fit of it around him as he skillfully brought order to the chaos of the road. What he (b) hated were the other drivers, and yet without them there was no way to demonstrate his prowess. Sometimes, he knew, his superiority at the wheel annoyed them. Yet in traffic, as in everything else, he saw himself as (c) the most innocent of men. It made him furious to feel (d) so guilty (e) so often.

Point C was his wife. Her car wasn't in the garage, so she was (1) still at the small shop where she and a partner sold fabrics, jewelry and expensive bric-a-brac from the Far East. It was only a short drive away, at the terminus of the elevated line in the next suburb north. Or she was (2) shopping for groceries or (3) having a drink at a friend's house, probably in that lush Millie's kitchen, or (4) on a buying trip to Bangkok or Lahore. Since her next buying trip wasn't scheduled until November, today it had to be 1, 2 or 3.

The effect of her absence was relative to her distance from home. Was she in Lahore? A chasm at his feet. Was she merely late getting home? The chasm shrank to a ditch. Either way, he was always uneasy, for she was the glue that held his life together. She was an attractive woman of medium height with a well-tended lissome body that fit his like a glove. He could put out his hand and she would respond, a perfect match. She had large hazel eyes, fine cheeks and a ready laugh, a woman who would never be untrue or even mean-spirited. Yet when she wasn't there he always had a sinking feeling, as if she had let him down. For one thing, if their children (a) were home from school, he would have to deal with them himself. If they (b) weren't, it would mean puttering around an empty house. He had beautiful children, an eleven-year-old daughter and two sons, twelve and fourteen, and he loved coming into a house with everything in full swing. Then he could (1) unload the burdens of the day, point by point, until (2) he felt that (a) life was worthwhile and (b) he had nothing to feel guilty about (c) that anyone knew of. No matter how cocky he felt at times, being alone instantly (a) heightened his self-doubt, and long periods in his own company (b) drove him to absolute despair.

His heart was a sponge. Every morning it awoke dry and empty, ready to soak up from others whatever was there, crankiness or mirth, self-loathing or courage. Without people around him from whom to draw, as Dracula might, his store of life-giving plasma, his heart absorbed like kitty litter whatever was there: stray aromas from the air, minerals from the water, chemicals from food. There was no joy in his heart then, and no sadness either. He was just a device of the computer age, a mechanical man waiting for someone he cared about to appear and give him vigor and comfort and happiness.

He hoped his kids were home. They were growing up as tall and healthy and successful as kids were supposed to be in his family. Not that he or his brothers were anywhere near as successful as his brother-in-law, but they looked the part. He knew that success wasn't everything. Christ, sometimes it wasn't anything. But success could make you smile, and wasn't it better to be happy? The trouble was, it was hard as hell to be happy for more than half an hour at a time. The Porsche made him happy. His wife and kids made him happy. Jimmy, his younger brother, usually gave him a lift. The others—occasionally. His father?

Staring out at the rain, he thought about his father. Right now, more than likely, he was sitting alone in his living room about three miles west, in the adjacent suburb of Skokie, probably doing the same thing he was, looking out a window streaming with water. If so, he was looking across the street at the park where his second wife had been found dead fifteen, no sixteen years ago. Natalie. How old had she been, thirty-three?

He had been twenty-four, the man in the garage. He had loved and hated her both. Hated her for marrying his father after his real mother died. Hated her for giving the old man three more children, his father's famous second family. Hated his father, too, for (a) marrying again and (b) having more kids. Loved his father, of course. Loved her. Why? He didn't know. Yes, he did. She was young and beautiful. He loved her for her beauty, just as his father did. When they were married, he was eleven. The night of the wedding, he dreamed about her naked body. He had seen her naked when she was staying at the house a few days before the wedding. He was going down the back hall from his room and her door was partly open. She was in the room with his aunt from Cleveland, getting dressed to go out. He heard laughter and turned to look, saw the flash of skin, her hands stretched high above her head. It had shaken him to his core, this Greek statue come to life, plaster turned to warm, pink flesh, breasts, thighs, brown triangular patch below her belly. That sudden waterfall of skin unleashed something in him that was both revolting and pure. She had seen him and covered herself. No one spoke of it, not ever. Did his aunt know? Did his father? Probably not, or something would have been said. He had told his brother Bryan a few days after the wedding, to illustrate his familiarity with marital sex.

"They get naked," he said, "and lie down. Then he puts

his thing inside her." He wasn't sure where, and Bryan didn't believe he knew anything at all. Bryan, repelled by the act he had described, screwed up his face like Fagin in *Oliver Twist*. So he added, as proof, "I saw her without her clothes on." Bryan's eyes widened and his jaw dropped. "I just stood and looked at her, and she didn't do a thing." Bryan looked away. They never talked about it again.

A gust of wind rattled the garage and rain tore at the window. He shook himself, staring out through the storm at three floors of fresh wet wood and soaked fiberboard and new glass that appeared to be afloat on a turbulent lake perhaps two inches deep. The addition had been under construction for seven months. It was Point D in the outline of his unease.

He had never been crazy about the house they had crammed themselves into for the past fifteen years. The rooms began and ended in the same breath. They led nowhere, like a cul-de-sac, or fooled you, like a maze. The addition would rectify all that. He and his wife had designed the floor plan themselves. The old rooms had been enlarged or turned into closets or speedways. The new master bedroom was so huge that their bed would be a king-size bauble. For the first time since high school, he would be able to roll over without banging into a wall. Best of all, the new traffic pattern would make going from the front door to the back yard like taking a chute. In the plan two streams of traffic met and angled past the new cooking island, then down one step into the family room, where sliding glass doors opened onto the most attractive part of the yard. It all worked like a charm.

So of course building it had become a nightmare. The contractor had gone out of control. He juggled costs and completion dates as if that's exactly what he was paid to do.

The owner of the house stared through sharp spatterings of rain and felt his resentment grow. He was proud of his powers of negotiation, and the contractor's intransigence was an insult to his integrity. The rain blurred his vision. His feet were wet. His back ached, and he pictured his wife having a martini in her friend Millie's kitchen while he waited for the rain to slacken. It wouldn't slacken. It beat down on his house, which the contractor would never finish, bleeding him dry and filling his head with vexation, rendering him helpless. He saw the glass in front of his eyes shatter and stepped back amazed. First, at the blood on his hand. Second, at his own fury. He had struck the window with his fist, and now his blood dripped onto the wet cement at his feet, draining away like his anger. He wrapped his hand in his breast pocket handkerchief. He felt the cut on the heel of his hand throb, but the pain he felt was just over his right eye.

He believed himself to be the most temperate of men, and his rage frightened him. Like the contractor, he had been out of control. That, he told himself, is how murders happen.

Staring out of the broken window, he felt his heart lurch. Something outside was different, and it took him a moment to figure out what it was. Jutting out into the yard was the raw framework of the deck, a truncated triangle twenty-five feet on each side. The deck was supported by a dozen or so stout wooden posts, rising out of the water covering the yard. It was like being in an ocean looking at the underpinnings of a great pier. Last week, to anchor the deck supports, workmen had dug a pit so large that the rear wall of the new foundation had been exposed. The pit had been there yesterday, the posts resting on concrete footings deep inside it. Now the pit was gone. It had not been filled in. The excavated soil remained beneath its giant tarpaulin on the far side of the deck like a great beast skulking through a rain forest. Clearly what had happened was that the pit had become a reservoir. It held the muddy runoff of a day of unceasing rain, the water climbing slowly up the foundation wall and the deck supports and overflowing the yard. In the rainswept garage, he stirred uneasily. He felt all at once like a drowning man. The pit had been dug to a depth of eight or ten feet. Now that it was filled with water, there was no way to tell it was there. Had he chosen to make a run for the house, he might be drowning indeed. Thank God his wife wasn't home. Thank God—

His children!

Damn! He cursed the weather, the house, the diggers of the pit, the contractor. When he felt himself trembling, he began breathing deeply until he grew calmer. The handkerchief around his hand, spotted with his blood, was like his soul stained by his anger. Afraid for his children, he was now doubly afraid, for himself. How long had he been in such a state? Was it a state of war, like the traffic on Sheridan Road? Might he at some point in their long dispute have killed the contractor? Had the contractor, by digging a pit in his back yard, tried to kill him? Had an angry God, by filling it with water?

He was of two minds about God. A, in his daily life he did not fear God, had no reason to. He told his children that God made the world wonderful, not only for Catholics but for everybody else who deserved it. B, in times of stress, like this, he feared God. This God was a vengeful God who, with a roaring and crackling of thunderheads, could bring on a biblical deluge like that tricky little ocean in his back yard. This sort of Jehovic fury was like his own. He felt terrified and depressed. The crash and rumble of the storm, the lake in his yard with its pit plunging to uncertain depths, the absence of his wife, the willfulness of the contractor, the combativeness of rush hour, the unresolved questions at the office and the bloodstained reminder of his own fury all were gathered together in a knot in his head. He felt stripped of his confidence and incredibly vulnerable. Bad thoughts multiplied. His heart, empty, pounded and gasped. He leaned back against the Porsche, but its elegance did not reassure him. Its skin was a dull, barely glossy black, like fine onyx. Not a scratch or a finger mark that he could see. Only a few beads of rain marred its smooth perfection. He wanted to take a chamois and make it spotless. He wanted to take a chamois and remove, swipe by swipe, the ugly imperfections of his immortal soul.

His growing desperation may seem unreasonable, even mad. Well, you had to be there. The fact was that he was right to be apprehensive. In the pit, after a daylong deluge, biblical or not, an upheaval was taking place at the base of the redwood deck. You may say that he could not possibly have sensed this, that he merely transferred to the pit the quakings he felt inside himself, and that the timing was accidental. But who knows the secret stresses and strains of new construction, any more than hidden shifts and shortfalls of the flesh? Especially of new concrete carelessly exposed to the vagaries of a northern climate, as the psyche of the innocent man lies open to evil? For months in the slow giving-up of winter, the frozen ground had softened and hardened, like a hand opening and closing into a fist. Even as late as April and May, its icy grip was still being pried loose, finger by finger, until it relaxed in a final thaw. Who could tell what flaws might have resulted from pouring a foundation or raising a frame or joining all those four-by-fours and two-by-tens and two-by-sixes and two-by-fours? If, in the midst of his panic (as if he had just invested a fortune in a strategic government bond fund), the man in the garage now feared the worst, he should not be condemned, even in the confessional that had become as familiar to him as a toilet stall. For his dry and palpitating heart had not deceived him.

Above the storm, a sharp crack.

It seemed to come from two places at once, (a) inside his head and (b) from the other side of the world. Moving to the window, he drew a ragged breath, like a symphony conductor who detects a sour note from the second clarinet. As he watched, six or eight supports wavered and twisted, sagged slowly to one side and sank into the waters of the pit as neatly as an entire string section fainting in unison, fiddles and cellos and bass violas, with all their delirious bows. A jagged line like a screech of woodwinds appeared in the foundation wall, which began to crumble. As the superstructure of the heavy deck followed the string section into the roiling, muddy pond, French horns, oboes, timpani and all, he heard the shriek of trumpets, the deep wail of bassoons, even the gurgling of trombones and baritone horns as they were mellifluously submerged. Perhaps, he thought, it was the gurgling of his heart as, like the pit, his chambered ticker soaked up a whole orchestra of woes.

But wait, there's more.

He was like a conductor standing at a podium, his orchestra gone, now seeing the stage itself begin to lose its tidy perpendicularity. The new addition, like a vast proscenium, leaned unexpectedly in his direction. There were grating, quaking sounds, perhaps screams in the audience and general pandemonium. He leaped to one side, thinking to protect not so much himself as the Porsche. A muddy wave launched from the inundated pit sloshed across the lawn and into the garage, eddying at his feet. Thunder crossed the sky as the house wrenched itself apart. Something horrible snapped in his throat, gagging him, as he caught a glimpse of his world caving in. Three floors of skin and bones and lath and plaster, wires and rods and timbers and sheathing and roofing and glass, in fact what seemed to be the last three decades of his life, were falling mightily toward him, an amalgamated avalanche of semiskilled carpentry, high hopes and missed opportunities. Something heavy crashed against the fifty-year-old garage, and he dove to the floor and wedged himself beneath the Porsche.

And still, in the quiet that followed, it rained. He could hear it clearly along with his dry, thudding heart as he lay beneath the car in an inch of filthy water, hoping desperately that none of his kids had gotten home too soon, that no one was in that awful thing when it fell, or beneath it now. In a moment he would go and try to find out. In the meantime, he tried to construct a thoughtful outline of a plan of attack, but the task seemed too formidable. As he listened to the first rising notes of distant sirens, he was unable to do more than consider the emotional impossibility of getting from A to B.

2

When the first cop arrived in the pouring rain, a drenched Marcus Franklin Gillespie, Jr., was standing atop the monumental debris of half his house, shouting the names of his children: "Lisa! Mark! Tom!" He had been yelling for several minutes like a man who was being murdered, and his voice was so ravaged the names were only guttural utterances: "Lee-ss! Ma-a-r-r! Ta-a-ah!" The cop thought he was barking like a dog. "He's gone nutso," the policeman said to himself. He called out, "Stand still! Don't move, I'm coming up!" Frank looked down from his perch in amazement. A young cop was standing near the entrance of the garage, and the wreckage of his house covered the entire back yard, ending at the cop's feet. Police and fire vehicles were being jammed bumper to bumper into the alley like a freight train, and from them poured uniformed men in slickers who quickly began to cordon off the area.

"My kids, for Christ's sake," Frank yelled through the rain. "They're under here!"

To the policeman, who was just beginning his second year on the force, it still sounded like barking. "Take it easy, wait for me." He clambered up the sloping floor of the third-floor master bedroom, leapt onto a broken staircase, slipped and fell, then, grabbing for a towel rod, crawled on his hands and knees up a tiled slab of wall from the second-floor bath onto the splintered chunk of roof on which Frank was standing, seizing him by the shoulders. Frank glared at him as if the cop were out of his mind.

"They're drowning," he shouted. "They're in the pit!"

He was still shouting as he was helped down off the wreckage to the shelter of the battered garage, where medics were setting up a first-aid station beside the shiny black Porsche. Someone wrapped him in a blanket. The cop, who still hadn't understood a word Frank was saying, was staring down at his own hand. It was streaked with red.

"Fuck," he said. "Now I gotta get tetanus."

A medic took the cop's hand and examined it. "Nothing here," he said. "You get cut?"

Frank nodded and held out his hand. The medic found the cut from the window and reached for his medical kit.

"Forget it!" Frank cried, heading for the door. The cop pushed him up against the car, opened the door and got him onto the passenger seat. A medic started working on the hand. A fireman poked his head into the garage. "Anybody under that mess outside?" he asked. Frank began shouting again, and the medic said, "His kids. Three of them." The fireman disappeared into the rain.

Outside, firemen and police, having confined the gathering crowd of neighbors and other onlookers to the side yards and the alley, began removing what they could of the wreckage while a crew started boarding up the back of the main house where it was open to the weather. A building inspector made a cursory examination and then entered the garage and began asking Frank questions. Blanketed like a monk and feeling unaccountably drowsy, Frank stared back uncomprehendingly until, over the throbbing engine of a departing fire truck, he heard his daughter's voice calling, "Mommy! Daddy!" and a cop unloaded her into his lap, an eleven-year-old tangle of legs and long yellow hair. Minutes later two teenage boys ducked past the barricade and ran into the soggy, rubberized arms of two husky firemen. Half an hour after that, they were in the back seat of the family station wagon with their mother at the wheel, on their way up Sheridan Road to their Aunt Clara's, two suburbs north. Frank, still holding his daughter on his lap, stared out at the rain as if he were stowed away on a voyage to the bottom of the sea.

"We can't just leave the Porsche there," he said, speaking slowly and with difficulty. "The garage door won't close. You'll have to go back with Don and get it." Don was Clara's husband.

"You won't need the Porsche," his wife said. She was driving and her name was Helena. "You're going to rest." She seemed unfazed by the disaster. She had clean lines and good bones and a gaminelike, saucy face. Clara, her sister, was the cherub of the family. Helena had been born for crisis management.

"Can't rest." It was hard for him to talk. "Client meeting tomorrow. Besides, they don't have room for all of us. I'll go down to Chicago and stay with Jimmy."

Helena laughed. "Go downtown tonight? In your condition?"

"I'll drive you down, Dad," his older son said. He was fourteen. My God, in a year he would get his learner's permit.

"Stop it, both of you," his mother said. "We're staying with Clara and that's that."

"We could stay with Granddad," the younger boy said.

"Your grandfather's not to know anything about this. It would just worry him needlessly."

For some reason, this amused Frank. "He'll see me on TV. He'll kill the contractor." He giggled.

"Don't joke," Helena said. "It's just what he might do if he gets upset enough. We'll clean up the mess and then tell him."

The older boy leaned forward, his eyes shining. "Dad, you were great on TV. Can we stay up and see it?"

Helena said, "You already have. Now let's just hope your grandfather doesn't."

The disaster had struck at 6:28 P.M. on the first Tuesday in May. An hour later, when they were driving to Clara's, it was not yet dark. So, three miles away in an adjacent suburb, just as his son had guessed, Marcus Franklin Gillespie, Sr., was sitting in a wingback calico-covered armchair not watching television but staring out a second-story window at a small park across the street. He was seventy-nine years old and was called Dutch because he had been Ronald Reagan's father-in-law's banker and the father-in-law had taken to calling him that. It had stuck. Dutch Gillespie was a big man, six foot three, with powerful shoulders, and his size, his vivid red hair and his intimidating expression always made him the dominant figure in a room. Now he was mostly skin and bone. Although his head still held massive amounts of gray, a dusting of red remained. These days his most striking feature was his eyes, which were as piercing as if he had just sunk a talon into your shoulder. It was this look Frank Jr. tried halfheartedly to imitate. Half-heartedly, because, after all, it had already been done.

The old man's eyesight was almost as sharp as it had been at fifty, but he could not see much through the spatterings and rivulets of rain on the glass. He sat at this window most nights now until it grew too dark to see anything except his own unwavering reflection, not even seeing that because it was not what he was looking for. He had always been obsessively single-minded. He had been nine years old when his father was killed in the first war. The eldest child, he had put himself through college and then gone to work in a Chicago bank in the worst year of the Depression. When the bank failed, he worked as a bookkeeper until he found another opening, and by the time he was thirty-two and, like his father, went to war, he was the president of a new neighborhood bank on North Broadway. He came home a captain, got married and gave his Christian names, Marcus

Franklin, to his firstborn, relieved, he said, that someone could share the weight of them. He had three more children, and when the last of these came along he was running one of the biggest banks in Chicago. Dutch's wife died when the fourth child, Jimmy, was born. Three years later, after a courtship of two months, he remarried. He was fifty. Natalie, his bride, was a dazzling twenty-year-old blonde from Northern California who had been married twice before. Divorced, became a backup singer in a traveling rock band called Aristocracy, then retired to marry a deputy sheriff from Skokie. Divorced him after four months and met Dutch at a party thrown by her high-priced attorney, who also handled estates. She had been married the first time at fifteen in California. She had a son from that marriage, Eric, a big, stubborn five-year-old with sun-bleached hair who reminded Dutch of himself. Thus he began his second family. The first Gillespie family of four was absolutely opposed to the marriage. They were obviously impressed by Natalie's silken-haired beauty, but their strange new brother-to-be aroused only hostility, at least in the older three. Frank Jr. was a robust eleven. Then came Bryan and Patricia. But Jimmy was two years younger than Eric, and thus would still be the baby of the family. In him there was not only hatred but positive dread. He didn't mind still being the baby, but he didn't want Eric standing between him and the others. Three days before the wedding, when Dutch introduced them to Natalie and her son in the big house in Wilmette, there was quiet panic.

"This is Natalie," Dutch said, daring them to contradict him. "She will be your new mother."

Spiritual consternation. The kids didn't move, and yet eyes and mouths and fingers spread riot through the room their real mother had once commanded.

"Your Aunt Nel is coming this afternoon from Cleveland," Dutch continued. "She and Natalie will be staying here so that we can all get better acquainted."

Disbelief, that Aunt Nel, a member of their father's own family, could be condoning this wrongful change. Horror, that the five-year-old monster clutching his mother's skirt, a boy almost as big as Bryan with a gaze as stern and unrelenting as their father's, was part of the package.

"And this is your new brother," Dutch said, dragging him before them. "His name is Eric."

Universal silent gagging. Eyes and mouths and fingers twisted in pain and anguish.

Dutch smiled a horrible death knell of a smile. "I know," he said, "that we'll all get along just fine." As he turned the full force of the smile on his shining bride-to-be, Eric wrenched out of his grasp and bumped against the glass-topped coffee table. A small, rose-petaled vase fell on its side, chipping its rim. Dutch stared, reddened, then laughed. The Gillespie children looked at each other with eyes that were endless dark tunnels of apprehension.

That night after everyone except their father and Natalie was in bed, Dutch's sister from Cleveland heard noises and found the four of them huddled on the bed in Frank's room, whimpering. Eric had been skulking at the door, the Gillespie kids said, threatening to turn loose his pet rats. They were terrified. Natalie was the soul of sweetness, calm and discretion. He had no rats, she said, and he had been wrong to alarm them. Dutch reported that the front door was ajar and that Eric was nowhere to be found. He was finally discovered in the garage, behind the wheel of the new Lincoln touring car. Asked to explain, he said he wanted to get away from the jerk babies and go back to California. Asked to come to bed, he thumbed his nose at Dutch, and Dutch put him over his knee and walloped him. The other kids heard his furious cries and went back to bed satisfied that at least their new brother was not going to be allowed to get away with everything.

Soon after the wedding, Dutch moved them inland from the rambling house they had always known to another one a block from the largest Catholic church in Skokie. It seemed unaccountable, leaving the lake and all that was familiar, but Dutch's bride had grown to like Skokie during her four-month marriage to the deputy sheriff and was certain it would be a good place to raise children. She entered all but the three-year-old Jimmy in school and joined the PTA.

Life for Dutch was perfect. Natalie was beautiful and right for him. He could refuse her nothing, and why should he? Then and later, she was, by any objective measure, perfectly formed and groomed, with perfect shoulders, perfect breasts, a perfect waist, a perfectly rounded bottom and perfect legs. Of average height, she carried herself with perfect grace. Yet her carriage and her body took second place to her perfectly molded face, and since she smiled readily, and in this way seemed accessible and welcoming, her perfect body did not seem awesome at all. Her face was like a medallion bestowed on the observer for bravery in battle. It was heart-shaped, framing large, blue, delicious eyes that looked out like perfect mirrors of her mind. The small, turned-up nose could quiver like a scenting device locked onto its quarry. The Cupid's-bow mouth seemed made for love. Natalie never fooled Dutch. Within this seemingly mild and accommodating exterior, he knew, there was a will of iron much like his own, a soft stubbornness that, when they made love, became for him a persuasive, all-encompassing softness. He knew that as long as she was his, she would be devoted to his health, his wealth, his causes and his children, and if anything ever came between them he would have no way to reach her, not with mind, body or material resources. She was a match for him, that was all. It was only a matter of time before his four kids would come to accept that fact and love her too.

Frank, the oldest, was the first to come around, and it did not take long for the rest to fall in line. In the first place, she was lovable, and in the second, it was plain to them that she loved children. She made it clear that she wanted more of her own, and that she always got what she wanted. She was irresistible. She liked being terribly attractive to men and loved falling in love, however briefly. Falling out of love, as she had in her two previous marriages, was painful to her, which was why she had never stayed married for long. But she was determined to make this marriage work, and somehow, partly through sheer willpower, she succeeded. Considering her several quick changes of heart before she met Dutch, it may be hard to understand how she could be just as single-minded as her new husband, never deviating from her course. It's true that she was obliging and unyielding by turns, as sweet and acquiescent at times as she was sweet and dictatorial at others. (Dutch never tired of her either way.) And the fact was that despite the many affairs and marriages before she turned twenty, she had not swerved from what she had set out to do when she reached Chicago: find lasting happiness with a man she could count on. The deputy sheriff was not that man. Dutch was.

Did she love him? Without a doubt. In the first place, she genuinely liked older men. Dutch may have represented the father she had no clear memory of, who had disappeared from her life when she was hardly more than an infant. But mainly she loved Dutch because she had made up her mind to do so, and her resolve was like a rock. If she fell in love easily and often, and dissolved these alliances after only weeks or months because the hard knocks of waking up to real life terrified her, she at least kept consistently to her main course. When she found Dutch, there was no question in her mind that she had finally found a fully reliable male. He was tall and strong. He had stamina. He was as stubborn as she was. He had money, he had power. He adored her for her beauty and her mind. He could give her a family. And all those things, she told herself, were really all she had ever wanted.

The first of their three children they called Hope. Emily was born two years later, and then, four years after that, Raymond. By this time she was twenty-seven. Dutch, of course, was still thirty years her senior. As far as anyone in the neighborhood could tell, they lived happily in the big house down the street from St. Matthew's Church, a house filled with eight children from the age of one to eighteen. Over the next few years, Frank Jr. and then Bryan and Patricia went to college. The last of the original brood, Jimmy, was sixteen when it happened. Eric, Natalie's own child, was eighteen. He was due to go to college that fall, but when his mother was killed he took off. He went to Phoenix, and that's the last anyone heard of him for a while.

Natalie's youngest child, Raymond, was just six when Dutch became a widower again. Until Raymond was out of high school, the family stayed where they were, with a housekeeper from Eastern Europe and a series of nannies from Scandinavia. Then Dutch closed up the big house, put it on the market and moved by himself into a nondescript but nothing-if-not-ugly flat-roofed apartment house across from the park where Natalie's body had been found. It was a weird thing to do, some said. Maybe it was. But it didn't seem weird or macabre to Dutch. He wanted to spend the rest of his life with her, and this, he had decided, was as close as he was going to get.

It had been a brutal killing. She was said to have been raped and strangled, her neck broken, probably in the car her younger daughters had seen her getting into that night. It was late August, 1972. Dutch had been gone that week. With the oldest three in college and Eric within days of going, he'd been thinking about early retirement. He had flown to Fort Lauderdale on banking business, in his spare time scouting property down there. Only the day before, he had phoned Natalie to tell her about a marvelous find, a house that backed up to the port, where you could watch oceangoing freighters and cruise ships churn by all day and all night. Having grown up in San Jose, Natalie loved the ocean. He was all set to buy it, wind up his affairs at the bank and move, taking the younger children with them. She had seemed eager to go. She had never looked happier.

A day later Natalie, who prided herself on her cooking, served the evening meal to the rest of the family but ate nothing herself. She ate like a bird anyway and never drank liquor, having a minor sugar imbalance and being extremely weight-conscious. But tonight, she said, she was taking a cousin from San Jose out to dinner, someone she hadn't seen in ages. She was obviously excited, and the two younger girls, sensing it, had been tumultuous. Hope was twelve and Emily ten. They helped her into their favorite white dress, shrieking so uncontrollably that she shooed them outside to play with their younger brother. They pretended Raymond was their cousin from California. They named him Bob and played a version of hide-and-seek, screaming, "Bob! Cousin Bob!" whenever they found him. Had she mentioned the name? Or had it just come to them as they ran outside screaming on that warm summer night so long ago? It was never clear.

At about eight-thirty, Natalie had come down the steps, all in white, kissed them good night and warned them to be in bed in half an hour and to mind Patricia, who was home from college and would be looking after them. Jimmy, who had just turned sixteen, had left the house after dinner to go to a movie with a friend. Eric was working late at the body shop, earning extra money for college, and had a late date with a girl he was semi-engaged to. He had grown up to be a favorite with Hope and Emily. Even though he wasn't there, they had giggled about his hot romance all through dinner. Even Bryan, home from the university for the summer, had been amused at their antics. Then he had taken the car to pick up Pat at the library. He had returned before dinner was over. Patricia, he said, had more work to do and would get a ride home with a friend.

When the car arrived, Bryan was in the basement and didn't see the driver. Natalie quickly got in and it pulled away. The two girls, who had just sent six-year-old Raymond into hiding again, were crushed. They had fully expected to be introduced to their mother's California cousin but got barely a glimpse of him, said they didn't know whether Bob was young or old, tall or short. Later the police would wonder about that because the two girls were terribly bright and yet told slightly conflicting stories. One said the late-model car was blue, for instance, while the other said it was green. Their confusion was understandable because it had been nearly dark and the nearest streetlight half a block away, and little girls who were terribly bright could be terribly imaginative anyway. Both had bad dreams for weeks, and severe headaches. It was generally accepted that Raymond, a shy, pale, thin little boy, would never get over it.

Sitting in his window with the rain streaming down, the old man sighed heavily, and as usual phlegm rattled in his throat. Great chunks of time, he reminded himself, had gone by since that night, yet it seemed the mere quiver of an eyelid. If she had lived, all would have been different. When he had quit the bank and moved his family to Florida, he and Natalie were going to travel. They would visit the Orient, which he had never seen, and India and Greece and Italy and Spain and France and then London, a city he had first seen during the war and had come to respect. By God, they knew how to bank in London! Dutch had no intention of forsaking banking altogether. One sound business reason for moving to Florida was that the bank he had worked to build was privately in trouble, the result of all those foreign loans he had warned them about. Well, now they could fight to hold on by themselves. Florida, he was convinced, would be the new center of banking and finance in America. Maybe when he and Natalie had had their fill of travel, he would get back into banking in Miami.

Drawing a ragged breath, he choked and spat into a handkerchief. When he thought about these things, he forgot how old he was. His love for Natalie surged in his loins. Pride in his life's work overtook him, and, momentarily, a feeling of youthful ambition. Then regret sprang up and smote him, and fury as well. Staring out the window, he imagined the park in the darkness beyond, and the killer who dragged or carried Natalie's body from the car and covered it with leaves, like carrion, destroying his family and emptying his future. He knew he was old. He thought sometimes that the anger and indignation flaming through his veins were what was melting his sagging flesh like candlewax. But old or young, at times like these he had it in his heart to kill. It seemed yesterday that the moon had sailed like a big bright orange through the clouds over sultry Fort Lauderdale, with the wind fresh off the sea, and he had tried to call her every twenty minutes from ten o'clock to midnight, poor Patricia's voice growing more and more strident with each call, and finally he had phoned the Skokie police, raising hell and more hell until at last they found the body, at four in the morning. There was no cousin named Bob from San Jose. That hurt him terribly, not just that she would deceive him but that she had lied to the children. Why couldn't she have told them that she was going to the damned PTA? That would have been a lie too, but somehow it seemed less devious. Or maybe it had all been innocent, maybe Cousin Bob was just an old friend—Dutch was willing to believe that. But if so, why hadn't she just told them who he was? Not that it made any difference in the end, but it wasn't like her to be frivolously irresponsible, having a lover pick her up at the house. It was as if she had lost her mind.

That's about as far as Dutch ever got pondering why she went out that night. Fright welled up and tied his brain in knots, and he had to admit he didn't want to know. Had she ever been unfaithful? Was she having an affair? If she was, was he partly responsible? He knew he had held her close. Too close? Like the three days in the seventh year of their marriage, when she had gone to the PTA convention in Springfield, the state capital. The baby was three months old, and since they planned to have no more children she had been thinking of pursuing a career. She wanted to run for state PTA office. He couldn't quarrel with that. She was so good at managing him and everybody else, he told her, that she ought to be in some kind of politics.

The banking business took him out of town a lot, but she had never been away from home overnight before. That was what had him fuming around the house that first night, and the next day he hired a private detective to fly to Springfield with a camera to track her through hotel corridors full of PTA ladies. She had spotted the detective right away and soon had him in earnest conversation. First she charmed him out of his socks, leading him on like a child. Then she lectured him sharply on the constitutional rights of women until, red-faced and stammering, he had pushed his way through a crowd of irate PTAers and fled the place. It was their first and only major row. Dutch had interfered with her chance, after seven years of marriage and motherhood, to lead an independent life outside the home, and she was sore about it. She withdrew her PTA candidacy and for a week flounced around the house, even keeping him out of their bedroom. She had never seemed more desirable. Suddenly, at the end of the week, she was all smiles, as if nothing had happened. He swore it never would again.

She said, "What won't, darling?"

Not a word was said about Springfield in her remaining six years of service to the PTA, not even when she ran again for state office the following year and lost.

Believe me, Dutch, he said to himself, watching rain course down the darkened window, you'll never see her like again. Nobody will. She had been as beautiful at thirty-three as she was at twenty. A bit of puffiness around the eyes and under the jaw and a little more roundness to her here and there, but the bright, vamping eyes and curved lips, the cute pink nose and tiny ears, the long, silken throat, and the rest of her right down from smooth shoulders to trim ankles were just as pleasurable to him after three more children as before, and as vivid to him now as when she was alive.

So the old man mused, looking into the storm, a man of means, a banker of stature—a cold man some said, known for a certain bitterness and a sudden, fiery temper if roused. Nobody dreamed that Dutch Gillespie could be so highly romantic a man. You can interrupt his thoughts as he sits there if you wish. Not me. I leave him there, partly because, like his sons, I am a little afraid of him, and partly because tomorrow he will face dreadful news, not for the first time in his life.

3

Everybody said how strange it was, how shocking. It was. First, the house, buckled and half demolished as neatly as if it had been booby-trapped. Then, the next morning, the girl's body, found floating in the flooded pond. How awful, how tragic. Yes, a stone's throw from the spot where they found her mother's leaf-covered body all those years ago. Wasn't it ghoulish, wasn't it macabre? It was. Was it the same killer? Her neck had been broken, just like her mother's. There was no way of telling if she'd also been raped. And wasn't it fascinating that the first wife, the original Mrs. Gillespie, the one everybody had almost forgotten about, had died unexpectedly, too, in childbirth. Undoubtedly true. It was strange and shocking, and was it also a family curse? That was a little harder to verify.

Of all the Gillespies, none had been closer to the two youngest girls than Jimmy, the baby of the original lot, not even Patricia, who had baby-sat them often enough. Patricia had a husband and two kids and a big, rambling house in Winnetka. Jimmy, thirty-two and single, lived downtown, on Lake Shore Drive, and since the girls shared an apartment only a mile or so north, on Pine Grove, he saw them once in a while. They were very bright. He liked them. Hope was blond, like her mother. Taller, with long legs, and skinny as a stick ("a sexy little twig," Bryan said in his clipped way). Quick and chattery, as if inviting all the world into the conversation. Emily was small and dark, intense, with little secret smiles, but when she saw you looking at her, a wide smile and glowing eyes that said her life was an open book. You knew it wasn't, any more than Hope's chatter revealed all she knew. Or if it was, it was a book held too far away to be read, the lines of print a tantalizing puzzle. Very tight, the two of them, very much a pair. Yet always glad to see Jimmy, and it had always been that way.

Jimmy, of course, was the one who had survived when his mother, the first Mrs. Gillespie, died. He had grown up to just under six feet, a husky young man, his blond hair turning darker and highlighted red, like Dutch's. Straight, short nose. Crinkles about the eyes when he smiled. A firm jaw that could snap shut like a turtle's when he was angry. Like Dutch's.

At one time or another while the rain swept the city that eventful night, flooding its low points, or the next morning when it stopped, all the Gillespies crossed themselves, like players at charades miming slitting their throats. All except Jimmy, who had left the church and its trappings behind. The ancient rituals amused him, he said, his jaw rigid with defiance. He had joked that having been born at the same time as the new Mass and the new math, he wasn't cut out to be either a Catholic or a mathematician. Actually he was awed and troubled by the church and its uncompromising mysteries, the body and blood of Christ, the incense, the plaster saints. Even seeing a man in black gave him a strangled feeling until he could see that there was no slash of white collar. Priests were one of the few things that scared him. Priests meant death.

Jimmy didn't remember his mother, of course, having been not even a day old at the time. But years later there had been a priest at Natalie's wake who had looked hard at him, this thin, scruffy high school kid, as if saying, "You killed your own mother, my son. Did you have anything to do with this?" Earlier, when he was just five and, as the youngest of the original brood, still thought of himself as the family favorite, he saw the same accusation in his father's eyes. An official of the church, a bishop maybe, had dropped by the house after mass to meet the family of one of the archdiocese's biggest contributors. Dutch presented Natalie and the children, and when he came to the youngest boys, Eric and Jimmy, he hesitated. Then, his eye on Jimmy and his smile fixed, he introduced Natalie's boy first. It hit Jimmy like a clap of thunder, being cleaved from his own brothers and sisters this way, his place taken by the seven-year-old intruder, Eric. The reason seemed obvious. He had killed his mother, that was the meaning of it, and his father's stern, unwavering, accusing gaze confirmed it. Jimmy's whole world felt shaken. That was the meaning of everything. His guilt was the meaning of his life.

That was a time of adjustment. Only two years had gone by since Natalie had brought little Eric with her into the marriage, a sort of California-style virgin birth, and relationships were still being sorted out. That wasn't all. The latest kid on the block was Hope, and Jimmy was already worried that this squawly one-year-old might replace him as the family spoiled brat. So why had Dutch pronounced him guilty before the bishop, this powerful representative of God? Jimmy was wounded and amazed and there was nobody to help him. He turned for reassurance to his oldest brother, the one he trusted most in all the world. Frank was a big-shouldered kid of thirteen who had learned long ago how to deflect the suspicions of fathers and bishops. He simply turned on them his adolescent gaze, an expression of attentive innocence that could be interpreted in any of several ways. Doubtless the bishop read it as humility in the face of his splendid authority. But Jimmy saw in it not only accusation but pity, and he knew he was doomed. Patricia, an eight-year-old beauty, red-haired like her mother, was no help either. In her eyes he saw only questions. Eleven-year-old Bryan wouldn't look at him at all. Bryan was easy but distant. He never looked directly at you except when he lied.

No one ever said Jimmy was guilty, not in words. But for years and years, maybe forever, when he looked into their faces he saw them accusing him. Sometimes the indictment was a banner being towed across the sky, sometimes a shooting star he wasn't sure he saw.

The priests were worse than anybody, for Jimmy saw them every Sunday and sometimes during the week, and they always had dire messages for him in their eyes. He avoided them when he could. He read his catechism without accepting a word. He went to confession, but never did one penance. He stopped affirming a belief in God. Nobody knew he did these things, least of all the priests to whom he silently admitted what they silently accused him of. So what if nobody said it aloud? It was self-evident, wasn't it? He was here and his mother wasn't.

Everybody noticed what a solemn boy Jimmy was, how sensitive and wrapped up in his thoughts. What could he be thinking of? What did he know? It made them self-conscious and some of them uneasy. Always, before he spoke, there was that instant in which he seemed to be measuring their worth in the world, their trustworthiness, their truthfulness, the value of what they said. Jimmy noted the effect. He was neither blind nor stupid. He saw how a single searching look could put others on the defensive. It turned them honest, or at least careful. Some it helplessly intimidated. He used this searching look on priests and teachers and friends and family, on everyone except Natalie's two girls. They never accused him with their eyes. On the contrary, they seemed to be conspirators, giggling and winking and whispering as if they understood what it was to lead a life riddled by guilt. When they were very young, they even shared his dislike of Eric, back when Eric hated everybody but especially girls. Eric didn't need a searching look, he was just naturally intimidating. Always big for his age, he glared and yelled and occasionally hit you. He was fierce. Once on the way home from grade school, he came up on Jimmy from behind and struck him hard on the side of his face, then ran. Jimmy chased him but couldn't catch him. His jaw was sore for a week. He hated Eric back in those days. Eric was impervious to the look.

Jimmy went on to journalism school at Northwestern, spending his summers on a newspaper in Cleveland, then got a reporting job at the *Chicago Tribune*. After three years he switched to television news, at Channel 2, and it wasn't long before he decided to become a TV anchorman. He saw how skillfully certain anchormen employed searching looks. David Brinkley was the master of this technique, even when he wasn't looking straight at the camera. The anchorman at Channel 5, to which Jimmy moved, was another. Both used expressions that were not only searching but skeptical, even wryly amused, and as a consequence both were respected and imitated by colleagues. The technique didn't work for everybody. Some TV newsmen wound up being merely confrontational, like Sam Donaldson, or oddly vulnerable, like Dan Rather. Jimmy knew he could master the skill. It had worked magically for him in newspaper interviews. The technique wasn't just self-serving, it could help sort out the truth, and the truth was what mattered to Jimmy. Every time he established the facts of a story it was like saying to Dutch, "See, it's true. I couldn't possibly have killed my mother."

After a year or so as a news reporter at Channel 5, he became the day assignment manager. His job was to move his staff around the city, collecting the day's events on tape that would be spliced piecemeal into the late-afternoon and nightly news shows. He could call on more than a dozen reporters and half a dozen crews in microwave trucks, those mobile TV studios that ran through Chicago like insatiable weevils. He could charter airplanes and helicopters. In the noise and heat of the moment, he could scream and curse. He ate, drank and breathed the life. He seldom made mistakes. He was fast and always in control, and he had streaks of unbelievable luck. At thirty-two he was as good at his job as anyone in the business. And he was a responsible person. He visited his father every few weeks, he participated in family gatherings, and he looked in occasionally on Hope and Emily. Once in a while he even dashed off a rambling letter to Raymond, the youngest of them all, who was still in college. But mostly he was caught up in his work and in the single life.

At five-thirty on the day of the deluge, while Frank was leaving his office for the parking garage to pick up his Porsche, Jimmy was driving his Ford Tempo through the pouring rain to his club. There he played tennis for an hour with Maud Leightly, a blonde he knew from college who worked in the governor's office in the Loop and was an excellent news source. By nine o'clock he had driven Maud to his apartment, cooked her a dinner of hamburgers and raw, biting onions and gotten her into the sack. Just about the time Dutch, up in Skokie, was turning off his living room light as carefully as blowing out a candle, Jimmy's phone rang.

Murmuring "Shit, what now?" he reached over Maud in the darkness to pick it up. He hoped it was the office. That would give him an excuse to remind her that he had to get up at six o'clock and didn't have all night. He crooked the phone against his shoulder, felt her nipple tighten under his touch and answered. "Yo."

"Turn on the ten o'clock news," Frank said. He sounded tired. Jimmy thought, Is this how it will be for me at forty? Maud slid one hand down over his stomach and moaned. Was it a real moan?

He said, "I always do, Bro. Got to check out my work." Her hand slid down farther and she moaned again. Even if the moan wasn't real, it was urgent. He glanced at the digital clock. Nine-twenty.

"Well, this is late-breaking," his oldest, most trusted brother said. "My house fell down."

"Your what?" Jimmy sat up, dislodging Maud's hand. She whimpered, a deprived sound full of annoyance.

"My house. It fell in the drink. The whole North Shore is floating away."

"Are you guys okay?" Jimmy swung out of bed, picked up his shirt off the floor and stuck an arm into it. He was unable to locate the other sleeve.

"Everybody's fine. We're all in Winnetka, at Clara's. Helena and the kids are going to stay here, but I have to be downtown tomorrow. Can I bunk with you tonight?"

"Sure." He sat down. "How soon will you be here?"

"An hour or two. I want to make sure everybody's calmed down up here. We're not telling Dad, no need to upset him, nothing he can do. Don's over at the house with Mike, making sure it's safe from looters and souvenir hunters and collecting my Porsche." Mike was Patricia's husband, his brother-in-law, and Don was married to Clara, even farther removed. But they were part of the clan, and the clan was rising to the occasion. "It's a fucking disaster, Jimmy. The main house is still there, but the new addition's gone, kaput. We'll have to start over on the damn thing."

"No one got hurt?"

"No one was home yet. I was putting the car in the garage when it blew. You've never seen such a mess."

"Jesus. Any camera crews there?"

"Oh, sure, that's why I want you to turn on the TV. I'm a celebrity. My fifteen minutes of fame."

Jimmy laughed harshly. "You'll be lucky to get twenty seconds. I hope you gave it all to Channel Five."

"I wasn't counting. Sorry."

"Listen," Jimmy said, "you want me to come out there?"

"No, I'll take next week off, when they start the repairs. Right now I need to be downtown. You don't mind?"

Jimmy felt behind him for Maud, connected with a slim, cool wrist and lay back, his head on her shoulder. "Not at all. I may be asleep but the door will be open. You can have the den. If I'm gone in the morning there'll be a key on the table. I hate to think what the newsroom will be like tomorrow if your experience is typical."

Frank laughed wearily. "Has it ever been otherwise? Look, I'm going out to try to get a paper. If there's any problem, I'll call you back. Otherwise I'll see you. And thanks."

Jimmy hung up the phone, checking the time. Then he rolled over, one leg straddling her. "My brother," he said. "His house fell down."

She patted his manhood. "House isn't the only thing," she said, still annoyed but smiling up at him.

He laughed and kissed her and then gave her the look. Her smile faded. Her eyes gazed steadily into his. Then she gasped and moaned a real moan and wrapped herself pliantly around him.

At 9:45, because there were no cabs in the rain, he took her home in his car. Ten minutes later, he got a beer out of the fridge and settled back on his bed to watch the ten o'clock news. It had been a busy night indeed at Channel 5. They had tossed out most of what he had done that day, of course. There was some tape of the early flooding, which plainly had gotten much worse. High water everyplace, power outages, waves lashing the lakefront, a couple of pleasure boats missing, extensive storm damage all across town, north, south and west. They led with the city, naturally. Michigan Avenue, live in the rain. Flooded viaducts. Earlier tape of rush hour traffic stalled on the expressway. Downed wires in the Lincoln Park neighborhood. Then suburbia. Islands of tract housing along the Des Plaines River. Crashing waves pummeling Winnetka's shoreline. The Coast Guard lashing down boats in Wilmette harbor. Then Frank's house in the downpour: glaring lights moving over wreckage that looked as if a 747 had landed in it. Then earlier footage, still daylight: faces in the crowd, bleary with rain. Frank, his hair pasted to his head, coming warily out of his garage carrying his eleven-year-old daughter, looking sheepish but giving a fair imitation of Dutch in a banking crisis, except it was taking him forever to say anything, as if his jaw was mush. "I just thank God nobody was home." A heavy sigh, a dazed look, then a smile. "God was looking after the Gillespies." Flashing a little Dick Nixon V-for-victory sign with a bandaged hand. His two boys in the background, ducking in and out of view, grinning and waving. It was a good cut, a scene out of the war on the home front. Jimmy watched the rest of the news, a full hour of it tonight, including that morning's interview with the governor in Springfield, on tax reform. Then he turned out the light and switched to the scanner radio for police and fire emergency reports. The phone woke him about midnight. It was Frank.

"Not tonight, buddy. There's no way downtown, all the expressways are flooded. Anyway, I spent an hour or so waiting at the railroad station for a paper, and I'm bushed. I'll see you tomorrow."

They said good night.

Frank. He loved Frank. He loved Frank's wife, had ever since Helena had invited him to bunk with them when he was starting at Northwestern. They had been married a year and she was pregnant. That first night in her yellow kitchen, all of them doing the dishes, he had described his summer as a cub reporter with the *Cleveland Plain Dealer*, and they had laughed till they cried. He had gotten the job through his uncle, a printing foreman at the paper whose chief bugaboo was typographical errors and such embarrassing inadvertencies as "Society Matron Ready for a Tramp in the Woods." Helena screamed at that one, but Frank stared in confusion, then giggled politely. Jimmy couldn't say he understood Frank completely. He thought he understood Bryan, maybe because there seemed less of him to grasp. Bryan was the only one of Dutch's children to follow him into banking, as vice president and chief loan officer up in Lake Forest, a truly elegant suburb. And he understood Michael Daugherty, Patricia's husband, who headed the Chicago stock-options exchange, a big, hearty man who, like his wife, was utterly without guile.

Banking and stock options both seemed terribly complicated, but in Jimmy's mind they held no mysteries like those of Frank's profession. Frank was a managing director for one of the world's largest corporate communications firms. Fells and Matthews had offices around the globe, and whenever Jimmy listened to the network news he wondered just how much of what was happening in London or Moscow or Beirut or Beijing was happening because this or some other public relations dreadnought had put the screws to somebody.

If Jimmy, as a newsman, dealt in facts, Frank dealt in legend. If Jimmy sought to discover what was true in service to humanity, Frank sought to establish the appearance of truth in the interests of a client. At its worst, Jimmy felt, public relations created propaganda, manipulating people's minds with half the facts. At its best, it used some kind of powerhouse magic he didn't understand to explore the avoidable consequences. Jimmy never got beyond such fuzziness in attempting to define it. It was like asking What is art? What is life? The only thing he could compare it to was what Merlin did for King Arthur's round table. Out of a few gaudy, evil-smelling knights clanking around in armor, Merlin built a legend that wouldn't quit. Who knew how he did it? He was a magician, for Christ's sake! But sometimes, like Frank, the guy must have driven the old king crazy. How much could you take of someone who held the secrets of the universe, made them palpable with a wave of his wand and yet, when he spoke of them, sounded like nothing so much as a garrulous gasbag in a pointed hat, courtesy of Walt Disney, full of solar wind, starshine and moonbreath? Maybe that's why there always seemed to be a side of Frank that remained a mystery to him, some troublesome gap between fact and fancy, truth and tintinnabulation, the difference between a look of instant reliability and Frank's sweet but impervious gaze, the one that always stopped priests and fathers in their tracks.

In the gray, sodden aftermath of the rain, the TV newsroom the next morning was a madhouse. All the crews were out taping storm damage, including more footage of Frank's fallen-down house. About nine-thirty the call came over the scanner radio: the body of a young female found in a park in

Skokie. Jimmy glanced at his assistant, a dark-haired young woman named Pamela, who was already on the phone to the Skokie police, checking out the report. In that instant he saw her as she might have looked lying strangled, covered with leaves, her agile flesh-and-blood features slack and white, just the way he had once imagined the dead Natalie. Then he shook it off and got on the radio to a crew returning from Highland Park on the expressway, rerouting it to Skokie.

"Unidentified white female about twenty-five," Pamela said, looking up at him. "Pulled out of a pond by firemen twenty minutes ago. Found by a fisherman. The park's about a mile from the center of town. The Skokie Swift goes right by there. Pants, blouse, no shoes. Five feet six, not much over a hundred pounds, that means thin as a rail. Blonde, blue eyes, couple of expensive rings. They're canvassing the neighborhood, and a diver is trying to find identification, a purse or something."

"Get the name of the park." He was hardly breathing.

She talked into the phone, then looked up at him . "Myrtle. With a *y*."

He said sharply, "Ever see it spelled any other way?" He thought, A park fringed by trees, and every so often the two-car commuter train hurtling by. A large, brown, L-shaped pond supplied by runoff, so the park was probably flooded. Maybe right now Dutch was looking down at it from his apartment across the street. He dialed but there was no answer. Must be over there, all the old horrors stirring. Memories. Poor old guy.

"Stay on it," he said. "And tell the truck where to go."

He had walked there lots of times with his father. Last year the park had been relabeled a nature preserve, which meant they had put a high fence around it and begun locking the gates at night to keep out the kids who went there to make out or raise noisy hell. It was Natalie's park, not because she had died there but because she had discovered it. He remembered when he was three or four. It was autumn and the leaves were dry and curled. Natalie had put a leaf into his hand and told him to put it carefully on the brown surface of the pond, like a boat. He had smiled up at her, unbelieving. Yes, she said, do it, it will sail. There was a brisk wind blowing his hair down over his eyes, and the leaf boat, its ends curled up like sails, moved slowly and erratically out over the water. As the wind caught it some more, it sailed faster, tacking at intervals, until it was far away and seemed to merge with the brown of the pond and finally fade from his mind. He went looking for another leaf, excited and strangely impatient, the kind of almost unbearable impatience he felt much later, in making love. He couldn't wait until the second leaf was out on the water. By now the other kids were looking, too, and soon a whole fleet of brown sailing ships had set out on a brown, endless ocean. It went on like that all afternoon until Dutch told them to come on, for God's sake, stop wasting his time.

There were particular leaves that sailed best, narrow little leaves without visible serrations, shaped like two lips, like the clever hulls of racing boats. Most of them curled back upon themselves, some in unexpected and humorous curlicues. Each sailed differently, depending on its shape. Tightly scrolled ones went in circles or stupidly went nowhere. Others raced off without stopping. Natalie said this was how cavemen got the idea of traveling by water. Dutch snorted, then admitted she was probably right.

These days, when he walked there with his father, they would stop and look down at the pond, not saying much. But always, eventually, whether the wind was right or not, Jimmy would put a leaf carefully on the water and watch it sail away, or not, as it chose.

He got on the phone with the crew. "We need identity, cause of death, time and all that. Get with the medical examiner when he gets there, but don't let him stay on camera indefinitely. Listen, Raz, did you ever sail leaves when you were a kid?"

"Good, Jimmy, very good. What are you smoking?"

"No, listen, when the diver gets out of there, try to get

some tape of the pond. Sun on the water, if there's any sun, with trees framing the shot. Quiet family park, all right? We'll build in the horror later."

"Sounds swell. Bucolic. Like 'CBS Sunday Morning.'"

Jimmy went over it with the producer. The shot would make a closer, perfect for anchorman to voice-over. Where she died was where hundreds of Skokie families had spent quiet afternoons watching the fishermen or sailing leaves. "Sailing leaves?" said the producer. "Never mind," Jimmy said.

Twenty minutes later, Pamela was looking up from the phone to tell him the body had been identified by a relative. When she hesitated, he shouted at her, "Well, have we got it on tape?" She said, "Jimmy, the relative says he's your father. Do you—did you have a sister named Hope?"

He sat back, suddenly tired of the whole day. People were staring. He said, "Tell the crew I'm on my way. Tell them to ask my father to wait there for me. Find out if he's all right. Look after him." He got up and spoke for several minutes with the producer while someone made notes of what he said. When he had told them all they needed to know about Hope and her mother, he headed for the newsroom garage to find a car.

4

Hope and Emily. So different from their mother, and in very different ways. One tall, blond and wide-shouldered, with darting movements and impulsive speech. One small, raven-haired and thin-boned, with Natalie's measured way of walking, the slow, back-and-forth princesslike sway. At first glance, seeing the three on their way to church with the blond Natalie in the middle, you'd have thought they were sisters sired by three different fathers. Hope and Emily. One with her mother's private exuberance, her tinkling laugh, her seeming ingenuousness. One with Natalie's highly proper public mask, perfectly made-up, a young lady without a glitch. So different from each other, the two girls, yet in some way Patricia could not fathom, together they made one Natalie.

She sat in a rock-solid New England rocking chair before a blank television screen, having seen enough news in the last few hours to last a lifetime. Over and over, the house, then the pond, then the police, then glimpses of Dutch slogging through the waterlogged park, avoiding everybody, and over it all mentions of bankers' wives, death, destruction, of her own husband, head of the stock-options exchange, of a clan shadowed by fate. Then, the TV off, making endless telephone calls, trying to find Raymond or Emily, the sibling survivors. Neither one on the face of the earth. But not lost forever, she thought, not like Hope.

Patricia looked like her mother, Dutch's first love. A beauty, with the same full-lipped mouth and wide jaw and fluted throat. Dutch had never liked Pat much, perhaps because of the painful memories her face aroused. There was a point when, however disapproving he might have been in her childhood, her father went further, suddenly dispatching her to some dark outer rim of his life, shutting her out almost completely. Something to do with Natalie, was that it? Something to do with the girls? She didn't know and had never asked him. In a way, now that she finally had her own life, it was a relief not to know. There were advantages in keeping Dutch at a distance.

Emily and Hope. They kept going around in her head as she tried to sort them out. Why was one dead and one alive? Hope, twenty-eight. Emily, two years younger. Both highly intelligent, both irrepressible, both susceptible to whim and to colds and headaches. Emily with her mother's mask. Hope with her impulsiveness. Both with her large, film-star eyes and her steely will. Emily, the little one, the one who was left, had Natalie's calm gaze, but it didn't lock on the way Natalie's could, and it didn't make rash promises it couldn't keep. Hope, who was gone, never looked at you longer than an instant. Yet she had made herself available, given herself more. Or had she? Patricia had never been quite certain. Was it that Hope had greater reserves of animal energy than her sister and therefore could take more chances? Emily, with the slow, tiny shoulders, seemed more vulnerable. She wasn't, though, was she? Hope, the tall, thin fighter, had been quicker, more elusive. Yet, as a child, she could be taken by the shoulders and calmed. Was she the more responsive? Outwardly, maybe. Emily, who seemed more cooperative, was often impossible to persuade, certainly not with any open, affectionate gesture. Put an arm around her and she slithered away. One sensed that Emily was more self-assured, had more spiritual resources. Perhaps. Which was the more diligent? Hard to tell. They had both worked like beavers on their schoolwork. Hope, though, had been a driver. She had the steam. When Emily wasn't asked for anything, sometimes she wasn't there at all. Now she was the only one who was.

Diligent? Resourceful? Hardworking? Yes, but was that all? Masked, too. Impulsive. Vulnerable. And elusive, yes. That's what was bothering Pat now. The elusiveness, the secretiveness. And sometimes a look of abandoned terror, after their mother died.

Pat remembered how they had looked that long-ago morning when Natalie didn't come home. As if they were clinging to rocks, terrified of being swept away but not daring to show it, as if they feared their mother wouldn't approve. They had gotten themselves ready for school without saying a word, Hope darting out the door first on her long legs, Emily scurrying to find a special notebook, then running down the walk after her sister. Hope striding ahead, not waiting, not hurrying either. That was the moment Patricia decided that between them they made one of their mother. They were Natalie's child, one Natalie, split in two. Two little beauties, together replicating their mother, and after that, carrying her memory between them as long as it would last. Now Emily would carry it alone.

She and Raymond. Raymond, the runt of the litter, the very last of Dutch's offspring. Bigger than Emily, because he was a boy. But just not there, just . . . gone, like an exploded firework. At twenty-two, he was a thin five foot six, as tall as Patricia. Yet so *not there* that you looked right past him. Or through him. Oftener than not, you found yourself looking past him at Eric.

Eric! Why did she always forget that Eric was part of the family, when he had always been by far the most noticeable presence in the house? He would carry Natalie's memory forever, too, like an Olympic torch that ran on acetylene. They had raised each other up, hadn't they, he and his mother? Three years after Natalie's first marriage, she and baby Eric had come all the way from California with the road band to entangle themselves briefly in another, with a deputy sheriff in Skokie of all places. The boy had been a tough, two-fisted five-year-old when Dutch finally got them, she a tough, fragile-looking twenty. My God! As always, Dutch got exactly what he bargained for, no more, no less. Except that somewhere Natalie went wrong. Or maybe went right. Patricia couldn't tell. Went back to her beginnings somehow, maybe to find herself, and lost herself instead.

Eric had stood by her all those years. Never really joined the family, stood aside, but firm as a rock. Fought with them all at one time or another, never gave in. Fought Patricia, naturally, when she baby-sat with the girls. He was only a year younger than she was. Fought with his mother when he got older, but always came around. Left Chicago right after the funeral. She pictured him running all the way to Arizona, or wherever he'd gone. She bet he'd come back someday like Daddy Warbucks and set everybody straight.

So now she had to find Emily, was that it? Before the kids came home. And she had to find Frank, who had found a way downtown and was meeting with a client, location unknown. Mike, her husband, was coming home early, and they'd get ready for what was to follow. The visitation wouldn't happen for a week because there had to be an autopsy. Or maybe it would take place on Sunday. In the meantime, to buck up the family, Jimmy was bringing Dutch over about six for dinner, and maybe Bryan would come along. Bryan had left the bank and gone to the park a little after eleven that morning, to stand by in case Jimmy couldn't manage Dutch alone. They were afraid the day would be too much for him. Not that their father was in poor health, but there were limits to a seventy-nine-year-old's stamina, even a man like Dutch. Frank and his wife and kids would come over from Clara's, at least that was the plan. They would have drinks. They would talk about Hope. And, inevitably,

Natalie. And their mother, their real mother? Maybe not. There was probably a place and a time for that. Dutch wouldn't bring it up, especially if Emily and Raymond were there. Where were they? It was nearly two o'clock.

Patricia didn't know where Emily worked—that was one of the problems. Jimmy didn't know. Nobody knew. Hope and Emily and Raymond still belonged to Natalie, in a way. They took care of each other and stayed apart from the rest. Emily was a legal aide or something in a middle-size law firm. Raymond was just home from college, with one more year to go. Had he been staying with the two girls? Everybody thought so, but nobody knew. Everybody seemed a little shocked that they didn't know. Shocked that the family had drifted that far apart without their realizing it. Shocked to discover there had really been two families all along, Dutch's first and Dutch's second. Hadn't Dutch kept track of his two youngest daughters? Why should he? He hadn't kept track of the first. Pat knew the two girls had been out to see him occasionally. He had called her once to say they were there. He seemed to be asking, Where was *she*? Saying, These two care about me, why don't you? Or saying, See, I don't care whether you do or not. Gloating. Saying, See, I don't need you, missy.

Pat had tried. She had him to dinner. She baked things and delivered them. She invited him to parties full of strangers—strange to him, that is, and certainly he strange to them. She inquired about his health, lecturing him about the food he ate and the medicines he took. She was damned if he was ever going to say she neglected him. She had even quizzed him about his preferences in nursing homes, wanting him to know she wouldn't desert him when he was helpless. She made him talk to her, and when he wouldn't talk she made him listen. Mostly he responded with his crusty old man's leer, a smug and crafty smile that enraged her, which was exactly what he hoped it would do.

He was punishing her. For what? Did he think she knew something about Natalie? Something she wasn't telling, some secret she had owed him for sixteen years? He had never been much of a father to her, didn't seem very good with daughters. He preferred the man-to-man stuff, knocking around with the five boys. Always so old-fashioned in some ways, acted almost scared of her sometimes. Was it simply that like so many fathers of daughters, he felt sexually attracted and hid himself away? If so, Natalie, thirty years younger, gave him the perfect out. Did he blame Pat irrationally, for being left in charge when he went to Florida and not keeping Natalie from being killed? Pat had been nineteen. Did he suspect that whatever Natalie might have been up to with other men, Pat knew and was somehow in league with her against him? Even egging her on? Did he blame her for leaving the two girls motherless? And Raymond, don't forget Raymond, though he's easy to forget. And don't forget Eric, motherless, too, maybe the most motherless of all. Dutch was probably capable of blaming her for all that. She didn't know for sure. They didn't really talk, and never had.

It was a pity. She had needed a father, and Dutch had been such a good one with the boys. He knew so much. He felt so much, she knew he did, damn it. He just had that in him, all that life, all that reaching out and drawing people to him, and doing things. Driving the van down to Mexico and putting it aboard a flatcar, and giving them all a look at the most unforgettable, most beautiful, scariest terrain. Fishing off Baja, fighting one single marlin all day, or scooping up sailfish off Cancún as if the fish had been trained to leap into the boat. Diving in the Keys, skiing at Jackson Hole, running down the Michigan dunes, whale watching on Cape Cod. Dutch was never still. Not like now. Now he sat. And remembered. And leered.

Well, she was remembering, too. Unwilling to be caught dead imitating her father, for fear he'd find a way of ridiculing her for it, she got out of the rocker and the phone rang. She went toward it. My God, didn't he know what a success she'd turned out to be? With her handsome, wealthy, fun-loving, serious, powerful husband? Two beautiful kids?

A great shock of her mother's gorgeous red hair, and as bright and attractive a woman as had ever been seen on the North Shore? Why couldn't he see her for what she was? Why wasn't it all right for him to love her the way he loved his sons? She picked up the phone and said hello. She was angry.

There was a long silence. Somebody breathing. She said hello again and stamped her foot. She was about to hang up when Raymond's thin, nasal voice gave her a hesitant, "Who is this?"

"Raymond!" she said. "This is Patricia. Oh, Raymond, how are you? Where are you? Where have you been? I've been trying to reach you all day."

"Patricia?" he said. "You didn't sound like yourself."

My God, she thought, who does he think "myself" is? Do any of us really know each other? "Raymond, I want you and Emily to come over tonight. We'll all be together, the entire clan. We want you both here. Where are you? What have you been doing?"

"I put Emily in the hospital," he said.

"Is she sick? What's wrong?"

"No, she's all right. I mean there's nothing wrong with her. She just went to pieces." His voice dropped to almost a whisper. "She's in the psychiatric ward."

"The psych—! Where? What hospital?"

"It's on the North Side, near Marine Drive. Lakeshore something. I took her there early this morning. Hope didn't come home and I went to bed but I think Emily was up all night." There was a moment's silence. "They were very close. My sisters, I mean."

"I know. God, Raymond, I know!"

"She's all right, they've sedated her. I just left there and she was resting. I didn't tell her about Hope."

Pat sat down in the nearest chair. "Raymond, let me get this straight. She doesn't know Hope is dead?"

She heard him fumble with the phone. "Well, yes," he said, "I guess she does, but I don't know how. I mean, I didn't tell her. I didn't know it myself. And later I didn't want to tell her, under the circumstances. She was already under sedation—"

She was beginning to be angry again. "When exactly did you take her to the hospital?"

"About six. I heard her screaming, and I—"

"But nobody knew!" Jimmy had called on the car phone after ten. "Nobody knew at that hour."

"She knew."

My God. "Knew about Hope? At six A.M.?"

"Well, it was like she knew something terrible had happened, something real bad. I thought it was a hysterical incident—"

Of course. Pat knew about those. That's something else Dutch held against her, creating a family problem by pulling a typical unforgivable female stunt, acting impulsively, hysterically, selfishly— She took a deep breath. "So you took her in at six. When did you hear about Hope?"

"On the radio. I went out to get something to eat, about eleven. I heard it then. You can imagine what I was feeling like. I felt like I already knew it, déjà vu, you know? I mean like Emily conveyed it to me some way. But she's okay. I just checked and she's still sleeping."

"Raymond, how are *you*?" Dear poor motherless familyless boy, she wanted to say. But they were all motherless, and Dutch seemed to like Raymond. After all, he was male.

"I'm all right. Feeling bad. You know."

"Why don't you come right out?"

"No. Thanks. I think I'll just stay down here and keep an eye on Emily. I'm going to look in again later, at the hospital."

"You shouldn't be down there alone. Someone will come down and be with you." She tried to think who. "Maybe me, except everyone's coming over. Just stay there and I'll make some calls. Are you at Emily's right now? Will you please stay there, Raymond?" Like a good boy, she wanted to say.

"I'll be here for a while. I'm pretty beat right now. I think maybe I'll get some shut-eye."

Shut-eye. That was Dutch's word. "All right." She tried to think what to do. "Jimmy," she said. Yes, Jimmy was closest to Raymond in age. "Jimmy can come down. He and Bryan are with Father, over in Skokie. Bryan can bring Father here, and Jimmy can come down. He'll go over to the hospital with you. What did the doctor say?"

"That she needed rest and quiet. He didn't seem particularly worried that I could see. She checked herself in, so she can check herself out."

"Good. Raymond, stay there and I'll have Jimmy call you, okay? Raymond? You know we love you. You know how much we loved Hope."

A long silence again. The end as in the beginning, she thought. Amen. Then she heard him crying as if his thin little motherless underfed-college-boy ribs would break.

"Raymond, stay there and wait for a call, okay?"

"Okay."

She hung up and leaned back in her chair. Cripes, she thought, a hysterical incident, and Dutch will never forgive me for it. Ran off and got married the year after Natalie died, while she was still in college, to a professor ten years older. Two kids, bang, bang. Then the professor grew a beard and went to California to check out the whales and the girls and the beaches. He wanted to live, he told Pat. So did she, damn it. Dutch had disapproved of the marriage, but he didn't get nasty until she cracked up. Spent three weeks in a psychiatric ward while somebody, maybe Helena, looked after the two babies, and he never said a word, never came near her, not even when Pat found a flat in Evanston and buried herself there for two years, day in and day out, with the kids and a brown dog she had found in an alley looking as lost as she felt, with tar on his front feet to prove it. And then one night a miracle. Helena threw a party and there was Mike. He came in with three other guys, dressed to the hilt, eyes shining, shouting, "Drinks on the house!" and all of them waving airplane tickets to Hong Kong. She went. It was her first night out in two years, and they were commodities brokers, wild men and proud of it, going short or long all week, raking it in, then going to Hong Kong or Indonesia on the weekends, throwing dollars around like yen or whatever they had in Indonesia. Three days into the following week, Mike proposed. She accepted. She loved him. He loved kids. She knew he'd never have to grow a beard. What she didn't know for sure was that he'd give up the life and go straight. Or that when he did he would rise liked a rocket in the LaSalle Street financial establishment.

She picked up the phone and dialed Dutch's number. "Jimmy," she said, "can you get away from there and go down and see Raymond? He's at Emily's place. Give him a call and tell him you're coming. Emily's in the hospital, the psychiatric ward. Nothing serious. But somebody should be with Raymond and I can't—"

"I'll go," he said.

"And Bryan's there? He can stay with Father?"

"Yes, he'll stay."

"And he can bring Father over later? And then you can bring Raymond?"

There was a short pause. "Patricia."

"Yes?"

"Stop with the arrangements. Relax. Everything's okay."

She put one hand up to her forehead, bent her head and cried. She thought, Oh God, I must sound like Raymond.

5

Rattley-trap, the train went. Rattley-trap-trap. Bryan was tapping his foot on the hardwood floor of the old man's living room to the rhythm of the train. Here and there were several worn Persian rugs of varying sizes, some of them vaguely familiar, as if he had first seen them in a previous life. Well, two of them he recognized as having once been in the old house in Wilmette when he was a little boy, especially the largest and most worn, which now occupied the center of the room. It reminded him of a boxing ring, with the old man sitting in one corner of it, in a high wingback chair like an old fighter who has been beaten many, many times, and him, Bryan, sitting in the other corner wondering, if he got up and went a round with the old man, whether the old man still had it in him to beat him. But he wasn't thinking about boxing, not really. Bryan was in a railroad mood. He was thinking, Rattley-trap, rattley trap-trap, as the Skokie Swift clattered past the far side of the park, beyond the budding fringe of trees. From the window he could see it go, the little two-car commuter train, scooting along toward the city. The old man sat looking balefully at nothing, or else at some figure in the old faded rug, probably not even hearing the sound of his son's tapping foot on the wood floor at the edge of the rug. The foot was keeping time to the distant clattering of the departing train. The Skokie Swift. Swift as an arrow, Bryan thought. Swift as . . . a swift. A bird. A noisy bird too heavy to fly, that had wheels rather than feet, that ran along on rails . . . swiftly. He told himself he didn't mind being alone with the old man, it was just that he'd have felt more comfortable with someone else in the house. Frank was unavailable, out somewhere with a client, Jimmy said. Jimmy had been on the phone with Patricia and then with Raymond. Then he had gone downtown, something about a psychiatric hospital and Emily, and now Bryan was alone with the old man and a whole hour passed. That's okay, he thought. Rattley-trap-trap. The Skokie Swift was gone. It was no more. He left off tapping.

He was a tall man of thirty-eight, as tall as Dutch, but without his heft. Handsome, everyone said so, with eyes a little too close together but of a very nice gray. Alert eyes, as if they were always listening. Large ears close to his head. A striking head of dark hair. Full lips that smiled well. A firm jaw that needed shaving twice a day. Something weak about the mouth. Or was it the eyes?

"Want anything to eat?" His voice was loud in the room.

The old man glanced up, but not at him. "What?" he said. "Oh, no. Nothing."

Bryan got to his feet. "I think I'll have another drink. That'll be two, but it's three o'clock. Cocktail hour coming up." Picking up his glass, he walked quickly past the old man into the kitchen and took down the bottle from the cabinet. It was a dusty, half-empty bottle of very old scotch. Dutch didn't drink much, never had. Bryan didn't drink much either, but he was drinking a little bit more every year. Today he felt like getting very drunk, especially now that he was alone with the old man. He hadn't been alone with him for years. Lots of years. My God, when it came to the old man now, years were all there was. He sipped his drink, looking out the window at the field across the way. Great big electrical transformers or something rose out of the field over the trees. A no-man's-land. On the other side of the field were a number of small, low-lying factories. Skokie was a city of light industry, nuts and bolts and gears and things. Bryan had never liked Skokie. With rare exceptions, such as the house he'd finished growing up in, the houses were like little rock forts, like caves. Rock fort, he thought, and smiled, remembering a meal at a country inn in France. Near Bordeaux, wasn't it? And the host, a banker from London, had the chef bring out a favorite dish. Melted Roquefort cheese, he couldn't remember what else. The man had pronounced it rock-fort. Sybil had laughed, and the Britisher asked her what had amused her. Rock-fort, she said, and tittered. Bryan had told her to shut up. Out loud, and his fellow banker had given him an approving glance.

Shut up, dear, he had said.

Ah yes, rock-fort.

He went back into the living room and stood looking down at the park. The flooding had receded since morning. The pond was resuming its former shape. An L. The body had been found at the crook of the L, along the bank among reeds, just thirty yards or so from the small tree where he used to see the fishermen when he went to the park as a kid. Quiet now. Nearly deserted, and closed to the public. Three or four cops, two in uniform, wandering over the soggy ground, looking for something. They had found her purse. Imagine, pulling out her credit cards and finding the name, and then the old man, who'd gotten through the gate somehow, telling them, Yes, that's my daughter. Saying to Bryan, "I knew it," later. Bryan had gaped at him, astonished. "I don't know how, I just knew it," the old man said, red-eyed. And then going on TV, making sure it was Channel 5 because Jimmy was coming out and he wanted to be able to tell him, Channel 5, that was it, damn it, I wouldn't speak to anybody else. And he didn't. The news bulletins on TV had said he was sixty-nine. Had he lied about his age, shaved ten years off it? Or was he just confused? Not likely. You had to give it to the old man, always thinking, as if he could get his job back if they thought he was only sixty-nine.

"You always were a supercilious bastard." Dutch's voice, behind him. He turned with a tight little smile, raised his glass and winked at his father. Dutch looked tired, his face a crag full of smaller crags full of the tiniest crags imaginable. Bryan drank. Dutch went on. It apparently was going to be one of those long speeches he occasionally felt compelled to make. "You always look like you belong, no matter where you are, don't you? You fit right in, that's what they always told me. When they were considering you at the bank, that's the second thing they said. The first was, He looks good. He looks good, he fits in, that's what they told me. The third thing was, He has a good background. First-rate, they called it. That's how they sized you up. Nothing about your other qualifications, your ability. Either they didn't care or they took it for granted."

Bryan said easily, "They checked me out. Bankers always do."

"Shut up," Dutch said. "You're drinking too much. What I'm trying to say is that you blend into the landscape. If it was the beginning of the world, you'd be the perfect picture of prehistoric slime. In a boardroom you look like every banker who ever lived. In that great big house you've got in Lake Forest, you're the lord of the manor. Look great in black tie, did you know that? Just like your old father used to. Wear it like a uniform, do you?"

Bryan smiled. "Borrowed for the occasion."

"Borrowed from me, the old family uniform. Yes, it got you into this racket, didn't it? Made you look good and fit in. They thought you took after the old man, that's what did it. Thought you took after the old man." He turned his head toward the window and shut his mouth as if he never intended to open it again.

Bryan waited respectfully for him to go on. When, to his surprise, he didn't, he said, "Don't you want anything?" They'd had sandwiches brought in for lunch, but three or four hours had gone by.

Dutch looked at him as if he might get up and go get the boxing gloves that used to hang in the back hall of the big house. That's just what he would have done twenty years ago, just for the hell of it. Just to remind them all that he was bigger and faster than any of them, although Eric might have been faster. "Yes," he said after a moment. "I want them back." His voice shook and sank to a rumble. "I want them all back."

Bryan felt himself shaking uncontrollably. He drank. He felt sweat on his forehead and his upper lip. Oh, Christ, now it was coming. Grief. The old man was going to go to pieces now, and Bryan had never been good at handling that. Like with Sybil. When she got emotional he'd give anything just to shut her up. Didn't his father know that? Why hadn't he gotten it out of his system when Jimmy was here? No, dump it on Bryan. Punish Bryan for being such a supercilious bastard. For fitting in. He gulped the rest of his drink and sat down.

Dutch had meant all the missing, of course. That's who he wanted back, his wives and now Hope. It was possible he might have meant everyone who had strayed from his hearth and left him here alone, all his sons and daughters and their several offspring. But it made more sense that he was speaking of the dead and not the living. It was more like him to demand not just the difficult but the impossible, and to demand it of Bryan, from whom he was least likely to get it.

With an effort, he said, "Father, I know how you feel." Of course, it was exactly the wrong thing to say.

"You know how the fuck I feel!" Dutch roared. Getting out of his chair, he went stiff-legged to the window and poked at the pane. "You see that over there? That's where she died, right there, killed by some bastard who was striking out at me. Why? I don't know. And you say you know how I feel! And Natalie." He was poking again, the thick, stubby finger looking as if it could break the glass like a hammer. "That's where she died, right there. Same thing. Striking out at me. Why? I don't know." He turned to Bryan. "And you say you know how I feel! Don't make me laugh!" He wasn't about to laugh. He looked as if he would never laugh again.

Bryan wanted to move, to get out of the chair. But he felt that if he did, his father might hit him. Most of all, he wanted another drink. Then he wanted to go home. He wanted to get out of this place, out of Skokie, and never see it again in his life.

He said, "Why do you feel"—and waited until it seemed safe to go on—"they were striking out at you, Father?"

Dutch shrugged, tired out. He moved slowly over the rug toward his easy chair. Bryan was suddenly conscious of two things. When his father shrugged nowadays, his hands dropped to his sides like meathooks, like the great heavy paws of a very old bear. The second thing was that he was wearing bedroom slippers, old cracked leather slippers that made him shuffle as he walked. Or he made them shuffle. Was that how an old man wearing slippers would walk? Bryan felt like giggling.

Dutch stopped in the middle of the room and said, "Why would they kill her here, unless they wanted to send me a message? Why here, practically in front of my eyes? Can you explain that, huh? Go on, explain that!" He went to the chair and sat down, glowering. "Explain that." He waved one arm. "Oh, go ahead. Get your drink." He was staring at the empty glass.

Bryan got up gratefully. He took his time in the kitchen. The old man was starting to bug him and he needed the respite. By the time the drink was made, though, he had more or less forgotten where he was. He looked out the window at the no-man's-land, sipping his drink contentedly, thinking of a day in Washington, D.C., some time ago now, when everything had gone well, almost seeing the Mall through the trees the way he had seen it from his hotel window. Then he heard the old man come into the kitchen and open the refrigerator, and when he turned to look Dutch was bending over, looking inside it, grumbling to himself.

He reached in for something, rejected it, then reached for something else.

"Hungry?" Bryan asked.

The old man pulled something out of the refrigerator and straightened up slowly, letting the door swing closed. He held out a thin slice of something. "Salami," he said.

"Salami?" He was surprised that his father ate salami. Shouldn't he have known that?

Dutch put it in his mouth, the whole slice, and chewed. It was like a bear raiding a camping site, taking his time.

"I didn't know you liked salami, Father."

Dutch didn't reply, since his mouth was full. He went over to the sink, turning on the water and letting it run while he found a glass in the cupboard where he kept the scotch.

Watching the glass under the tap fill up, Bryan said, "I ate salami in the army, or something like salami. The first night they served it frozen. We got in at midnight, just raw recruits, and they served us frozen salami. I never got used to it. I mean, even unfrozen. I hated it after that."

Dutch said, "You get used to it." He shut off the faucet and chewed some more, then drank. Bryan watched his Adam's apple move up and down as he drank it all. The glass came down on the Formica countertop with a brittle clunk. It was a plastic glass. Bryan hated drinking out of plastic. "There," Dutch said, and looked over at him. "Does watching me eat salami disgust you?"

Bryan shook his head, startled by the question. "No."

"Well, it does me," Dutch said. He leaned against the counter. "Not the eating and drinking. Just doing it here, in this house, on this day, and nothing is like it's supposed to be." He straightened up and began rubbing his back with both hands. "You don't understand that, do you? With you, it's all the way it's supposed to be, a fine house, a fine job, a fine wife, no kids, no mortgage—"

"I have a very large mortgage." Bryan smirked.

"For tax purposes, oh yes. A fine car, a car, another car, that's three cars. A house, a house, that's for the house at

Lake Geneva. What else? Everything you want. Don't you?"

Bryan raised his glass and smiled. "Do I?"

"Do I? Do I?" Dutch bared his fangs, and they stared at each other. In the living room, the phone rang. Dutch looked away. "Get the phone."

It was Frank. He was out of breath. "My God, I've been out in the country since eight-thirty. Is it true? How's Dad taking it? Does he need a doctor? God, Bryan, this is awful, and I didn't even know. I'm out here in God's little green acres, out by Galena. I can look down the damn hill and see the Mississippi River. We flew out of the downtown airport at seven-thirty. I'll never know how I got downtown, the traffic was terrible. This client has a time-share deal going, a whole forest of condos with ski lifts and everything. How are *you* doing?" Bryan, startled by the sudden silence, tried to remember some of Frank's other questions so he could answer them all. He couldn't. He said, "Fine." Frank went on. "I just spoke to Pat, and she says Emily's in the hospital. Have you heard anything from Jimmy? Are the cops there? What did they say? Was it really awful? Listen, I can't talk now, I've got to get off the phone, I'm sorry as hell I haven't been there to help out, I know this must be a horrible burden on you, but I'll see you at the house tonight, at Pat's, right? As soon as I can get myself out of here, back to Chicago. I asked Pat to put in a call to Helena. Let me speak to Dad, just for a second. Christ, I would have to be out here on a day like this. Bryan, you there?"

Bryan put all the questions out of his mind and got Dutch on the line, and then he walked into the kitchen for one more drink. He could hear Dutch's end of the conversation, conducted mostly in monosyllables. He sat down on a kitchen chair, a hard-backed model that went with the ramshackle table and dug into his spine, and stared out the window at the gray, forbidding afternoon sky. There wouldn't be any more rain, would there? There couldn't be. He couldn't stand any more rain. He wouldn't drink any more either. He would positively, absolutely decline any drinks before dinner. It was imperative now to keep himself fit and ready for any further emergencies. And he wanted to be absolutely sober in front of Sybil, or the rest of the family, or the authorities if they came back. The detectives had been there about noon and Jimmy had handled them, a hard-nosed Germanic type and one with a Hispanic or Italian name. They had been very polite, very considerate, considering. They had asked a few routine questions, made a few notes, hadn't even sat down. They said he might see them later, he being Dutch. They might have more questions. Bryan had tried to be helpful. He had made sure they knew he was a Lake Forest banker, the kind who went home every night and went to bed early. He could see the image register in their minds: the big house in among the dark trees, the glittering cars in the drive, the fancy neighbors, the right schools, church on Sunday morning, the paneled office he entered every day after parking the car in his private slot, the quiet streets everywhere, the exclusiveness of it all. He had his first drink right after they left. But it had been all right. He looked good, he fit the part, he had a good background. He was one of the family. He was one of the bereaved.

He could no longer hear Dutch's voice. He became wary, as if someone might be prowling in the parlor. It was not an unusual feeling. Unless his father was right there in front of him, smiling or shouting, it had always been that way. If Dutch was in another room, or upstairs, or in the basement, or out in the yard, anyplace but right there and visible, Bryan had always been alert, ready for anything. It was like being in the North Woods with a bear in camp. Just a bear somewhere outside the cabin, prowling. Night or day, it didn't matter. He had always had trouble doing his homework with Dutch somewhere else in the house. It was hard to describe, the feeling. When he tried to think what the feeling was, there was just this big blank, as if a light had flashed in front of his eyes, blinding him. When he tried to explain it, he saw how ridiculous it was. Only it wasn't, not really. Because it was so real, the feeling. Almost a kind of terror, as if his father might come lunging in from the next room, even through the wall, and attack him. Dutch had never beaten him up, of course, had only struck him a few times, always pulling his punches, sometimes afterward even demonstrating a rare fatherliness. Roughing him up gently, rubbing his knuckles hard through his hair or getting a viselike grip on his biceps and squeezing. Fondly. Feeling the merchandise, seeing what this son was made of.

So where did it come from, this fear? Bryan laughed softly to himself and poured one more little shot from the bottle of scotch. Fear? It wasn't fear! How could it be fear?

It was, though. The only times he wasn't afraid with Dutch somewhere else in the house was when he was able to put it out of his mind. Forget his father was there. Bryan could do that, just forget where Dutch was or that he even existed, just forget everything except what he was doing, like his homework. It had started with a maid they'd had once, a Polish woman with the face and form of a potato who spoke very little English and therefore rarely said anything at all. One day, bright and early, she saw Dutch drinking orange juice in the kitchen and spoke. She said, "Juice? Never!" Dutch had looked up with a puzzled frown and glanced at Bryan, who was making a sandwich at the sink, for his junior high school lunch. Between them they got out of her what she wanted to say. She had never permitted her kids to drink fruit juice. Why not, they asked. "Why not?" she said. "Evil! Whiskey!" Dutch had quizzed her relentlessly until he understood. She had a theory that if her children never drank juice they would never get drunk on whiskey.

At school, Bryan couldn't get the conversation out of his mind all morning. It seemed absurd, and yet the more he thought about it the more it began to make a weird kind of perfect sense. At its simplest, it came down to this: Don't drink and you'll never be drunk. And it had all kinds of applications: Don't eat and you'll never get fat. Don't breathe and you'll never smoke and get emphysema. How simple! In reading class, he wrote down all the ways in his notebook.

Don't move and you'll never get tired. Don't let your heart start beating and you'll never have a heart attack. And the best one of all: Don't live and you'll never die! Just for a moment, sitting there in class behind Priscilla Schmelzer and her long straight hair, he began to imagine that his heart wasn't beating, that he wasn't breathing, that he couldn't move. He knew it was, he was, and he could, but for a little while it seemed to be true: He didn't exist. At lunchtime when he had a Coke, he told himself he hadn't. He denied having had lunch. He skipped his first afternoon class and went for a walk, being careful to keep to the alleyways, where he wouldn't be so easily spotted. He sat down in the shade of a factory wall and told himself he hadn't been born. It worked. He felt great, and suddenly free. For the first time in his life, he had nothing in common with all those about him who ate, drank, breathed and moved, or with their fathers who got fat, got drunk, smoked, coughed, and were dying of heart attacks. Nothing unexpected or upsetting or frightening would ever happen to him again.

That night, looking at his father across the dining room table, he told himself he had never come from those randy old loins. How could he, if he'd never been born? Because he hadn't, he was immortal, and impervious to pain. And the formula came to him, the most important formula in the world: Don't feel, and there'll be nothing to dread. No pain, no fear, no heartbreak. The old Polish woman had it right, and now, twenty-five years later, Dutch was the proof of it. His father wanted to live, and he had wanted his wives to live, and of course they were dead. He wanted his kids to live, and one of them was dead and eventually they would all die, along with Dutch. It just didn't do, to want to live, when the answer was so simple. You just denied that you were alive. Just the way, when Dutch was somewhere else in the house, he had discovered how to get his homework done. He simply convinced himself that he was alone and the only person on earth. And he was.

He didn't really believe all that, of course. How could anyone believe such nonsense? Besides, if he believed it, it wouldn't be true, and he had to admit that he wished it were true. Well, if you wanted something to be true, you simply didn't believe it. I mean, he told himself, there it is!

Sometimes, though, the formula didn't work. Like now. In spite of everything, he found himself listening for a sound from the next room. And hearing nothing, he felt his hair slowly rise up on the back of his head, as if it were listening, too.

Then he cursed himself for being a fool. Dutch was probably sitting in his chair, having put down the phone. Maybe he had even fallen asleep. Old men did. Even young men. Even kids, if they were tired enough. But it was undeniable: There wasn't the slightest sound. And Bryan was afraid that any minute his father might come busting through the wall between the kitchen and the living room and beat the hell out of him. He tried to prepare himself. He listened, hearing his heart beat in his ears. How could it be fear, he asked himself. And he replied, Easy.

He picked up his glass and drank until there was nothing left, and no sound at all in the apartment except the rattling cubes of ice. Going rattley-trap. Rattley-trap-trap.

6

Frank got out of the Porsche, pulling the soft, padded cast with him. Leaning against the side of the car, he wrapped it around his left leg, over his pants, and pulled the straps tight. It went all the way from his ankle to his crotch. It held the leg straight and was supposed to help keep the swelling down. Right now what he needed was ice, lots of ice.

He pushed off, stiff and sore, and went slowly up the walk toward his sister's house, which was a huge white shape looming in a night full of crickets. His brothers' cars were already at the curb. In the darkness they glittered with the light from massive windows designed to show off great staircases and enormous Christmas trees. He loved Patricia's tall, white-clapboard New England house, always felt welcome in it. The only thing that made him glad he didn't live there himself were the two spindly pillars absurdly placed astride the entryway as if they were meant to support the entire structure, like thin little crutches holding up a mountainous figure swathed in bandages.

His swollen leg hurt like the devil. His chest felt as if there were a steel band around it. He puffed as he pulled himself along. Forty was getting to be a touch too much. First the leg, and then the phone call to Pat, asking her to tell Helena that he'd be late, and that was when Pat told him about the two girls, one dead and one in the hospital, and that was when the steel band started to tighten and throb and the little lights came and went like a marquee in front of his eyes and he wondered how he could tell Bennigan he was falling apart, right there in little old Galena. He hadn't even told him he'd hurt his knee, though Bennigan must have suspected something, the way Frank had staggered in the doorway, coming in from outside.

Bennigan was the client. The client was never supposed to know anything was wrong. Only Bennigan wasn't the client yet. He still hadn't made up his mind, and that was the other reason Frank was getting palpitations.

The truth was that his whole day had been wretched: A, early morning, he had learned that it was possible to drive downtown on Sheridan Road and the Outer Drive along the lake, so he'd left about six and made it to the office in just over an hour, a miracle considering the traffic and the fog. B, the limo was waiting as he slid the Porsche into the garage beneath his building, and the driver, Marty, a solid hunk of a man, a baked squash of a man, snapped at him because he was twenty minutes late. Marty had been an enlisted man at Iwo Jima and had vivid memories of cleaning up Japs with flamethrowers and hence had little regard for public relations executives with commuting problems. C, as they dipped into the lower level of Wacker Drive, Frank got Bennigan's office on the car phone and told them he was on his way to Meigs Field, an airport for small planes that lay like a carrier on a spit of land off the Loop, in the lake. Bennigan's secretary told him not to hurry, right now Meigs was fogged in. How was Mr. B, he asked her. She laughed. "Oh, he hates fog," she said. He said, "Does he hate it worse than somebody showing up late?" She laughed again.

Terry Bennigan was a great big guy with a paunch and thick thighs, a former pro football player who was the acknowledged king of the time-share business, a *Wall Street Journal* profile and all that, having built or taken over huge recreational apartment complexes mainly in the South and West, wherever there was a patch of water, and more recently in cold country, New Hampshire and Montana and Colorado, wherever there was a hill of snow. From the first, Frank felt they had much in common, Notre Dame to start with. Bennigan was seven or eight years older, probably class of '62 or '63. He'd grown up on Winnetka real estate money, his father having been a builder of great subdivisions in prairies north and west of Chicago in the postwar reawakening. After a dozen years as a defensive tackle with the Pittsburgh Steelers that got him a gimpy hip, he'd hit the ground not even limping, taking his father's business nationwide and reshaping it completely. Frank had always dreamed of doing something like that but didn't know whether he had the right stuff. Watching Bennigan at the last meeting, though, as he towered over the long, shining table in the firm's most elegant conference room, an interior space redone as an Edwardian dining room, he thought maybe he had. Like Bennigan, he liked moving at a fast, post-Edwardian pace. Frank had played a lot of soccer at Notre Dame, and his father had made loans to Chicago's postwar subdivision barons. Sitting at the dark, glossy conference table, he glanced down at his own hardly visible paunch, his own stout thighs, and he knew that he and Bennigan were alike. The sooner Bennigan knew it, the better.

Of course, the whole thing was tricky. There were others in the room who wanted a piece of Bennigan, and the stakes were high. He had to be careful because he was not among equals. There was Hyatt, the new head of the Chicago office, who had never quite warmed up to Frank. And Zelda Cameron, the catlike, carroty-furred colleague Hyatt had brought in from Indianapolis and made a vice president. Technically she was Frank's superior, although if he managed to win Bennigan's confidence she might just fade out, she and her Cheshire smile. The third honcho, Charlie Crane, wasn't really in the running. He was too shy, too indirect, too intellectual, and too vain. He'd never played soccer or football in his life. For that matter, neither had Hyatt. He wasn't too sure about Zelda. If he could score with Bennigan, he could blow Crane and probably Zelda out of the water, because he was here as the representative of his friend Criswall in L.A., the head of the firm. It was the old Notre Dame connection. Criswall was class of '70. If Bennigan signed, Criswall would give him the moon and the stars, and a chunk of the sun. Maybe even a raise.

The deal was this: Bennigan was in the process of opening up another time-share complex on a promontory overlooking the wide, brown Mississippi River at the northwestern corner of Illinois. It had some short ski slopes and a couple of other lures, like riding trails and souvenir shopping in nearby Galena, a century-old lead-mining town whose houses cascaded down a picture-pretty river valley. Ulysses S. Grant had once owned a house there, and so had one of Frank's great-grandfathers. But Bennigan was worried. Not only was this his first project in his home state, but in his mind it was tied directly to the success of a much more important venture. Bennigan was going to run for Congress, and he was determined to win. The Galena property had become one with his political future, almost one with his idea of himself. If it fell, so did he. To Frank, this line of reasoning, skipping straight from A to Z with no intermediary points of consideration, was tantamount to madness. Nevertheless, the firm had made its bid for Bennigan's business. It was pledging its resources—those that Bennigan was willing to buy, anyway—to enhancing not only his investment and his reputation, but also his somewhat shaky self-image. The risks had been calculated, the decision made. Now all Bennigan had to do was sign. It would be a business marriage, for better or for worse, for as long as the money came in. But now the builder, who had entered the room like a bridegroom, was getting cold feet. When he got cold feet, he stood up and ranted. Not five minutes into yesterday's meeting, he had begun pounding the conference table, making the chandelier jump.

Frank jumped, too, to his surprise. Zelda, across the table, widened her yellow feline eyes at him. He had often imagined her in bed. Though her tiny body was both smooth and willowy, almost devoid of body fat, he was not altogether sure he liked the idea. Would she claw? Would she spit and yowl?

Before he could speak, she said, "Mr. Bennigan," her voice half scratch, half meow, "first things first. Why be concerned about this now? You're on schedule, your investment's secure. You have lots of room to maneuver."

Bennigan looked down at her as if she were road-kill. He said huskily, as if he were swallowing something unpleasant, "But not lots of time, lady." She blinked, but he was already walking around the room. "I'm not worried about the condos. Just between you and me, I'm already half sold out. I made sure of that before I went into this thing. It'll pay off, but will it pay off big? That's my only question."

He meant big politically. Frank moved in. "Well, there you are then," he said. "Terry, Zelda's right. Even if Galena fell short commercially, which it obviously won't, there's no way it's not gonna move you along to where you want to be. Listen to what she's saying. Galena's the perfect fulcrum to make you a winner."

If Bennigan knew anything, he knew fulcrums. The word stopped him cold, and he sat down, still burning with impatience but ready to listen. Frank saw Zelda's huge sunshine eyes sweep over him gratefully as she turned to the big guy and began her spiel. She growled and purred irresistibly through the rest of the meeting, and when Frank offered to make the Galena trip she did not resist. There was no way anyway that she was going to stand with Bennigan on a windswept outcropping of Illinois and discuss running him for high office. She was a long-haired cat who liked to cozy up by the fire.

That's all Bennigan really wanted, of course, that damned seat in Congress. His football prowess and his father's regular contributions to the party coffers had made him a comer in local politics. The leader of the Chicago delegation in the House knew his father from real estate zoning trade-offs of old and had been badgering the younger Bennigan for years to take the plunge. The campaign had finally begun more than a year ago with the negotiated retirement of the North Side's veteran congressman, a clockwork liberal so routinely reelected that he had been gradually elevated to sainthood by the voters and forgotten. But now that the balloting was only months away, Bennigan's panic was at fever pitch. It was up to Frank to convince him that the firm, with its troops of experts in Washington and the rest of the computerized world, was all the army he needed to take Capitol Hill. Bennigan's Rough Riders. Bennigan's People. The next best thing to the Pittsburgh Steelers. Better than that, unless all you were after was a Pro Bowl ring.

Marty got the limo to Meigs Field in five minutes. Bennigan, obsessed with the drifting fog, did not notice that he was late. When it lifted, they took off for Galena, Bennigan busy with a fine cigar he swore was his last and Frank with his calculator. He was figuring costs for routine campaign items: staff, transportation, mailings, that sort of thing. He came as close to final figures as he dared, making his points succinctly. First, he said, a massive research job, the emphasis on the demographics of Bennigan's likely support; B, a saturation mailing. He stopped, nonplused. Had he really said "First," then "B," when he should have said either "First" and "Second" or "A" and "B"? He blushed. Bennigan noticed and smiled wickedly.

"Following your lead, Frank," he said, "*A*, let me check your figures with my people. *Second*, let me cost out the research end of it. I know you're going to want to do it, but maybe I can get it cheaper through the party." He stood up, wincing. "Damn hip," he said, referring to his old football injury, and went forward to talk to the pilot.

Frank sat back, astonished that Bennigan (A) had a mind quick enough to catch an almost imperceptible error in outlining, (B) that he cared—no one else ever had—and (C) that he had taken the occasion to (1) kid him about it and (2) question the research angle, the one thing Frank had wanted to nail down. The firm was affiliated with a top research outfit, and Hyatt, the head man in Chicago, had instructed him to get them a key role. Was Bennigan this aware of everything? If he was, getting him to sign was going to be harder than Frank had thought.

Nevertheless, when Bennigan came back and sat down, Frank took him effusively and in detail through an old sports injury of his own. It had occurred in the miracle play of his life in a Notre Dame soccer match, in which he'd made the winning goal with a dislocated shoulder. Bennigan, smiling slightly and still smoking the cigar, watched him through half-closed eyes. Shit, Frank thought, does he think I'm an idiot because I say "First," then "B"? Or did he, like so many Notre Dame jocks, just think soccer was a sissy game?

They were in Galena by eight-thirty. Gray, lowering skies. By nine they had looked over a model third-floor apartment and a model penthouse suite and were out on the ski runs. Frank plodded alongside the big guy over the soggy slopes above the river a hundred yards and then another hundred yards, and it was tough going. Did Bennigan really have a bum hip? Or was it just jock talk, a way of keeping his fairly remarkable sports legend alive? There was no good reason to be out here slipping and sliding up and down hills that hadn't seen a skier in months and wouldn't again until the election was over and Bennigan would be setting up shop in D.C., a fledgling congressman, one more sure shot for the Washington real estate lobby. Meanwhile Bennigan was keeping an eye out for deer, as if that's what they'd come for, a look at the Galena wildlife. Another hundred yards farther from the apartment complex, he began relating a Notre Dame adventure of his own, involving a priest and a visiting junior-college bimbo Bennigan had tried to sneak into his dorm. Frank, laughing appreciatively, lunged upward after him, placing one foot on a hummock of grass that broke off suddenly under his weight, giving him the sensation of falling into the sky. He lurched downward, turning his body in an effort to stay upright, and came down hard on a twisted left leg. He felt something pop alongside his knee. Bennigan, well into his college reminiscence, didn't notice a thing. He kept going, and Frank staggered quickly up after him. At the top they stood for a long time near a fringe of pine, looking for deer and surveying the expanse of brown, turgid river and green hills and woods. The leg didn't hurt much, but the pop made Frank queasy. He felt himself go paler and paler with some inexpressible dread. A light rain fell as they finally made their descent, and by the time they reached the office he was limping badly except when Bennigan was looking.

If Bennigan noticed the limp, he didn't say anything. Frank made his phone calls to Patricia and then, somewhat hysterically, to Bryan and Dutch. There was lunch, and an hour or so of strenuous negotiating. He rode to the airport and all the way back to Chicago scarcely breathing and not at all certain what he'd promised. In his stubborn pride, he could not bring himself to tell Bennigan about his leg, which was now throbbing with pain and swollen beyond belief, nor about Hope, who was dead, or Emily, who was incapacitated. Partly pride, partly an irrational fear that to mention any of this would be admitting a profound weakness in himself and the structure he had built of his life. Bennigan must have wondered why he'd gone so pasty, but maybe not. The big guy was so full of himself and his own concerns that Frank felt he could have leapt from the plane and Bennigan would not have noticed. Maybe that's what he should do, he thought. Maybe in Galena he had botched up everything. He found himself wishing the cat lady had been there instead. Zelda would show him no pity if he'd screwed up.

Marty was waiting at the airport, and when they'd delivered Bennigan to his apartment house off Michigan Avenue and reached the office at last, it was after five. Marty opened the rear door of the limo and Frank said quietly, making it sound like a threat, "Help me. I can't get out." He saw the smirk on the chauffeur's face as he pulled himself into the

Porsche. By using his leg like some sort of external appliance, he drove north, stopping off at Evanston Hospital for an X-ray and an ice pack and the soft cast, which he had to remove to get back in the car.

Patricia met him at her door. She stared. "Frank! What's happened to you?" His face must be a beacon of pain, he thought; she hadn't even noticed the cast yet. He smiled, to reassure her. It was an effort. Standing between the ridiculous pillars listening to the shrill pulsing of the crickets, he resisted the impulse to let himself fall into her arms. It would have been so comforting, just to collapse, just to say, Here I am, I've had a hell of a day. Maybe this was how Emily had felt this morning. Maybe at this moment she was resting comfortably, regaining her strength. He wanted desperately to regain his, if only he could remember where he'd misplaced it. He said, "Well, here I am. It's been a hell of a day," and sagged against her. She cried out, and in the ensuing silence the crickets went crazy.

Jimmy came and got him and half carried him inside. They put him in a little room just off the living room, Jimmy and Mike and Bryan, in a leather chair that held him cupped upright, his leg up on a hassock. Somehow they had got him out of his pants and into a robe that covered his leg, and his hands were holding something that held brandy. His entire being seemed contained within his monstrously swollen knee. His cheeks felt hot, even his eyeballs seemed swollen. Jimmy's hand guided the brandy to his lips, and he felt it burn all the way down like swallowing a dagger. The ice clutched his left leg in a glacial grip. He could hear Dutch someplace, giving orders. What had he told them? God, he thought, I'm home, I'm going to recover. God, don't let Bennigan see me now.

Remembering Bennigan made him remember Zelda, whom he'd promised to call. Somebody got him a phone. Helena, who'd been upstairs with Pat's kids, sat beside him with her head on his shoulder while he dialed. The cat lady answered the call brusquely and he jumped. "Zelda," he told her, "Bennigan's in good shape. I'm not. I fell over a hill. I've got a sprained knee and won't be in until Monday. Nothing's broken, thank God. He's ready to deal, I think. He's got some questions in the research area, but if you can get him in on Tuesday I'll be ready for him. Think you can do that?" She clucked and sympathized and said she'd handle Bennigan. He said he was sure she would. Helena got rid of the phone.

Suddenly he felt very brave and in control, despite everything. He got the ice bag from his knee and put it on his head, where it seemed to make a world of difference. Helena took his temperature, and he heard her telling somebody he was coming down with the flu. He had to laugh at that, it was so silly. Somebody put a blanket over him, all except the knee. The ice bag was down there now, searing his skin like a hot iron. That was his last coherent impression for a while.

When he awoke they had turned down the lights. From somewhere he could smell mingling aromas of hot food. Something rapturously Italian. That would be for the younger crowd. His father wouldn't touch the stuff. Instead Pat would have prepared something just for him—a tiny chicken perhaps, maybe fish, maybe a small, very lean roast.

A single small lamp was lit in the corner of the room near a small TV set, and just to the left of the gray screen was Raymond's thin face looking at him through smudged, pale-rimmed glasses. The face was as gray as the television screen, and as dim and blank. My youngest brother, he thought, the last-born.

"Raymond?" he said, suddenly wondering if there might be more of him than his face, and the face grinned and said, "Hi."

He raised himself up a little in the chair and saw Raymond sitting there with his legs crossed. "Good," he said, "you came out. How's Emily?" One of Raymond's hands went up to his forehead as if to ward off a blow.

"She's okay," he said. "She's resting. They wouldn't let me see her, maybe tomorrow. How's your leg?"

He looked down. The ice was gone. He pulled the robe

away and his knee stared back at him, a truly enormous knee. "Fine," he said. Without weight on it, the leg didn't hurt at all.

Mike poked his head in, his great Irish face glowing. "How are you feeling, Frank?" God, he had a marvelous buoyant voice. All that energy! "I heard you took a header."

He smiled gamely back. "Never fell down. If I had, I'd have rolled all the way to the river."

They both laughed at that. Even Raymond managed a wan grin.

Mike said, "We're all in the dining room. If you want, we can get you to the table, but I thought you'd want to take it easy in here. Pat will get you a tray." He looked over at Raymond. "You sure you've had enough to eat?" He said to Frank, "Raymond's not feeling so great either. Listen, I can get you more ice any time, we've got plenty. You can stay overnight if you like."

Frank said, "Thanks, I'll have something later. Raymond, why don't you go in?"

The kid shook his head. "No, I've had enough. I'll stay here with you." He looked up at Mike. "I'm okay, really."

Mike said, "I'll get that tray," and ducked out.

He looked at Raymond. Thin college boy, glasses, dark hair down over his forehead, a red and blue plaid lumberjack shirt, jeans, old scuffed hightop yellow shoes. No socks. Big silver Mexican belt buckle thumbtacking him to the chair. Little leatherbound notebook in the pocket of his shirt. Not so different-looking from the way he himself had looked, home from college for the summer. Different era, though. Then it was riots and civil rights and assassins, changing the world by killing those who might want to make it different. Now it was free agents and inside trading, the Bennigans on the move again, back in control.

"One more year of school, is that it?" he asked. Raymond nodded. "I'm sorry about Hope. I know you were closer to her than anybody, you and Emily."

From somewhere Pat's voice said, "Raymond says Emily

knew Hope was dead at six o'clock this morning," and he looked around to see her leaning against the wall beside the door, a vivid wine-red sweater picking up the red highlights of her hair. "That was hours before anybody else knew. Was it some kind of out-of-body experience, Raymond?"

Raymond's hand went up to his glasses. He looked frightened. Patricia pulled a chair up next to him and put a hand on his arm. "Oh, Raymond, I haven't wanted to ask you about it until we were alone, but Frank loves you, too, and we have to know. Can you tell me about it?"

Raymond stared from one to the other, and Frank said, "What is it? I don't understand." He didn't, either. He was trying to adjust to the fact that Pat was in the room. Had he fallen asleep again? Why was she speaking with such intensity? She was scaring Raymond out of his wits.

"Tell us," she was saying. "You got up at six. Why?"

Raymond said, "Actually, it was about four. The girls were out, I mean the night before, and I went to bed early. I didn't hear her come in. I didn't hear anything."

"The girls went out," Pat said. "You went to bed. You don't remember anything until Emily came in, about four?"

"No, she came in earlier, maybe eleven or twelve. But I don't think she slept at all. About four she came into my room and said Hope wasn't coming back."

Pat said, "Then something happened last night. What was it?"

He was looking at the floor. "I don't know." His voice was expressionless, like his face. "She and Hope got separated, and she came home and sat up waiting for her. She was afraid Hope—" He stopped.

"Wasn't coming back," Pat said. "Or that she was dead?"

He was staring at his sister as if she had hit him. "I don't know. She was screaming and everything. I tried to get her to eat something, but she wouldn't listen. I finally just got her in the car and drove to the hospital."

"But—" Patricia turned to Frank. "So it must have happened last night, and maybe Emily saw it."

"No," Raymond said, "she didn't see it."

Frank was growing weary, trying to grapple with this mystery. "Raymond," he said. He didn't look at the kid. It was all he could do to keep his eyes open. "Tell us as clearly as you can what it was you think Emily did see. Did she mention the park?" He pictured the park, a few acres of dark trees, and the rain coming down.

"I think she did. She said she climbed the fence, I remember that. It was all mixed up. She was hysterical. She was fighting me there in the kitchen."

"Yes, but how do you know she didn't see what happened?"

His brother was silent for a moment. The park closed at eleven. If she climbed the fence, it was after that. "Well," Raymond said, "because she didn't seem to know what had happened to her. All night she'd been waiting for Hope to come back, she was expecting her back. It was like they got split up, and she was just lying there waiting for her."

"And then at some point, about four A.M., she gave up."

"And just went to pieces, like I said."

Patricia said, "The police talked to Raymond this afternoon, just before Jimmy got there to pick him up. Then the police went downtown to talk to Emily. I don't know if she was in any shape to see them."

Frank said, "Have you told all this to the police?" He looked up.

Raymond was shaking his head. He looked as if he might cry. "Not all of it. They didn't ask me all of it."

Suddenly Frank felt very angry. He wanted to shake the kid, make him cry out, anything. He had never really been able to talk to Raymond. Raymond always seemed to be half there, and pervious, like a sieve, threatening to drain Frank's energy, taking and never giving back. And just as suddenly he was ashamed of himself. The kid was a kid, that was all, the youngest of his father's second family, Dutch's last. There would be no more of Dutch's children. Frank had always felt that after Dutch had sired his first family, his genes had more or less run out. How old had his father been by the time Raymond came along? Nearly sixty? By then his rampaging sperm must have dwindled, shriveling like tiny plants in the dark. That was silly, too, Frank thought. Raymond had his own strengths, and Lord knew the girls had. One of them was an innate sweetness that might someday become charm. Lots of kids have it these days, he said to himself. It's called youth.

"Okay," he said. "Now, where did the girls go last night? Did Emily say anything about that? I mean, what in God's name were they doing in Skokie?"

Raymond shook his head as if it was all a puzzle and said, "She said Hope had a date."

"A date?" Frank felt outraged. "This happened on a date?" He saw Raymond slump down in his chair, withdrawing, and realized he'd been shouting.

Pat said, "That's enough grilling. Let's stop now."

Frank put his head back and closed his eyes. He opened them again when he heard her say, almost immediately, "Oh, that's sweet of you, dear, but I don't know if he wants anything." Bryan was standing in the doorway, holding a tray of food.

"That's okay," Bryan said, grinning down at him. "I just came in to see what all the yelling was about." He put the tray down on a tray table.

Pat got up. "I'll go check on the others."

Something intensely Italian on the tray made Frank's stomach do a flip-flop. It was so Italian he didn't know how he'd live another moment without it. "Your lasagna," he said to his sister. It sounded like a starving man's last sigh. She smiled and went out.

He picked up the linen napkin and tucked it under his chin. Bryan sat down beside Raymond, glancing curiously at him. Frank picked up his fork, cut into the lasagna, and lifted a steaming chunk to his lips. He paused, looking down at it, while his stomach did another half-turn.

"So," Bryan said to Raymond, "your sister had a date, is that what you said?"

Frank put the bite back on his plate. The sensation of melting, bubbling Italian cheese soaked in oregano was nearly overwhelming.

Raymond nodded.

"Who with?" Bryan said. His face in the soft light looked taffy-colored. He was wearing some sort of high-necked shirt with broad, varicolored, horizontal stripes.

Raymond shrugged.

"Did she know the man?" Bryan said.

There was a sharp silence that dug into Frank's ribs. He saw Raymond look at him, his eyes full of some unspoken knowledge.

"I think so," Raymond said, and dropped his eyes.

Frank felt his stomach heave. He sat forward and leaned toward the tray, taking his left leg off the hassock to brace himself. As it struck the floor an arc of pain shot along it, and he vomited into the tray. He heard Bryan say, "For Christ's sake!" Someone's arms were around him, a cold hand cradling his forehead, and someone else was running from the room.

7

For Dutch, lying in the big bed in the principal guest room, it was a night of familiar and unfamiliar faces, welcome and unwelcome, the living and the dead. The first group of these were scattered across the darkness roughly the way they had appeared earlier, in the dining room: Mike at the opposite end of the long table where Dutch would be sure to see him, Jimmy next, so that he and Mike could talk sports and the other news of the day, Patricia, midway between Dutch and her husband, where she could keep an eye on them equally, and then Bryan next to Dutch—for what purpose, to keep the peace? To watch over him, keeping his bib properly tucked in? Bryan had watched after him all day, had driven him here, was sleeping now in a bedroom down the hall and would drive him home in the morning, as weary of Dutch as Dutch was of this banker son to whom he had taught nothing but the value of money and the means of managing it for himself and others.

Patricia had a keen organizational ability and a sense of fitness. She had placed Mike opposite him deliberately, bound and determined that her father wouldn't fail to notice her husband's hearty, handsome face, the smiling symbol of his success in the financial world and of her ultimate personal achievement against all the odds. Dutch knew she blamed him for all the rotten things that had happened to her growing up, the motherlessness, the loneliness and fragmentation, the beautiful young stepmother, the alienated boyfriends, the desperate marriage that failed, the children who had no father to speak of until Mike came along. They had looked bleakly into each other's faces down dining room tables often enough, and he had seen the pale glint of accusation in her eyes, which were gray green like her mother's, had felt his own craggy, sour expression clamped on his face like a mask, to spite her. He refused to give in to the guilt she showered him with, therefore kept himself stern and unbending. So Mike, her unexpected achievement, was her way of reminding him of how it might have been, how he might have been, had he had it in him all those years. She dangled Mike's bright Irish face down the table from him like some golden Celtic gong which every once in a while she struck, getting Dutch's attention, asking for his recognition and remorse. Well, he would give her her due, that's all. Mike was an incredible success at his age, bigger than Dutch, bigger than the rest of them put together—this house was proof of that. He was also a decent human being, something like Frank without Frank's foibles. He would never arrive crippled at dinner and go off by himself like a pitiful, wounded deer, although thank God Raymond, the whelp of the family, had something to occupy himself with instead of sitting at the table like a mope, appealing for sympathy when they were all in need of it and stifling conversation.

On the other side of the table, Helena, Frank's wife, then the kids, four of them, Helena's and Patricia's, all except Patricia's youngest. Towheads, mainly, teenagers or else getting to be, already older than the adults at the table had been when their mother died, the first Mrs. Gillespie, the earth-mother, the wife he had taken to bear his first brood. Dimly, lying in the big bed, he could make out her face before him at the end of the table between Mike and Jimmy. It seemed so like her to choose to share space in his thoughts with the son she had died giving birth to and the son-in-law Dutch could not fully accept because he was like some leprechaun in an Irish fable who had brought a rainbow and a pot of gold out of nowhere, and what had his daughter done to deserve it? Appearing between them as if she were determined to give them her support, saying, "See, Frank? This is the son I gave you with my very last breath, and this is the man our daughter wished you to be." Forgiveness all around, was that what she was asking? The face wavered, as if underwater, as Dutch felt himself rebel.

He had forgiven Jimmy long ago for being born, if that was what was needed. And he had accepted Mike into the family gratefully, relieved that Patricia could now turn her energy elsewhere and not pour it all into hating him for the way her life had turned out. Now, in the darkness, it surprised him, seeing his first wife's face at the table in that particular guise of judge and redeemer. He had gotten used to believing that he had never felt that about her while she lived. But maybe he had, in a way. Their marriage, postponed by the war, had not begun until they were both in their midthirties, and although it had been a joyful union she had been embittered by the long delay, blaming not just the war but him, too, for it had been his choice. What if he were killed, he had argued, leaving her widowed with children? The truth is, he had prized his wartime freedom, never having known any before. He had liked both combat and the intermissions of war, liked the camaraderie of so many men, liked and been amazed by the love of so many women. But none of these faces appeared at the table, only hers, wavering under his uncertain gaze. She had long, gorgeous red hair and large eyes, green and flecked with gray, and at thirty-five still had a freshness about her that would not begin to fade until she was forty and the rest of the babies were coming along. By then he had taken on so many responsibilities that she began to represent them in his mind. He had always known that this was the way it was meant to be in life. Job, marriage, family. And the family the end and be-all, the reason for work, for giving up freedom, for the disappearance of easy camaraderie and irresponsible love. She came to represent all that, too: duty and deprivation. Their romance, begun feverishly but caught in the coils of delay, resumed with a spirited wedding but stifled by work and domesticity, seemed to thrive only when there was a semblance of combat—ambitious family trips, the logistics of house-buying and birthing, ceremonial attendance at the illnesses of children and the deaths of parents. Otherwise she was as he saw her now, a judge presiding over a family jury, all of them measuring his worth, his guilt or innocence in the conduct of his life. It had only been ten years. Deprived of her, he saw her then more as she must have been: beautiful, wondrous even, capable, loving, and herself deprived of what he might have given her beyond respect and faithfulness and a distanced, unromantic love. Romance, excitement, adoration, the thrill of the chase and capture? How shockingly had his life turned over when Natalie arrived.

Natalie.

In the darkness of the bedroom her face obliterated all the others. Not at the table, not anywhere. Out there, in the still, black chaos beyond his closed eyes. Or rather not beyond but within them, inside his skull, inside his brain. Not so much a memory as a part of him, as real as his arm or his leg. Or more like an internal organ that kept him alive, functioning, and would be the last of him to die, the very last face to blink out.

Her face had a perfect symmetry, each feature of a higher order than the last. The nose was his sentimental favorite, neat, small, tipped slightly into pug and, when she smiled, twitchable. She could twitch it like a rabbit. The ears were small and delicately formed, like fine china; the eyes, merely dazzling, but when stared into long enough they became dark tunnels into which he was drawn so deeply it was like a free-fall. He had never taken drugs. Neither had she, she hated drugs of any kind, even medicinal. Yet, having seen her eyes lock on to his like that, he knew what it was to be gripped by a force far more powerful than he was, and to fall into them inexorably. In lovemaking, her lips were like that, holding him to her as they fell farther and farther out of sight into each other. Yet he liked her lips best in repose. Then they were perfectly matched petals to which his own clung like dew—

Damn!

He sat up, his stomach muscles knotted, and passed his fingers through his hard, twisted hair. The memory of the kisses was what always got to him. He could always remember them beginning, the first light touch, her soft moan, but he could never remember them ending. And knowing that he would never kiss her again drove him wild inside and, pretty regularly, made sleep a joke.

Irritably, he twiddled the fingers of his left hand. The circulation had shut off because he had been lying on his side with his fist clenched beneath his cheek, knuckles digging into his cheekbone and temple. He always went to sleep that way in strange houses, where the pillows offered his head no support. For years he had slept on special pillows contoured to his neck, which otherwise got bent out of shape and started the pain going, down between his shoulder blades. Patricia always gave him the hardest pillows in the house because once, when she awakened him, she had found a tightly rolled blanket beneath his head, but all of Pat's pillows were useless, not just soft and plump and silky but faintly perfumed with a scent he would not have minded if he could have identified it with Natalie.

He pulled back the drapes so that he could wake to sunlight, hung them over the chairs on each side of the large window. Through the tall trees, he could see the broad facade of the house across the street, one of the massive old cottages built by nineteenth-century city folk who drove out on Saturdays to be by the shore. His father had grown up in one in Winnetka, a red barn of a place built on a wooded knoll set back from the northernmost beach. Cross Sheridan Road and there the water was, if you knew where to look.

The lake lay at the bottom of a whole hill of trees, the path curling down through them toward glittery little patches of rippled sunlight. That was summertime. In winter, the cold wind blasted through tall, empty branches like a North Atlantic gale through ghostly ship's rigging, and the lake turned to ice in front of your eyes.

His head fell back on the pillow, turned away from the windows this time, his other fist tucked uncomfortably beneath his head. The next face was harder to picture because it had changed so quickly over the years, going from childhood to womanliness in a rapid series of flashes. It was easier to picture her if he kept her at twelve, the age she was when her mother died.

Hope, at twelve.

Long blond braids, the way she looked in the mornings when she and Emily finished Natalie's final inspection and shot out the door to school, Hope always first, her long, nimble legs seeming too skinny and gangly to carry her ten feet without getting entangled, Emily moving after her sedately, her head set straight as a ruler, princesslike, while Hope's swiveled and yawed as she chattered and giggled, skipping backward and urging her sister to hurry up.

Natalie dead. Hope dead. He was thankful that Natalie didn't know. He had never seen Natalie totally distraught. Only once had he seen her even mildly hysterical, the night the girls were very young and she made one of her rare miscalculations, leaving them without a sitter. It had been their ninth wedding anniversary, and they had gone downtown to celebrate. Dutch still had his Chicago apartment, a perk of the bank's where out-of-town customers stayed sometimes, and where he did when business kept him downtown too late to drive home. They had gone to an early concert, always her favorite thing because it meant being cultivated and being seen being cultivated. Once in a while she had to prove to herself that she could hold her own with the culture crowd. He didn't blame her for that. He knew she was as good as any of them, and so did she most of the time.

Only occasionally, when something reminded her of her roots, did her feelings of inadequacy surface. Then she needed a jolt of self-esteem from somewhere outside herself and him.

Afterward they'd had supper and gone dancing. She was musically talented and a natural dancer, maybe a little stiffly self-conscious on the floor of a first-class hotel with pink lampshades on the tables and the orchestra one of those tight-assed society jobs. But she hadn't sung with the rock band for nothing, and back in San Jose she'd even worked for a while as a go-go dancer, in a cage, very young and supple, proud of her flawless body but too proud to comply when told by the management to bare her breasts to the crowd. Naked in public, even half-naked, wasn't her style.

That anniversary night they'd wound up at the apartment, and he lay naked on the bed watching as she stripped to her underwear—yes, by God, that was the way he wanted to remember her! When you came down to it, that was what he had seen her as finally, his own perfectly formed, pink-lipped, wide-eyed go-go girl. Not a wind-up toy, not a plaything. Made for love, but not just her perfect body, not just her perfect face. As much character in that face as in his imperfect, aging one, and each variation of it a thing of wonder, a new way of seeing her, a subtle shift in the pattern of his love, reaffirming it, restoring his faith in himself and in her. My God, she was incredible! My God, you had to love her!

Who cared if she didn't know who her father was? Childhood legend had made him a state legislator from the Northern California uplands, one of a steady stream of boyfriends and husbands her mother had swept through over the years, none of whom, Natalie said proudly, ever forgot her mother, including the nationally known country music star of the old school who was said to have composed half a dozen plaintive ballads in her memory, before she died at the age of thirty-eight in the hallway of a motel in Arizona, in the spring of the year.

Natalie didn't look at him as she let her bra flutter nonchalantly down her arms, although she knew she was being stared at. She liked having her body admired. But this time the bra didn't drop to the floor. Instead it hung from her wrists, and he glanced at her face just in time to see the cognitive thunderbolt strike. For an instant she was powerless in the grip of it, and then the straps settled back on her shoulders and she slammed the bra shut over her breasts like a cupboard door and reached for her gown.

"Come on," she said, her voice sandpapery, the way it got when she was very nervous but had made up her mind. "I'm sorry, darling, we've got to go home."

By the time they had dressed and ordered the car, he had the full story. The boys were all away, the younger ones off at camp, one in Wisconsin and the other in Arizona; the other two, just home from college and off on midnight forays of their own. That left Patricia, a high school sophomore, as the designated sitter, and for some reason she couldn't fathom Natalie had forgotten to designate her. She appeared to be calm, but inside, he could tell, she was going crazy with guilt, almost with horror, at what she had done or failed to do. It seemed to be true that there had been times in her life when she did things impulsively without remembering how they had occurred or what decisions had gone into them. They just happened, that's all. Did she have a lingering fear at those times that her life had suddenly gone out of control? It appeared so.

He said, "Why don't you call, right now, just to be sure?" and that made it worse because there was no answer on the other end of the line.

"Why? Why?" she kept asking, out on the expressway, one hand wrapped tight over her eyes, her mouth trembling. "What happened to me? How could I not have told her? The girls were playing in the television room and I guess they thought—I thought—" Her voice had that shrill, flat sound she saved for emergencies or unconditional disagreements, and her feet were planted as if she were driving a runaway buckboard.

They stopped halfway, pulling off into a no-man's-land of shuttered brick factories and railroad sidings, and she ran to a phone booth outside an abandoned gas station with a great flap of siding torn away. She came slowly back to the car and got in, putting her head back and shutting her eyes, her hands twisted in her lap.

"Well?" he said.

She sighed. "They're all right. Pat just got home. Bryan's been there for a couple of hours." She didn't move.

"Why didn't he answer the phone before?"

"Oh, he was down in the basement. He said he couldn't get upstairs in time."

He smiled. "So why aren't you celebrating?"

She kicked off her shoes and brought her knees up under her chin and hugged them. "How could I forget something like that?" she moaned. "What went wrong, Frankie? It's just a blank. Why can't I remember?" She put her lips to her knees and kissed them, like a child with little hurts.

Dutch was nearly overwhelmed, partly by her calling him Frankie, which she almost never did, but mostly by her doubting herself, punishing herself. Tears in his eyes, he put the car in gear and pulled it around the sagging gas station wall, locked the doors and took her in his arms. They made love, just after midnight in the tenth year of their marriage, in the front seat of a magnificent touring car made in the U.S.A., in the last decade of the American century.

He had never made love in a car before, but she had. That was how she had come to fall in love with Burt, she told him, not at all abashed. Burt was her previous husband, the deputy sheriff with the father in county politics, the man who had introduced her to Skokie and then lost her. Burt loved cars. He bought a new one every six months through a rental agency downtown, had it washed nearly every day. He drove cars all over, he arrested people in cars, made love in cars, chased people in cars—

Lying there in the big bed, fist digging into his cheek, the familiar ache between his shoulders, one hip wrenched awkwardly beneath him and his stomach protesting the earlier invasion of rare beef, Dutch scowled. Burt's face was unclear, like that of a bandit in a silk-stocking mask. That was appropriate, for he thought of Burt as a bandit. He hadn't seen him in years, not since the night of the car chase.

It had happened three weeks after Dutch met her. Her brief marriage to Burt had been over for nearly a year, but Burt still loved her, she said, still pursued her, still, once in a while, even managed to date her. She might go through men almost as quickly as her mother, but like her mother she never entirely let them go. If once she'd loved them, they continued to be important to her, and if, afterward, they remained jealous lovers, that seemed to sweeten it all the more. So somehow she encouraged them to maintain an interest, and Dutch never could figure out quite how she did it. Never with outright sex, he was sure of that. Once love was over, sex was over. And besides, sex wasn't necessary. They might carouse, they might live with somebody, they might even remarry, like Burt, but they kept coming back. Having had their turn in line, they simply went to the end of it.

Burt had stayed as passionately possessive as the day they were wed. He was a big man who, like most cops, kept guns around the house and spoke occasionally of the necessity of breaking people's legs. He seemed to be much more than a law officer, and much less. He seemed not to have either a neck or a waist. He was tall and round and heavy and jammed together, not a fat man but a solid one, and when he walked up to you with his hands in the pockets of his cream-colored wool overcoat he looked like an enormous pale egg in a crocheted egg jacket. You stared, and you just hoped he might not be the last person you saw on this earth. Dutch was taller and leaner and, he believed, meaner, but nevertheless he found himself sweating a little when, as he was letting Natalie out of the car in her driveway after their second date, Burt suddenly strolled around the garage toward them. Natalie reacted angrily, but it was an anger that had no real edge, as if it had been blunted by extreme curiosity over what would happen next.

At this time, Burt might still have meant more to her than Dutch, who was something of an unknown quantity. She stood on the other side of the car and watched, making an occasional remark or gesture of intervention, half protesting, half inviting the two men to have at it—verbally, of course. Dutch, verbally confronted, said little, not even when Burt moved past him, reached into the car and felt around in the darkness for the keys. Dutch was amused when he failed to find them. Did he mean to turn off the engine? Pocket the keys? For what purpose? It occurred to him then that Burt didn't really know what he wanted to have happen, maybe didn't care, and that this wasn't a man given to making clear plans. Such a man, he figured, couldn't really be dangerous. Except a man without a plan might still become violent if nature was any guide—red in tooth and claw; he could be an accident waiting to happen when no one expected it, least of all himself.

They talked, though God knows about what. Dutch could never remember. At the time it seemed more important just to stand his ground and keep things sort of neutral. Burt, it turned out, had come over that evening, unbidden, to see young Eric. He'd served as his father briefly and they liked each other. Burt was known to the sitter so she'd let him in.

"Well," Natalie said finally, "you've seen him. Now it's time for you to go."

Seen who, Dutch wondered. Eric? Or was he the one Burt had really wanted a good look at? Intimidation—feigned or not—seemed to be a specialty of his. Two weeks later, Dutch left Natalie's and stopped at a light six blocks away. Another car pulled up behind his, its headlights practically inside his front seat, it seemed, like arc lights inside a darkened theater.

When the light changed, he turned and headed for the expressway, and the other car followed. He turned onto the expressway and it did, too. Damn fool, he thought. He accelerated and it stayed right with him, slowed when he slowed, sped up when he did, changed lanes and passed when he did, changed lanes again, right on his tail. He settled back, his breathing measured carefully, kept the needle on fifty-five, looked straight ahead. There were few other cars on the roadway so there was little hazard, and no police cars, of course. He had never believed in car phones, but now he wished he had one. Dial 911, and maybe he could at least confound the guy. Get him off his ass.

It didn't really get sticky until he approached the turnoff at North Avenue. He was in the middle lane, his turn signal going, when Burt got on his right and stayed there, his chubby, bland face plainly visible. Did Dutch imagine the smile? He slowed, to try and get in behind him to make the turn, and Burt slowed, too. That made it dangerous, or would have if the expressway had been crowded. He swore and blew his horn until finally the other car slowed way down, allowing him to move in front of it, and then he pulled off and drove the last mile to his apartment building, where he was spending the night.

He left his car in the building garage, relieved. But as he approached the doorman inside the building he saw Burt's car double-parked across the street. Suddenly his temper flared. He ran past the doorman and across the street, shouting as he ran, "What the hell do you want?" He stopped ten feet away, Burt looking back at him. When there was no reply, he said, "Nothing? It's a long way to come for nothing," and turned on his heel.

Burt yelled something after him that sounded like "Nothing from nothing." That reminded him of old Edward G. Robinson movies. And then Burt called out, "Good night, old man," and that enraged him, but he went back into his building without breaking stride and went right to bed.

There were phone calls after that. Never when Natalie was

there. But on those occasions when he stayed and she drove herself home, often there would be a ringing when she'd gone, sometimes in the middle of the night. He'd answer and hear a click. It was upsetting. It was infuriating. But after the wedding, when he went downtown less frequently, it stopped. Never did it happen at the Skokie house. Apparently Burt had a reason for that, maybe something to do with the sacredness of the family. Dutch was simply grateful that it was ended.

Burt had been questioned by the police after Natalie's murder. He had been cooperative, the detectives said, and had looked and acted stricken. Dutch didn't know how they could tell, but probably he would be in mourning even if he'd done it. By this time he lived in neighboring Morton Grove and had two kids. Dutch hadn't seen him since that drive downtown and didn't miss him.

Dutch rose shortly after dawn, exercised his lungs while hopping up and down for fifteen minutes in front of the open window, and after breakfast had Bryan drive him home. There he pored over several phone books without success and finally called the sheriff's police on Milwaukee Avenue in Niles and left a message. About noon his phone rang. It was Burt, his husky voice empty even of threat.

"Good of you to call," Dutch said. "I need to see you."

Burt came by at three o'clock in one of his usual late-model Detroit cars. Dutch, who was waiting at the curb, got in and began coughing right away, even though the windows were open. The car was full of cigar smoke.

"Have the police called you in?" he asked.

"Not yet." It looked like an expensive cigar.

"You and the police seem to get along just fine," Dutch said. "In fact, as I recall, you're sort of a cop yourself."

"I'm a sheriff's deputy. It's official. I've got a badge."

"You don't wear a uniform."

"I do sometimes." Burt glanced at him, a rolling motion of the eyes that gave Dutch a sensation of seasickness. The man had put on weight. He wore jeans and a light woolen sweater with nothing underneath. "I have a regular job, but I'm available for special assignment when they need me."

"What do you do for a living?"

It was a moment before Burt deigned to reply. "I manage a chain of liquor stores. I mean I own them. It keeps me busy, checking on them."

"Can a cop own liquor stores now?"

"This one does."

Dutch sighed. He jabbed a finger toward the park. "That's where it happened."

Burt looked but didn't comment.

"Both of them," Dutch said. "Sixteen years apart."

The other man nodded, then turned his head to look at Dutch and shrugged. He said something and looked away.

Dutch leaned toward him. "What?"

"I said I'm sorry. Sorry for you, old man."

Dutch bridled at the "old man" but held his temper. He said, "She was beautiful."

Burt kept looking out the window.

"She was beautiful," Dutch said again. He seemed to have to say that, and to want it confirmed. Recorded for eternity.

"Yes," Burt said huskily. "She was."

Dutch sat back, satisfied for the moment. Burt smoked. "Burt," he said finally.

"Yeah?"

"Do you know who killed them?"

Burt took his cigar out of his mouth and gave a harsh, mirthless laugh. "No." He looked around at Dutch, smiling and scratching his cheek. "You know, that's funny, both of them. You think one guy killed them? And it's especially funny coming from you."

"Why?"

"I don't know, it just is. I mean, what are you anyway, the Avenger?" He shifted in his seat, in order to face him. "Well, look at it my way. I've got no reason to kill anybody, and if I did it wouldn't be her, or her kid. And then again, even if

I did, what would you do about it? How could you prove it? I mean look at you, there's nothing you could do. That's funny."

"I'm not accusing you."

"Oh no, not much you aren't. Do I know who did it? Are you kidding me? Don't make me laugh, old man."

Dutch thought, Well, if he keeps calling me that, I can always get out of the car. He said, "Back then, I thought you might have killed her."

Burt stared out his window at the park, slowly shaking his head.

"I couldn't see how it could be anybody else," Dutch said. "All those phone calls back then. Following me downtown."

"Yeah," Burt said, his voice barely audible, "I'm sorry about that, I don't know why I did that." He sighed, a fat man's sigh. "Look, that was a long time ago. I've got two grown kids now, I'm practically a grandfather myself. Life is good. I'm happy. I wish you were happy, too. I wish Natalie was happy and alive. And her kid. I don't have an enemy in the world." He looked at Dutch. "Why would I kill anybody?"

The look was unblinking, but there was just a hint of a smile.

Dutch looked down at his hands, at the large gold band on one finger. "I thought you might know something."

"Yeah," Burt said, "and in a couple of days, just like the last time, I'll get a request to make a statement, and I'll make it and that'll be that. I can't help you, old man, it's all a mystery to me."

Dutch spread the fingers of his left hand, and the gold flashed in the sun. "Nothing at all? You're sure?"

"Nothing."

Nothing from nothing, Dutch thought. "Did you see her again, after that night you followed me downtown?"

Burt stared at him. "No."

"You did, didn't you? She told me you did." That was a lie, but Dutch was sure he was right.

"No, I said no." Burt kept looking at him. "Why? Did she say she saw guys or what? I know she saw guys. It wasn't anything, nothing happened, nothing important. You don't want to get into that."

"Who did she see?"

Burt stretched, and his hand went through his graying hair. What was he, fifty? Why didn't he lose some weight? "Oh, look," he said, "I'm talking twenty-five, twenty-six years ago. There was this guy from California, I don't know if she was married to him or just knew him, but he came through town and she had dinner with him. And there was this other guy, a baseball umpire she said, who'd call her up sometimes when he came in for a Cubs game. She had dinner with him, that's all. Other guys, maybe. One was a lawyer. She sued somebody once, and they were friends. And there was you. You were just a joke. I didn't think she'd marry you, of everybody she knew. You were old, for God's sake."

Dutch said, "This was while you were married to her? And afterward?"

"And before. Mainly before. There was nothing I could do about it. And nothing happened." He threw his cigar out the window. "There were rock guys, guys from the band, I guess. They were just friends."

"How do you know that?"

"She told me so."

"You believed her?"

"Sure. Didn't you?" Burt sounded amazed.

"Have you told the police about these people?"

"Who? These guys twenty-five years ago? Why should I?"

"It could be important. The lawyer. A local lawyer?"

"Yeah, he got in a jam not long after that and went to jail for a while. I don't think he's around here no more."

"The referee—the umpire, what about him?"

"Probably still working. He'd be fifty, fifty-five, sixty, who knows?"

"What was his name?"

Burt laughed. "How would I remember that? She called

him Doc or something, some cartoon name, like one of the Seven Dwarfs."

"Would you recognize it if you heard it?"

"What are you, a cop or something?" He laughed again, ending in a little wheeze. "How come you don't wear a uniform, old man?"

Dutch got out of the car. "Thanks for coming by. If you remember anything else, let me know. You have my number."

"Oh, sure." Burt ducked his head so he could see him through the window. "I've got your number." His voice was flat again, noncommittal.

Dutch stood looking at the park long after the car had disappeared, the faint smell of cigar smoke still in the air from the butt that still burned in the street. It all seemed clearer now, no longer so foggy, this dread suspicion he had. The murders were connected with the past, something in Natalie's life that she had never managed to untangle herself from, maybe something she couldn't even remember how she had gotten into. Something that had just happened, and that had grown to unbidden proportions, and that somebody had believed couldn't be put to rest any other way.

And did that apply to Hope, too? Something that had gone on even after Natalie's death, and Hope entangled, too? He started across the street toward the park, buttoning his jacket because he felt a chill.

8

It was a night and a day and another night of phone calls and conversations, just one message after another, as if all the information Jimmy had ever wanted had been held back until now and was suddenly released, the way he had often worked on news stories, digging and digging, all seemingly unrelated facts and unsubstantiated rumors, and then finally, through one lucky break, they came together and started making sense and then there was no stopping them, they just poured over the dam and inundated you until you wanted to yell *Stop*.

There were half a dozen messages on his answering machine when he and Raymond got in from Wilmette about one o'clock in the morning. Two were from Maud Leightly, the first an invitation to the governor's fundraiser Saturday night and the second a frantic apology for just catching up with his sister's murder and a fumbling reissue of the invitation, if he just wanted some friendly cheer. He was grateful for the second message; it made it unnecessary to answer the first. Three of the messages were from the newsroom and would wait. The sixth was from the Chicago Patrolmen's Association, asking for his annual twenty-dollar donation. He hoped all police record-keeping wasn't this bad, because he had already paid it and then, forgetfully, had paid again.

By that time Raymond was already in bed, and they lay in the dark, dredging up childhood memories, how for instance he had walked his little brother to school right after Natalie died, dropping him off at his second-grade classroom on his way to high school, Raymond carrying his little red lunch bucket and impulsively chasing squirrels, and Jimmy calling him off, afraid he'd get bitten.

"I walked you to school all the way through third grade, when I left for college. I remember you were getting to be a good reader. You told me once about having to read this passage from *Tom Sawyer* aloud in class and how the teacher said you were the best. Pat said you were going to be an actor when you grew up."

Raymond was shy about recalling the past, which was where his pervasive feeling of loneliness had begun, but in the darkness he had warmed up to the conversation right away. The idea that his older brothers and sister had looked after him, had cared about him all those years ago, must have startled him. Somewhere in the night a siren sounded. "I remember the play," he said.

"What play?"

"The Christmas play in third grade. We did it for the high school. I knew you were there someplace, out in the audience, but I couldn't find you." Jimmy racked his brain. He couldn't recall the play. "All you guys hooted when this girl and I hid under the blanket, when Santa Claus came down the chimney."

Jimmy laughed. "Oh, yeah, I remember." Funny, not to remember that at all.

Raymond sat up and punched at his pillow, then lay back down. "I'd probably be a good actor. I'm good at going on stage and turning into somebody else. Lots of actors start that way."

Like Bryan, Jimmy thought. Bryan had talked once about how you could hide from yourself, turn into somebody else.

It had never made much sense to Jimmy. If you couldn't be yourself, who were you? But he said, "Sure, you could do that. You'd be good at that, Raymond."

After breakfast he spent nearly an hour on the phone with his producer, telling him about Emily being in the hospital and last night's family gathering, working out possibilities for interviews when the time was right, a little family documentary on Channel 5. It depended mostly on Dutch. Was there any way his father would sit down in front of a camera and submit to questions? Maybe if he could be persuaded that it would help catch a murderer. Maybe not even then.

He found Raymond lying on the living room couch, looking through an old textbook on crime reporting, his yellow boots up, one hand under his head. After last night's conversational binge, he was talking only in monosyllables.

"We'll go see Emily at the hospital tonight," Jimmy said, sitting down across the room. "Thursday night is visiting night, you said."

Raymond pushed his glasses up on his forehead and rubbed his eyes. "Seven to eight. You can't get in just anytime."

"How did you know where to take her?" The glasses came down and Raymond looked at him, puzzled. "The hospital, I mean."

"Oh, everybody goes there," Raymond said. "In high school, half the kids I knew got a shot at it." He went back to the book.

Jimmy called Pat. She'd been upset last night, sitting with him on the bed in one of the spare rooms, a blue room, talking and talking, waiting for the others to shut off the television downstairs and come to bed. They'd gotten Frank back to Clara's, scooting him into the back of Helena's wagon with the kids. Raymond had driven the Porsche, excited by the power beneath his fingertips, and Jimmy had brought up the rear in the Ford Tempo so they'd have a way back to Wilmette. Now Raymond and Mike and Bryan and Dutch were all downstairs watching David Letterman on TV. Dutch said Letterman had spunk. It wasn't clear if Dutch knew he was a comedian. He was big and he was outrageous, that was enough. Letterman even looked a little like Dutch, but when he wasn't grinding his teeth he was more like Mike, fast-talking and confident and persuasive. Raymond seemed to be only mildly amused by him. Bryan was sitting there completely missing it all but trying to fit in. And upstairs, Patricia was sitting on the bed in her winey cardigan and stylish black cotton slacks, finishing a drink and smoking a cigarette from a pack she had fished out of a dresser drawer.

"I try not to do this," she said. "I'm trying to quit. But this is my smoking room when I've just got to have one. I haven't smoked for two weeks, not even this morning after you phoned me from the car with the news. Not until five o'clock, when Dutch was due to arrive. Then I turned off the roast and ran out and bought a pack. Now I've got two kids in there who won't go to sleep and keep giggling like simians and a father downstairs who won't turn off the TV, and we're all tired out but won't give it up and go to bed. Maybe this wasn't such a great idea, a family dinner right now. I'll tell you what, if you can take Raymond home with you tonight, I'll look after Dutch. He's gotten his second wind but he's running on empty. He looked positively glassy-eyed at dinner, and I don't think it was the wine."

She lit a second cigarette from the first.

"I've got to stop this or I'll be sick. Tomorrow I've got to go see a house with Helena. Bryan thinks he can find something for her in Kenilworth." Kenilworth was a rich man's suburb tucked in between Wilmette and Winnetka, but west of Green Bay Road there was a pocket of moderately priced houses, some of them rentals. "They just need something for the duration, until they can move back home. But everything's so damned expensive and they need every penny right now. They don't pay Frank half enough down there. Anyway, Bryan knows this bank customer in real estate, an expert in rentals. If he can reach her tomorrow, I'll go have a look with Helena. She's beside herself."

"She looks okay."

"She always does. But Frank's incapacitated, and he doesn't even know it. He's bound to be home for a couple of weeks at least, and they can't stay forever at Clara's, not with the kids."

Now she said, on the phone, "We're going over to see a house this afternoon. Bryan took Father home this morning and went straight to the bank and called his real estate contact. Oh, he stopped off at Field's for a shirt and tie. He says he just loves living out of a suitcase, you know how silkily sarcastic he can be when he's angry and upset. He's had his fill of Father for the moment. He said isn't it great, not knowing what little emergency is going to happen next, like being back in the army with a war going on. You know how he hated the army. Anyway, this real estate person says she has the perfect place, it just opened up so we're going to look at it. Helena may need some help with the moving, she can't do everything herself. It isn't furnished, of course."

That afternoon he took Raymond to his health club, and they ran a while and then did some laps in the pool. Raymond was bug-eyed at the sight of all those female shapes in leotards and swimsuits.

"You like older women?" Jimmy kidded him. Raymond grinned and blushed.

They sat down and had a drink in the bar with Sheila Henderson and a friend of hers, a thin-faced young woman who looked Grecian, tiny-boned, beautifully formed, even her fingers, a little like Emily. Her name was Jan and she worked in the state's attorney's office. Sheila wrote a chatty, know-it-all column for the *Sun-Times* that Jimmy could never bear to read, but she was bright and friendly enough, and of course she was curious about these two brothers caught up in a family tragedy—grist for her mill. Jimmy laid down the ground rules immediately.

"We don't want to talk about that, okay?" he said, and

Sheila, nodding sympathetically, backed off. Raymond was enjoying himself in what he must have thought of as this glittery domain of the rich and famous. He leaned back as they talked, his legs outstretched, one yellow boot resting on the other, and looked down his nose at Jan, smiling, lost in a postathletic haze of well-being. He still wasn't saying much, but Jimmy was astonished at his boyish aplomb. Maybe he wasn't a hopeless nerd after all. "You've got a way with women," he observed in the car.

"They're all right," Raymond said modestly.

"Yeah, but I think Jan really liked you."

"Do you?" His brother frowned, as if this was vital information he was getting.

"Yes, I do. Don't you know that? Can't you tell?"

"No," Raymond said. "She's so much older."

"She's maybe four years older. Maybe five. She's probably tired of sophisticated older guys, especially the kind you meet in health clubs. After all, she's interested in getting into public-service law."

Raymond thought for a while. "You think she'd go out with me? I don't even have a job."

"Sure. Call her."

"I don't have her number."

Jimmy smiled. "I'll get it for you."

They stopped off at Ditka's for steak, and Raymond ate ravenously. When they reached the apartment, the answering machine was blinking again.

"Hi." It was Emily's voice. "It's Thursday afternoon. I'm out of there. I'm home. There's nothing to eat here. I don't have any money. I have to go to the cash station. Where's Raymond, do you know?" The voice sounded small and thin, like Emily. "I'll be back later, after I get something to eat. I tried to call Patricia but she's out. God, where is everybody?"

Jimmy phoned but there was no answer. They drove over to Pine Grove and sat waiting in the kitchen. It was a large room with a twelve-foot ceiling, the way buildings used to be. Two tall, double-sash windows showed them a fire escape and a bricked-in view. The windows were trimmed in an off-green paint that seemed to have hardened as it dripped, like old candles, covering the wood cabinetry as well. The walls above the stove and countertops were papered in a lighter green thatched pattern that, like the paint and the floor tiles, looked many-layered, as if there was much to hide from the years gone by. Here and there were lively touches, the quilted hot pads on hooks beside the stove, the colorful decals on the broom closet door, and the silvery pull-down light globe over the knobby table and chairs, which seemed to be out of a farm-country setting, painted also to within an inch of their lives, a solid-looking blue.

Jimmy went into the living room and called Pat.

"She is?" Pat exclaimed. "And you're over there right now? Thank God you're on the job! What will you say to her? I mean, is she all right? How's Raymond? Oh, Michael just walked in the door. I've been to Kenilworth, and Helena's put down a deposit on the place. It looks lovely. I mean it will, when it's occupied. I hate empty houses, don't you? Bryan's friend met us there. She's something! Wild red hair like mine, only frothy, blue eyes that rocket you across a room. She knows her business, all right. She had Helena pegged even before they met. Tall cathedral ceiling, fireplace that looks like it was out of a castle, stairs going up on one side of the living room, dining room where you can see the fire, family room off the kitchen. Not a lot of room, though. They'll be cramped, a little. Just barely enough bedroom space for the kids and not enough baths, but a big balcony in back that'll be great this summer. No back yard at all, but two enormous oak trees and a big front yard. Quiet street. Lots of turnover in the neighborhood, all divorcées and their kids, just hiding out until the worst is over and they can get back on their feet. It's a tall stucco, vaguely Tudor. You'd love the agent. She's about your age, a bubbly redhead in a matching red dress, looked like a burning bush. Not bubbleheaded, though. Married. Oh yes, she kept saying, very married. Her name is Molly Haverford. I liked her, and Pat likes the house, so that's that. Frank can recuperate in the family room without having to climb the stairs, and she'll be able to drop the kids off at school on her way to the shop every morning. No, actually, they can walk! I forgot, it's only blocks!" She paused. "They seem to be very good friends."

"Who?"

"This Molly Haverford and Bryan. When I mentioned him she seemed about to sizzle and leave the ground in a shower of sparks, like a firework. She said, 'Oh yes, isn't he brilliant!' She said she meant banking and investments, but it was more than that."

"Pat, are you getting at what I think you're getting at?"

"Well, she doesn't know Sybil, didn't even know who Sybil was. Such amazing blue eyes and ruddy skin. That's when she told me how happily married she is."

Jimmy laughed. "For Christ's sake, you think they're lovers?"

"Well, it has happened, a straitlaced, astringent banker having an affair with a buxom sun goddess who colors right before your eyes." But Pat laughed, too. "And the strangest thing is, I don't believe she's a fool, at least I hope she's not. Though I couldn't help feeling a little sorry for her, I mean if it's true."

"It's not true."

"Of course not. My imagination."

"And anyway, why feel sorry for her if it is?"

"Oh, Lord, Jimmy, it's not like you single folks. Forbidden married love can positively kill you. All that silent hankering and anxious hiding away together. It'll bust a gut. I know there's nothing to it, of course. Only I keep remembering the way she looked at me when she told me how married she was, as if she knew I knew, and she was even pleased I knew. Oh, Jimmy, tell me I'm wrong."

"It's not true because if it was, Sybil would know it, and Sybil would have had Bryan's hide by now."

"If she knew."

"She'd know. Sybil knows everything."

"Well, maybe you're right. Anyway, Frank and Helena will be moving, and Emily's out of the hospital, and now I've got to go serve dinner. Call me and tell me how she is."

"I will."

"Good. Thank you, Jimmy, for looking after things. Oh, and Father called a little while ago. He wants you to call him."

When he returned to the kitchen, Raymond was brewing coffee in an automatic coffeemaker beside the stove. "Emily uses filtered water," he explained. "Best coffee in the world."

It was good. Well, better than most. He carried his cup back to the living room and called Dutch.

"I'm fine," the old man said. "I took a walk in the park. I even did my exercises."

A key rattled in the door. It opened and Emily came in. "Dutch," he said, "hold for a minute. Somebody's at the door."

She looked even smaller because she was all in black, black turtleneck, black skirt, black tights, and she stared at him as if she had never seem him before, then broke into that isn't-life-marvelous smile that meant absolutely nothing you could count on. He put down the phone and went over and hugged her. She came up just to his chin. "Glad you're home," he said, smiling down at her. "Raymond's in the kitchen. I'm talking to Dutch."

She nodded and went toward the kitchen. She looked pale and tired, but her walk was as springy as ever. Should he mention her to Dutch? he wondered as he picked up the phone. Emily's face was marvelous—a model's face, formed so delicately that you wanted to stare but didn't dare to, not the way you could look at her mother without caring if she noticed. What was the difference? He couldn't tell. Maybe it was her size, as if someone so petite should be a child, with a child's unformed features. Or maybe it was the need for attention one saw there, an expression asking What will happen to me next? Natalie's face had made no requests. It had simply stated the fact that she was there, and acceptably beautiful.

"Dad?"

"Who was that at the door?"

Oh, what the fuck, he thought. "That was Emily. I'm over here on Pine Grove. She came home today, just now."

"Good. Don't let her go back to that place."

"She seems okay. Raymond's here."

"Good. Tell her I'm glad she's home. Tell her to call me when she has time. We'll have a talk." He cleared his throat. "Jimmy, now listen. Did you ever know of a baseball umpire named Doc? Albert Hemphill, now retired. Lives in Arizona. You're a baseball nut, have you ever heard of him?"

"No, Dad."

"I've told the cops about him. He knew Natalie. I hate to say it, but he may have hung around Natalie, seen her from time to time after we were married. I told the cops he lives down in Tempe, Arizona, and they ought to pick him up and question him. I don't know if they will. If they don't, I might just go down there and look around. You want to come along?"

"Dad, what do you have on this guy?"

"Nothing. Just some information that he and Natalie knew each other. It isn't much, but it's a lead."

"What do the cops say?"

"Nothing. They never say anything. I talked to that Spanish one. Very polite, won't say anything, but thanked me for the information."

"Where did the information come from?"

"From a police source. You remember Burt, the deputy sheriff? I talked with him this afternoon. He called me back with the name."

"It's not much, is it?"

"No, but it's something."

"I'll call you back later, Dad. I think I'd better go talk to Emily."

"Don't mention this. It'll just upset her."

"I won't. I'll call you later."

Always protecting each other, and for what? Dutch wasn't to be told about Frank's house falling down, but he was already working on the murder. Natalie's murder. Sixteen years had gone by and it was still fresh in his mind. Newly fresh, after Hope's death. There was no need to protect Dutch. Probably Emily didn't need protecting either.

When he walked into the kitchen, they were having coffee, sitting in the old, high-backed chairs the way they had as children in the big kitchen at home, waiting for the next thing to happen. Raymond looked up. "The police were there this morning and talked to her. She says she told them everything."

He looked at Emily blankly. "Everything?" He sat down.

"They made me talk to them." She glanced at Raymond. "The sergeant was cute. He was Latino. He asked me for a date." When Raymond looked startled, she said, "Well, he was just kidding around. He was nice."

Jimmy said, "What do you mean—everything?"

She sipped her coffee. "Why not? I have nothing to hide."

"Well," he said insistently, "like what?"

Her complexion was pink, like a child's, but under the light he could see that there were circles beneath her eyes. She said, "Well, you know how it was. It was raining like hell and we were shivering, soaked through. Wet T-shirt night. Hope said we might as well take off all our clothes."

"Wait a minute," he said. "You were in the park?"

But Raymond was staring at her in horror, and she laughed nervously. It was a burst of laughter, almost a shriek. "We didn't take off our clothes, Raymond, it was just a joke!" She glanced at Jimmy and said, as if Hope were still alive to worry about, "Raymond always worries about us," and suddenly, realizing what she'd said, didn't know where to look. "Yes, in the park. Hope went off toward the pond with this guy.

They were going to fool around, she said, so I could go home." Her face had turned pale.

"What guy?"

"Just a guy. He has nothing to do with anything, just some boy from school. He's not involved."

"How do you know that?"

"Because I know." She shrugged. "So I climbed the fence and came home. That's all."

Jimmy sighed. He got up and poured himself some more coffee. "This is what you told the police?"

She nodded. Raymond looked up at him, dismayed, waiting. Jimmy said, "Is that how you got into the park, climbed the fence?"

"No, we were there when they locked the gate. We hid."

"Why did you get so upset that night?"

"Well, she didn't come home. Naturally I got upset."

"Did you give the police the guy's name?"

"Look, I told you. He's nobody."

"Why did you go into the hospital?"

"Raymond took me. I was upset. I thought I wouldn't have to talk to anybody there."

"About what?"

"About anything." She looked at him anxiously and her lip quivered. "My God, I wouldn't have told you I was out if I'd known you were going to grill me." She sounded hurt and angry.

He sat down. "Just what were you doing in the park? Hope had a date with this guy?"

"Yes. It was just a lark. It seemed like fun."

"In the rain."

"In the rain."

He let a few seconds tick off. Then he said, "How do you know this guy didn't kill her?"

She stared down at her coffee cup, her lips tight together. "I checked into the hospital because I didn't want to talk about it." Her voice shook. "I just don't want to talk about it. I checked out so I wouldn't have to talk about it anymore.

Isn't there someplace I can go and just not say anything?" Her voice seemed to run out. She said faintly, "Can I have some more coffee?"

He looked at Raymond, and Raymond got up, brought the glass pot to the table and filled her cup. Watching him, Jimmy suddenly remembered his conversation with Dutch. "Raymond," he said, "have you ever heard of a baseball umpire named Doc?"

Raymond shook his head. Emily jumped up, took the pot from him and put it back on the coffeemaker. They both watched her standing with her back to them, leaning against the stove with both hands as if she were trying to keep it from sliding across the room. Was she just stressed out, he wondered, or had the name struck a nerve? Raymond sat down.

"He lives in Tempe, Arizona." Jimmy spoke slowly, soothingly. "The police think he might have something to do will all this. They're thinking about picking him up."

There was a split second when he wasn't certain she had heard, but then Emily whirled around, looking frenzied, as if the stove were electrically charged. She reminded him of a kitten that had been scared out of its wits. Raymond was half out of his chair.

He kept his voice calm. "The Cleveland Indians have gone to Tempe every year for forty years, for spring training." He leaned back, trying to look casual, smiling up at her. "No, hell, I'm no baseball expert, but I spent several summers in Cleveland. Bob Feller is one of their heroes, one of the all-time great pitchers, maybe number two, did you know that?" She was biting her lip, close to crying, but she shook her head. "He won two hundred and sixty-six games, something like that, back in—oh, way before you were born." He turned and looked at Raymond. "Bob Feller. Remember him?"

Raymond shook his head too, looking scared, his shoulders peaked up close to his head, his long, white, narrow fingers cradling his cup.

Jimmy looked back at his sister, feeling completely relaxed.

"Look," he said gently, "we're family here." He watched her relax a little. Then he said, "Emily, do you know anything about this guy Doc?"

That was all it took. That, and the look he gave her. An unblinking, sympathetic, searching look.

9

Jimmy came out about eight o'clock with Emily and Raymond in tow, what was left of them. It was hard to believe. Here they were, the two youngest kids in the family, looking like lost, bedraggled pups hauled inside for the night, glad to have someplace to be but not sure they belonged anywhere really. Jimmy had explained some of it on the phone. Emily was talking at last, he said, and now she needed her older sister to lean on while she went through the rest of it with the police, the reporters, the other authority figures who would ask her why she had done what she had done, and while she wrestled with her guilt, deserved or not. Well, Patricia thought, why not? She had always been the official sitter, the one who took care of whoever needed looking after. The house was the size of a small hotel anyway. Seven bedrooms and only four of them occupied, most nights not even that, Michael Daugherty being an adoring husband.

She thought about that. They had separate, adjoining bedrooms but yes, she decided, adoring. She was lucky. How many of the women she knew could say that after ten years? Helena, yes, but then Frank was such a baby. Not Sybil, and certainly not if she was right about Bryan and his human Hot Flash. Molly Haverford? Had she even been married ten years? Dutch? He had been deeply attached after a decade of marriage, but what man wouldn't be, with a woman thirty years younger who might just as well be up on a movie screen? And did Dutch know what love was, any more than Bryan? She gave it up. Who knew what love was? Besides, they were looking at her, waiting for her to say something. Anything.

She went to Emily and took her in her arms, motioning for Raymond to for God's sake stop standing in the doorway and bring inside the pitiful-looking little suitcase he was carrying.

"Oh, you kids!" she cried. "Come on in. And Jimmy, make some drinks or something. Come on, precious, we'll get you settled and then we can talk. What did you have to eat?" She looked at the young men, her brothers. "Have you two eaten? Come on, tell me what's been going on."

They went into the living room. Mike was upstairs with the children, aware that his somewhat unfamiliar presence might make Emily uneasy. She sat them all down. "Now, what can I get for you?"

"We ate on the way," Jimmy said. "We stopped at the Chinese place on Green Bay."

She had never seen him so uptight. "Don't ever do that again," she said. "You know I have nothing but food in this house. Well, Emily, dear, let's have a look at you. Are you glad to be home?" What was home? she wondered. Out of the hospital, she meant. Would the Pine Grove apartment ever be home for her again? Was she home now?

"Oh, yes," Emily said, and glanced at Jimmy. She had obviously been crying, and now she was sunk back in the biggest chair in the room, Mike's leather high-top, nearly lost in it.

"Well, tell me," Pat said again. How many times did she have to say it? "I'm sorry, maybe it's too soon to talk. Does anybody want a drink?"

Jimmy got up and went to the bar. "I do. How about you, Emily? Raymond?"

Raymond shook his head. He seemed to be in mourning.

Emily said, "Scotch. With an awful lot of water." She looked at Pat. "Do you have an aspirin?"

So were the headaches back? While Jimmy tended bar, she got the aspirin and called up to Mike, checking on the kids, checking on him, really. They were quiet, he said, standing at the top of the back stairs. He looked so tall and comfortable, and so sexy in the white shirt. Pat held up the bottle of aspirin and smiled, as if to say, What did you expect? Then she returned to the living room.

"Now then," she said, settling back, "tell me what this is all about." She said to Emily, "Then we'll get you to bed. You must be exhausted."

Emily was clutching her tall drink tightly, as if it might jump out of her hands. Jimmy said, "Pat? Anything?" and when she declined he went over and sat down. "Emily," he said, "it's still family. Why don't you just tell Pat what you told us?"

Emily said, "Well," as if she were about to begin a long story, and then she was overtaken by a deep, involuntary breath and shuddered, then sighed. She put her glass on the coffee table and sat back, wiping her eyes. She looked exhausted, all right. Then she put her fingers to her lips, still calming down, making little twittering sounds that Pat was amazed to realize was laughter, little bursts of nervous laughter.

"Take your time," Jimmy said.

She said, "No, it's all right. It doesn't matter." She looked at Raymond, a longing look, as if she wished they were small children again. Then, with a sidewise, unfocused look at Pat, she began. "There was this man." But she was silent, not looking at anybody.

"Tell us what man," Jimmy said, with a glance at Pat.

Emily's eyes were heavy now. She took another gulp of air. "We were ten. You know, tennish. Hope was older, a little." She tried to focus on Pat. "We weren't children, not really, not little children, not like Raymond. I don't think he saw who was in the car at all." She glanced at him. "You were too little to see what we saw." To Pat she said, "The man in the car, who picked Mother up that night."

Pat said, "From San Jose, your mother said."

Emily shook her head. "Yes. Wherever. It was a green car. I imagine it was rented."

Feeling dumb, Pat persisted. "Her cousin?"

Another shake of the head. "We knew who he was. We'd met him at the pizza parlor. You remember the pizza parlor? You took us there sometimes, when you were sitting." She turned to Raymond, who sat staring at her. "You remember, with the clown and the air mattress you could fall down on without hurting yourself, with all the bouncing balls? A huge place, and the kids shouted and screamed so you couldn't hear what the person right next to you was saying. You remember, don't you, Raymond? We used to go on Saturdays, and one day he was there? We had pizza. Nobody could hear anybody. It was that kind of place."

Jimmy said, "And you heard his name."

"Doc," she said. "His name was Doc." She looked at Pat. "He lives in Arizona."

Jimmy said, "And he was the one who picked up your mother that night, in his car."

She nodded. "It doesn't matter now." As if in explanation, she said to Pat, "Hope's dead. It's no fun anymore." Her shoulders shook, and she began to cry.

Pat got up and pulled her up out of the chair. "There, there," she said, her arms around her, "it's all right. That was a long time ago." When she stopped crying, Pat took her to the couch and sat down beside her and held her. She said to Jimmy, "Maybe Mike should come down now."

Jimmy said, "There's a lot more."

Emily looked up at her, a child. "Where is Mike anyway?"

Patricia smiled and patted her. "Upstairs. He's putting the kids to bed. And working. He has a meeting tomorrow with some men from the SEC."

"Like the cops."

Pat kept smiling. "Like the cops, exactly. They don't mean

any harm, just asking questions. Do you want to tell me some more?"

Emily was silent. Pat said, "Raymond, did you know about this?"

He nodded. "Some of it. She was talking a lot the night . . ." He was trying not to say "Hope." "The night I took her to the hospital."

Emily struggled out of Pat's arm, sitting up straight, suddenly animated. "Raymond was too small. When Mother got killed, we played a game. Hope made it up. We pretended the man in the car was Cousin Bob, from San Jose, just the way Mother said. I said the car was blue, Hope said green. She got to say green because she made up the game. We said he was younger, younger than he was."

"You made him up," Patricia said.

"No, we made him the way Mother said. She said he was her cousin, so that's just what we said."

"But why, if he wasn't?"

"Because that's what she wanted!" Emily sounded angry, but her eyes were innocent. She glanced at Raymond. "Raymond, you remember." He shook his head. "Yes, you do. We couldn't tell anybody about Doc, not after Mother died. If she had wanted people to know about Doc, why did she say he was her cousin? She knew we'd see who was in the car, the man from the pizza parlor." She looked at Patricia anxiously, explaining again. "If she didn't want us to tell, we couldn't tell. It wasn't a lie. It was just not telling."

Patricia waited, not sure what to ask. "You've never told anybody, all these years?"

"No, not anybody. That's how she wanted it."

Jimmy said, "You thought." She stared back at him until he looked away. "So," he went on lamely, "this was your secret, you and Hope. What was the rest of it?"

Pat wasn't sure she wanted to know.

Emily said, "The rest of it was, when we were in college Hope saw him on TV."

"On TV?" Pat said, feeling stupid again.

"We never watched baseball. But one night the game was on in the students' lounge, and Hope said, 'Look.' It was Doc, just this one quick look, standing behind the plate and whipping off his mask to yell back at an angry manager. I told her she was imagining things, I couldn't believe it was him. But she wrote to the TV station and got his address. It was the umpire's association or something. Al Hemphill. We wrote him a letter, just for the fun of it, and got one back from Tempe, Arizona. Well, not just for the fun of it. We had other reasons for doing what we did."

"What?" Pat said. "What did you do, and what were the reasons?"

Emily leaned back and moved closer, so that their shoulders were touching. She began chipping away at a red fingernail. "We decided we were going to be rich," she said.

Pat had the oddest sensation whenever she recalled that night, as if afterward she had flown through the house like a bird, flitting into this room and that room, her children, her husband, Emily tucked in bed, her brothers taking their leave with wan smiles and tired good nights, the kitchen, turning out the downstairs lights, Emily awake, standing in the hallway, Emily with her headache, herself getting into bed and holding on to Mike, the lights from the street coming in the window, making odd shadows on the wall, a car going by, herself standing in the hall outside Emily's room, hearing her weeping, wanting to make sure she was all right but not daring to go in, and all like a bird flitting and soaring, seeking something. What was it? Escape? Yes, but not entirely. Wishing this were not her responsibility, not any of this. Wishing she were back in her mother's house, the house she barely remembered except it was exact and precise and everything was planned and accounted for and taken care of. Yes, all of that, but more. Searching through the rooms of her house, for what? For the family? For her father—where was he? For her brothers? For Natalie? Maybe even for Hope? Wanting to put them all back together, the way a bird builds a nest to put her family into. Yes, maybe that was it. Had she dreamed being a bird? Or was it just her wish, to fly endlessly, gathering everything together, making everything all right? One big, giant, happy aviary, full of bright colors and chattery noise.

The truth was she couldn't bear what was happening. Death, yes. Horrible, horrible. Violation and disaster. Rain and flooding and Frank's house falling down and he lame and a dead little sister drowned in a pond, and another little sister fucked up by fate and facing some kind of atonement, God knows what it will be. Crazy, crazy things.

Murder and death and blackmail, my God.

And Michael Daugherty, loyal, loving husband, asleep in the bed while she stares out the window wondering what will become of us, what will he think of me now?

She shook it off in the morning, got him off to work, got the kids off to school, let Emily sleep, hoping she'd sleep a long time. Sitting on the sun porch with its multiple yellow couches and rug, and its round white tables and walls all windows with sunlight coming in, thinking, Well, this is how the day begins and so what? We'll face it. We'll just use it, make it work for us.

Blackmail? Who would have believed they could have invented the game they did, those two bright little girls? Something like Bryan's playing with fire. She was sure of it now, he and Molly Haverford, Molly obviously with a lot to lose—happily married, she said, very happily. Bryan? For a long time it had been clear that his marriage, at some undetermined point, had gone down the drain and was stuck someplace not far from the bottom. Sybil, Pat had always believed, was an ass, smart, sophisticated, cold, calculating, with a spiteful intelligence and a withering wit. Yet she wasn't wholly to blame, perhaps not even by half. Bryan was all those things and more. They deserved each other, but neither deserved the lives they were leading in a marriage that was little more than a corpse. So Bryan, unlike Molly, for instance, had little to lose except perhaps financially, and he could always make more. Molly? If she should lose the husband who loved her (if he really did), she might not even get Bryan, which might be better than if she did. She was too nice, too bright, too competent, too deserving to deserve this. My God, Pat thought, I have to talk to Bryan. Threaten him might be more like it. Or blackmail. She'd never thought of blackmailing anyone before.

It had begun with Jimmy's call, saying that Emily had finally talked. What should he do? Bring her out to stay in the suburbs? Would Pat take her in? Raymond could stay with him for the time being. Maybe Raymond would wind up going back to school, he said, hang around Cambridge for the summer. He liked it there.

Her immediate reaction was not what she thought it would be. Yes, of course, she found herself thinking, somewhat desperately, send them all to Patricia, all the failed mortals of this earth. She was the flesh and blood Statue of Liberty, her torch held aloft, beckoning them home. Emily? Of course she wanted Emily. She was practically her own child. So what if she didn't know her, didn't understand her? They were strangers, yet perhaps no more strangers than many real mothers and daughters, especially the unluckiest, who are prevented by an illness of the mind or spirit from communicating except in shouts and threats and beatings, physical or emotional or both, but must for some reason, rational or not, keep together or else at least one of them goes under, lost absolutely. Emily must not go under, not while she had a chance.

So now Emily slept, in the small pink bedroom, unable to talk anymore, her headache gone, marvelously serene. She had spoken after sixteen years of silence, she had spilled her guts. How much closer to real life she must feel now, having spoken. To Pat the longest distance was silence, it could keep people so far apart. What was needed now was spiritual surgery and long, long rest.

Jimmy would talk to the police today, and then to his producer. And maybe the detectives were already on their way to Arizona to arrest a retired baseball umpire for the murders of Natalie and her daughter. And maybe it was all over now, except for what they would all carry around in their bones, especially Emily.

She could hear Jimmy now, going over it in a corner of the newsroom, telling his producer the whole story from beginning to end, and sounding like some long recapitulation of a very old crime as told in the Sunday tabloids, the way reporters are supposed to talk to each other:

"They actually blackmailed the guy, can you imagine? Can you picture these two sweet young things threatening him with exposure unless he forked over—what was it, three thousand dollars three times over, and more to come, they thought? Knowing about him when they were still in grade school and keeping it in all those years? Christ, I can't imagine how you could do that without going crazy, can you, and I can say that because I don't think she is, she's functional, and that's a miracle, thank God for that. Maybe Hope was a little shaky. There was a time Pat was worried about her, thought she should get counseling. Emily, too. I don't know what a psychiatrist would say. Technically, maybe they did go a little nuts. But I don't think Emily's unsalvagable, not by a long shot, do you?

"It's amazing. First they keep it a secret because they believe Natalie told them to. Don't tell, they thought she said, it's our secret. They remembered the guy from the pizza place just the Saturday before, the kids' place over on Oakton. They'd met him once before that, maybe a year earlier, out by the airport. A well-known umpire. I don't remember him at all, but I must have seen him work half a dozen times those summers I spent on the *Cleveland Plain Dealer*. You know, you never really see umpires as individuals unless you're a student of the game. I was never that close to it, although I played some in high school and college.

"So they saw him in the car, all right, and they thought they'd been told not to tell, and when Natalie didn't come home they didn't know what the hell to do except keep quiet. So they did what they thought she wanted, made up the rest of the story. Talked about the cousin from San Jose, told confusing stories about the car, even said it wasn't her ex in the car, though how could the police have accepted that since the girls said they couldn't really describe the man in the car? The cops wanted to get him off the hook if they could, I guess, since Burt's a part-time cop.

"And they kept the secret. It was to protect her. Forever, Christ Almighty! Protect her memory, keep the vow, whatever it took. What a life sentence she left them with. And she'd been killed! Maybe it also occurred to these two scared kids that if they told they'd be killed, too. And one was, because she threatened to tell. The blackmail.

"And all the time they didn't have the vaguest idea who he was, not really, not until college when Hope saw him in the game on TV. They got his name and address, and then another six, eight years go by. Can you imagine what they're thinking about all this time? He killed their mother. He should be punished, right? But if they tell, they break a pledge made in life, a pledge extended after death out of respect for her memory. They loved her. She was everything to them. She still is. She was their mother! And besides, violating her secret might get them killed.

"So what do they do about this guy? Well, maybe there's one thing they can do, and maybe it's something their mother might even approve. They can punish him by threatening to expose him and making him pay for their silence, which, unlike their mother's silence, would be voluntary. Seemed fair to them. Maybe even to him, in the beginning.

"So they got up their nerve and wrote him, and he sends the money, the first three thousand dollars. Think about what he's going through now. Emily said it took quite a while to get the money that first time. He didn't take it seriously. They had to get downright insistent. They even sent a lock of Natalie's hair, some old keepsake, which must have had a terrific psychological effect. They described his car, his license plate—they even had most of the number! They described him down to a T, and they told him they had a third witness. They didn't say it was a six-year-old brother who had almost no memory of that night at all.

"So he gave in, and he made two more payments, and then he decided he'd had enough. He made arrangements to make the next payment in person, or else that was going to be it, he said.

"Now these were two tough young ladies. Oh, they were nervous and even squeamish, and they were still thinking of it as a game, in some ways like a childhood game, like Hide and Seek. And it was exciting, and they were also frantic because, after all, it was their mother this was all about, and her death at the hands of this man. He was a murderer, and they must have felt she was crying out to them from the grave!

"So they did two things. They said, Okay, leave the money in a package in the park where their mother's body had been found. Leave it and take off. See, they did want to punish him. If this was to be the last payment, they wanted him to pay emotionally, too. They wanted to bring him back to the scene of the crime, make him remember, make him sweat. And the other thing they did was to split up, for safety. If he chose violence, he still couldn't win. He wouldn't dare to kill just one of them because the other would still be alive, could still make him pay.

"Hope said she'd go get the money once he'd left. Emily was to hide, keep out of sight, and watch to make sure he didn't come back. It would be dark, there were woods to hide in and houses just across the street. My God, my father lived right there! And it seemed safe enough to them. Christ, it seems like orchestrating your own nightmare.

"Only it was worse than that because it rained all day and flooded the damn park, and then they waited and waited and the park crew arrived and locked the gates, and still nobody came, and there they were, trapped at night inside a fenced compound in three inches of water that was rising all the time, because the rain was pouring down and this was a natural drainage area, and they must have wondered if God or their mother had decided to take a hand. Had they done the right thing in her memory or had they broken some moral law and were now to be punished for it? Emily didn't put it quite that way, but it must have been terrible, what was running through her mind.

"Well, he came. And when he couldn't get in, he threw the package over the fence and drove off. Hope ran to get it, or rather slogged through three or four inches of water, because it was slow going. Neither one saw him come back until he was over the fence. Emily was hiding, and she saw and tried not to see. She couldn't see him clearly, but it couldn't have been anyone else. She was petrified. She may even have fainted, for all we know, because she had no idea where to look for Hope by the time it was over, and she has no idea how much time elapsed. She got over the fence somehow and drove home, looking behind her all the way, utterly terrified. How she got through the next four hours I'll never know. Well, obviously she didn't quite. Raymond tried his best to calm her and must have known something was desperately wrong, but he finally had to give it up and take her to the hospital. End of story."

Patricia got up off the yellow couch and walked over to the window, where she could see the back yard where the roses would be coming into bloom. In the sunlight, the grass looked exceptionally green. Like a cemetery, she thought, that's the way it grows when it's got to cover everything over, all the things you can't possibly understand, like dying and families and the human mind. She pushed open the door and went down the steps into the yard. In the garden house she found some thick cotton gloves and pulled them on. Then she took the spade and marched across the lawn past the rose bushes and the apple tree, just budding, and began to dig up the grass. She was going to make a vegetable garden. They'd never had one and she didn't know how big it would be. Maybe it would go all the way to the fence. She didn't care. It just seemed damned appropriate, and the best possible thing to do.

10

Friday morning. TGIF. Bryan got out of bed and looked in on Sybil. She was asleep in her fiery web of white, the four-poster bed all draped in thin, glimmering swaths of white cotton that seemed to come from everywhere and be inextinguishable, like white-hot strands of fire, and the white sweeping curtains that crisscrossed at the windows, burning gently with soft sunlight, and the off-white walls and ceiling and the white, deep-pile carpeting and the crystal chandelier whose tinted prisms glowed with secret little flames of their own, like chemical reactions, and deep in the tunneled web of her bed her long black hair spread over the pillow, a spider that lived at the center of all those slow-burning filaments of white ash. He closed the door without a sound.

Still in his pajamas, he got Molly on the phone at home, so he wouldn't have to go through the switchboard and pretend to be a real estate customer. "Coffee," he said.

"Yes," she said brightly, "all right, I'll be there." He could picture her husband at the other end of the room, before the mirror, putting on a tie. "But you know they're not going to come down much on the price. Just so you understand. Goodbye."

Twenty minutes later he was out the door and in the car,

heading for the expressway. It took him ten minutes to get there. It was just at the edge of downtown Winnetka, and at this hour there was usually a place to park at the curb. Inside it wasn't much, a seedy little Greek cafe full of construction workers and elderly types, where the eggs were always flat and overdone and the hash browns barely heated through. Nobody either of them would care to know ever went there, which was why they did. He went up the steps into the back room and slid into the last booth, facing the door. He insisted on that, said his radar was perfect, he could spot the enemy, whoever it might be, instantly. If she got there first, he told her, she was to sit there, too, but she never did.

"I don't want to know," she always said. "It makes me too nervous."

So, arriving after her, he would see her shock of burning red hair in the last booth, and go up the stairs and slide in on the other side and pick up the menu, smiling over it at her. He always ordered the same thing: eggs, bacon and wheat toast, dry, with jelly. It always came with the half-cold hash browns, which he ate anyway. Since he hadn't ordered them, he thought of them as free.

Molly usually had grapefruit. And hot, creamy coffee.

God, she was beautiful! It was the hair and the blue eyes that did it. He kept track of her hairdresser appointments, eager to see the result, whether she left it long and flowing or wore it seasonally shorter, close to her head, in soft curls. It was her hair he loved most. In the car he nuzzled it. When they made love he swam in it, closing his eyes and going in face first, following it over her ears and around the nape of her neck until she screamed with pleasure. Molly loved his lean body. She said she had never felt any skin as smooth. That had been a revelation to him. He had never thought of his body as attractive, not naked anyway. Nor had he thought women cared much either way, as long as you had a stiff cock and made the right moves. She even thought his cock was beautiful. She held it in both hands like a museum treasure, some ancient Venetian vase she knew was valuable beyond price. Until she got excited. Then it might have been a dangerous rodent she was trying desperately to throttle, before it was too late.

Today he was early. A young, skinny, slovenly waitress who everybody else seemed to think was God's gift brought him his coffee and a newspaper. He didn't know her name, though God knows he had seen her often enough on an empty stomach. The coffee looked perfect, black and steamy, but he was surprised that it had no taste. Was it always like this? Why couldn't he remember? Molly, probably. She completely distracted him from everything else around him, even the financial pages. Patricia said the financial section was all he cared about, that he was a nut that grew on the money tree, the way moss grows on a live oak, and something else, something about DNA. Oh, yes. She said he was like a cell in the organism of the capitalist system that got its instructions from the financial pages, like DNA. What about Mike, he said, her brilliant husband, the stock-options king, doesn't he deal with numbers all day? Doesn't he read the financial section? All the stock market is, he told her, is betting on which company will make money, like a day at the races. She said, Oh, Mike. If you were musicians, she said, Mike would be a rock guitarist, playing to the joyous common herd. You'd be a cathedral organist, sitting all alone in your tower, scattering numbers like notes high across the vaulted ceiling and dropping them into the deeps of religious mystery. When I hear you talk about numbers, she said, I get the bends. Pat had never liked him all that much. All she ever saw in him were numbers clicking through the interstices of his brain, drying him up, making him more rigid and less caring than she thought he ought to be, locking him away like hard cash in an airless vault. God, if she only knew!

A flash of red appeared above the stock tables as she sat down, and he looked up and smiled. She smiled back, glowing, getting settled, and the blue eyes seemed to drive him deeper into the tacky Leatherette seat. She looked ravishing, an absolute knockout. "Good morning," he said.

She said, "I can't see you tonight," still smiling and barely moving her lips, as if she had merely breathed.

"What?" he said in alarm. In alarm, hell—in pain.

"I can't see you, not tonight. Clark won't be going out of town after all. I'm sorry my schedule's so unyielding right now."

He smiled, trying to pass it off as if it didn't matter, and said lightly, "I'm glad it's your schedule that's unyielding. I was beginning to think it was you."

Her smile bobbled a bit. "I'm sorry," she said again, looking at the menu. "Maybe toward the end of next week. I think he still intends to go." Loudly, she said, "I think I'll have the grapefruit. How about you?"

Clark Haverford. How he detested the name. Some sort of editorial director for a publishing house downtown. Always going out of town to meet with agents and writers. "I've been thinking about Clark," he told her. She looked up, frowning, warning him to be careful what he said. "It's all right, just a joke. Ask him this when you see him. The world is in such terrible shape you have to wonder, If God is the author of the universe, then who in hell is the editor?"

He laughed. So did she, after a moment. Then the waitress came and they were suddenly all business, as if they hardly knew each other.

He loved meeting her like this, almost as much as meeting her in private. It had begun in an unlikely way, with a phone call to her home—on banking business, of course. They had known each other slightly for a couple of years, ever since she had acquired her real estate license and begun sending him customers for land trusts. When he called, Clark happened to be away so she was in no hurry, and something he said reminded her of a story. They fell to bantering. Finally, he suggested they transact their business over lunch. To his astonishment, she accepted. It was, for the most part, a very straightforward business lunch.

They didn't see each other after that except occasionally in the bank, and he called her once in a while, again always in the line of duty. One evening he offered to deliver some papers to her house for a closing the next day, and there were drinks and some pot, and before he knew it they were rolling together on the floor, laughing uproariously. They had sex. They met again three weeks later in a motel in Morton Grove. It was fantastic. He had never had sex like that before in his entire life.

He began making phone calls to her describing how he felt in her naked company. He recalled the process of lovemaking in detail, from removing her clothing to the ultimate spasm. To his amazement, she responded. "My God, I'm wet!" she said. The next time he called they took turns describing the experience exactly as if it were taking place at that moment, the disrobing, the discovery of skin, the hugs and caresses and nibblings and pawings. "We can do this, I'm sure of it!" he exclaimed, and she didn't think it was mad. To him it was simplicity itself. It was an extension of his time-tested method of not being there, only in reverse. He wasn't there, but he was. He wasn't touching her and being touched, kissing her and being kissed, fucking her and being fucked—but he was! This kind of cooperative, creative phonic intercourse was absolutely new to him. He was thrilled.

Although they met secretly every few weeks, in the interim the telephone became their principal means of sexual communication. The silence on the line was their love for each other, their voices its means of expression. His voice was his cock, each intonation, each gasp, each colorful phrase a nuance of sexual love. As long as he could call her nearly every day, he discovered, he didn't miss her at all. Soon she seemed to be with him constantly, in his mind, and as time went on she came to be almost as vividly present on the phone as in actuality. By now she was far more real to him than his wife. Except when Sybil shocked him by something unexpected she said or did, she hardly existed at all. The outside world had faded into nothingness beside the sweet, ineffable source of all his happiness, Molly Haverford, her hair, her eyes, her lips, her body, all of which came to be encompassed in her voice, as if lips and tongue and throat were completely vaginal and his, courtesy of the phone company.

The fact was that he had not loved Sybil for years. It wasn't that they were all that ill suited to each other. It was just that his wife no longer gave him that extra bang he needed to overcome the pain he felt in this life. The pain had always been with him, it seemed, at least ever since his first run-in with Dutch. Only it wasn't Dutch, it was his mother, the first woman with glorious red hair whom he had loved. She was the one who, when he was five, had threatened to cut off his head if she caught him playing with his cock again—that's what he heard her say whether she said that or not. Only it wasn't his mother but Dutch he blamed, for his father had merely stood by, silent, hard-eyed, perhaps amused, as his wife, in her mild, insistent way, scolded her little boy for doing something she feared would get him into terrible trouble someday. It was she who cared about him, wasn't it? His father seemed not to care at all.

And so, plunged in despair, he secretly fought back. He didn't quite know why. At five he knew nothing of sex, of course. It had something to do with a deep, abiding concentration on the other person, such as romantic heroes, knights in armor and all that, displayed toward certain women to whom they were mysteriously bonded. A little later he discovered that it also had something to do with people taking off their clothes. He learned that when he was nine. Frank told him. Frank knew. He had seen Natalie naked. Natalie was new in their lives, an untouched, unsullied, untested, virginal force for good or evil. Their new mother. To Bryan she was all right to fantasize about because she wasn't his real mother and therefore not really his father's wife. In some strange way, she seemed to belong to Bryan—not his wife but nevertheless his. He had seen his sister naked, had seen the crack between her legs, so he could imagine Natalie naked. He tried everything to see her without her clothes. He walked into her bedroom when she was dressing, then stammered and backed out. He abruptly opened the door when she was taking a bath. But somehow she always covered her nakedness before he could see.

By the time he was eleven, he had a treehouse where he would sketch naked female figures on a pad of paper, dazzling and titillating the boys who made the climb with him with drawings of rather disorderly, ovoid-shaped bodies, two dots for women's breasts and scratchy V's where they legs were joined, barely recognizable females caught by surprise and transfixed on paper, like butterflies in a collection. The treehouse had been nailed together board by board in the crotch of an enormous tree catercorner from the house of his beloved, a scrawny girl in his sixth-grade class with long, dark, tangly hair and a narrow face and sensuous lips that were constantly sucking her teeth like hard candy. He adored her. It never occurred to him to imagine her naked. By the time he entered puberty, he was trapped sexually somewhere between treehouse art and outhouse reality, and not especially attracted to either. He was extremely cautious about being passionate in public. Privately, in his room, he masturbated, he was sure to excess, but once out the door he maintained an aloofness toward the girls he dated that marked him as pathologically shy. On the day in high school when he discovered how to beat death and danger by not breathing and by not letting his heart beat and by denying that he even existed, he knew he had also conquered sex. It didn't matter. It didn't exist. He stopped masturbating, he stopped having erections, he felt nothing at all.

When he grew up, having managed in adolescence to put his body out of his mind, he married a woman as nearly like his mother as he could find, someone who could keep him from ever becoming the kind of accelerated sexual being his mother had warned him about. Sybil was it. She looked nothing like his mother and had none of her softer ways, but she had his mother's implacable stare when she was crossed. He knew she was it because whenever she frowned he apologized, whenever she spoke harshly he cringed. In this way he knew he was safe, for he was observing the letter of the law. They had sex, of course. That was permitted because it was behind closed doors. In fact, Sybil was wildly and athletically passionate. She screamed when she climaxed, lying beneath him in the white cocooned center of her white-hot bed. At first her behavior startled him, but he soon grew used to it, and he found that he could climax without feeling much of anything at all. Sybil didn't notice. As long as he was there, inside her, his cock stiff and pumping, she was content to play out her fantasies alone. They had no children, of course. They desired none. To Bryan, it seemed criminal to bring a child into the world. He could not forgive Dutch for bringing him into it. Sybil had no time for having children. She served on a great many civic and community boards, and she said she had all she could do just bringing opera to Chicago.

Five or six years into the marriage, he began to wonder what real love was like. Almost immediately he found himself magically involved in a series of on-again-off-again liaisons with a number of women from whom he got great joy and much grief—the joy because they were flattered and sought to please him, and the grief because they were never willing to share his life. If they had, would he have divorced Sybil and married them? Probably not, but that wasn't the point. They eased his pain, a pain so profound and long-established that it had become as much a part of him as his cock. Probably he had chosen them deliberately, knowing that he would continue to be safe with Sybil because none of these others would have him. For one thing, they were all at least fifteen years younger and much too bright to get involved with a high-profile banker in a messy North Shore divorce. For another, they were put off by his eccentricities, by his anxieties, even by the very thing that had made them so responsive in the first place—the shrill pitch of his passionate search for true love. All except Molly, and she was inextricably attached to someone else. She claimed she loved them both. What she meant, of course, was that both her husband and Bryan gave her happiness by taking away some of her own pain. Both of them gave her an obvious reason for living, which otherwise she lacked.

He told himself that he loved Molly more than he had the others because she had revealed his sexuality to him. For the first time, he realized how much the rest of his life resembled a prison. Waiting for her in some hotel room, he saw how the room was like a cell and the waiting like an eternity. His work was a prison, his sleeping and waking. Being apart from her was serving time on a chain gang. Even the phone calls, delicious as they were, were only a temporary release from bondage, and an entire day in her company was merely a brief parole. The feeling that she could be with him around the clock, in his mind, became inadequate. He wanted more.

He tried to give her up, but it was useless. He always had trouble giving people up, even Sybil. It seemed to him that his falling in love, his habit of losing himself in others to relieve his pain, lasted longer than other people's, probably because his pain was more intense and more protracted. His need was greater, his desire was stronger, and therefore his ability to end a relationship was practically nil. But no matter how protracted and painful recovering from an affair was, he always got over it. Not with Molly. Each time he left her, he came to feel that he had died. He entered a profound emptiness, losing himself in the very kind of mindless void that until now had been, he felt, his salvation. By emptying himself, he had beaten death many times. Separated from Molly, he found both emptiness and death. Only through her, he decided, could death really be overcome. In his previous entanglements, years after they were over he had experienced recurring periods of longing and attachment, times when he could have instantly resumed an affair just as if it had never ended. But returning to Molly each time was like conquering death for good, like being born again, a new, perfect soul returning to earth.

Loving Molly, he thought of himself as a rock resting comfortably in the stream of life, washed by rushing waters and made smooth. Nothing harmed him, no hammer could touch him there, he was safe. What he forgot was that if a rock could be cracked by a hammer, it could also be cracked by ice.

At the bank, in midmorning, he got a call from Frank.

"I've got this ringing in the ears, probably the flu," his brother said. His voice was raspy. "Listen, I got a call from Pat. Jimmy's gone to the police. Emily's home, and she's talking about a baseball umpire who knew Natalie pretty well and was the man in the car, and they were blackmailing him for years, she and Hope, and Tuesday night they met him in the park and he killed Hope, honest to God this is true, and the police have gone down to get him. In Arizona. Are you following me? It sounds crazy, I know, but they're bringing him in and they're going to be questioning everybody to make sure they've got a solid case against him. Where were you Tuesday night?"

"Home," Bryan said. He knew instantly it was a mistake. He'd told the police something else. No, no he hadn't. Had he? No, he was sure. He had told them he was home. It hadn't seemed important at the time.

"So was I, but listen. I went out in the rain to get a paper the night Hope was killed and was gone for over an hour. Wait'll they find that out. Can you imagine what they could make of that?" Frank laughed, then went into a hacking cough. "I've got this cold." His voice was almost unrecognizable. "And now I can't hear. I called the office this morning but I can't find anybody to talk to. On the phone, everything sounds funny. I ought to be down there dealing with this client, but I can't even walk. My knee is still swollen. Bryan, are you there? You should call Dad. He wants to go to Arizona personally and take charge of the case. You know how he is. Pat says he's been walking in the park, looking for clues. He needs to be watched, I mean he forgets he isn't as young as he used to be, you understand me? I'd call him myself but I'm helpless. I can't even go to work, and somebody might have to go over there and sit on him. Call him, will you? Before he takes off by Greyhound or something."

Bryan dialed the old man's number. Very slowly. And when there was no more numbers to dial, he hung up. He called Molly.

"Hello?" she said. "Baird and Warner, what can we do for you?"

"Molly," he said, cupping the mouthpiece with his hand. His office door was closed, but he was taking no chances. "It's me. Just listen, don't talk. The police are picking up somebody in Arizona in connection with the murder. The next thing they'll do is bring everybody in for questioning again, to wrap up the case. Now listen, I want you to tell them I was with you that night. I told them I was home, but I wasn't. I was down here working, but I don't have any way to prove it. The place was empty."

"I can't tell them that." She sounded incredulous that he would ask her to.

"What? Why not?"

"I was home. So was Clark."

"Oh." He was dumbfounded. He should have anticipated that.

"Besides, how could they suspect you?"

"How would they suspect anybody? But I lied. And Frank, my brother Frank, he was out for an hour that night. They'll suspect anyone who hasn't got an ironclad alibi, you know that."

"Then ask Sybil."

"What?" She had never said the name before.

"Ask . . . Sybil." Her voice was cold. It was a completely unfamiliar tone, as if he were talking to a stranger. He found himself shaking.

"Sybil?" he said.

"Your wife. That's her name, isn't it? Look, I can't talk now."

"Molly, wait. You're right, I'll ask Sybil." He sat breathing, unable to think of what to say, and then he heard a click and the tone. She'd hung up.

He dialed his home.

"Yes?"

"Sybil. If the police ask you where I was Tuesday night, tell them I was home. It'll be simpler that way."

There was a considerable silence.

"What's the matter," she said at last, "won't she tell them where you were?"

Something froze in his gut. What did she know? Was she tapping every phone in town?

"Sybil," he said. "I don't know what's in your mind, but I have no idea what you're talking about. Who's 'she'?"

"Kim," she said. "The waitress."

"Waitress? What waitress?" He could see the girl's thin, slatternly features. Was it possible that Sybil thought he and this little package of dynamite were having an affair?

"I think you know, Bryan. Coffee every morning? Tea every afternoon? What do you have at night, something stronger? Kim called me last January, the morning you forgot your briefcase. We got to chatting. I wondered what you were doing, slumming in Winnetka. She told me."

The briefcase. He had remembered it and gone back and picked it up. The slut hadn't even told him about the phone call. Neither slut had.

Sybil said, "I think it's time you gave it up."

He felt the emptiness opening up before him. He pretended he hadn't heard. "I was working, Sybil, only I lied to the police, that's all. Now what will they think? I told them I was home. I wasn't home, I was at the bank, but no one was here to see me. Sybil." He leaned harder on his elbows, steadying himself. His voice came out almost in a whisper. "It isn't much to ask."

"Well," she said. It was a kind of exclamation, uttered in a ripe melonish tone, as if a revelation was now complete. He could picture her icy smile, and he knew exactly what she was going to say. When she did, it was like hearing an echo in the emptiness. "Why, of course, Bryan, you know I'll say whatever you want."

He said, "Thank you, Sybil," and put down the phone.

So she knew, and it was over. She would say he was home that night and never let him forget it. Molly. It was over. He thought he was going to faint.

It. Give it up. It was over.

All because of "it." And "they." Not to mention "and then . . ."

It seemed to him that his whole life was summed up in those words. "It" meant all the material things he had ever known, all his life long. The house, the cat, the dog, his bike, the school, the church, his little red wagon, the hat his mother wore lying on the floor of her dressing room, where she would never come back anymore and wear all those clothes, those soft, silky, long dresses that were so voluminous and smelled of dust and perfume. "They" meant her, and his brothers and sisters and grandparents and uncles and aunts and cousins, and yes, the postman and the grocery clerk, the junior high school principal, the gas station operator and yes, yes, yes, even his father who when the old man came into a room shut everybody else out because of what he represented and what he could do, his anger and his silence, his power, his approval or disapproval, his contempt, his way of absenting himself and withdrawing—not his love, for there was never any love, but his protection, the possibility of his protection, and the awful, debilitating withholding of his protection, not to mention the withholding of his love. "And then . . ."

Out of the "it" and the "they" grew what happened next: the "and then" that was so inevitable and so irreparable. You couldn't go back and undo it. "And then" was like the coming of war or famine—it just happened and no way to prevent it, it was like growing up and outgrowing the kid in you before you were ready or even had a chance to get really acquainted, he was gone, left behind like a pair of old tennis shoes on the floor of your room, and here you were in this tall frame of a body, not prepared for this but drawn without a pause into the "and then" that happened before you knew it, not even time to wish it away. You were almost glad it came, glad to have it over with so you wouldn't have to think about it anymore.

He sat staring at the door of his office, surprised not to see it banging in the wind. Of course there was no wind, no rain, no hurricane, no abyss.

Maybe that's why he had been drinking more lately, anticipating the end of it. Give it up. It was over. He was safe with Sybil now. But already he missed Molly like the devil.

11

Marcus Franklin Gillespie, Sr., picked up the phone and called his eldest son, Marcus Franklin Gillespie, Jr., about five o'clock, sounding crabbed and vindictive and churlish. Whatever cheer he might have felt earlier in the day seemed to have vanished. No, the old man said imperiously, he had heard nothing from Bryan. Bryan never called anyway, he was undependable, how could he make a reputation as a banker if he treated customers this way? Customers and family were exactly the same. If you didn't follow through with one, you didn't follow through with the other. People found out about you, they took their business elsewhere. Bryan may think he had it made, being Dutch's son, but you had to make your mark on your own, you couldn't sit around trading off your father's reputation forever. But that wasn't important. Dutch cleared his throat and spat, presumably into a handkerchief. The important thing, he said, was finding the goddamn killer.

Oh, Christ, Frank thought, Dutch was accumulating suspects like baseball cards. Why hadn't Bryan taken care of this? Frank was in the sitting room upstairs while below the kids were yelling and running in and out of the house, Clara doing her best to keep them out of trouble, but the kids were cousins, distant cousins, and they had never really liked each other. Now, living in the same house, they were starting to get on one another's nerves. Between the racket downstairs and his father's monomania and his own tiresome physical afflictions, Frank was feeling miserable. He had this inflatable knee that was blown up to the size of a small wine cask, the flu was making him achy all over, and now the hearing loss he had experienced for years without really noticing it had shut down his left ear. Helena said it was more than a hearing loss this time, it was an infection. Whether it was or not, he had an appointment with the doctor. He held the phone in his right hand so he could hear and tried to sound like a solicitous, fully competent elder son.

"Dad, the police are on their way to Arizona to pick up this guy, didn't Pat tell you that? It's all over, the whole sixteen years of it. So relax." He put his hand over his eyes. He shouldn't have done that—given his father a direct order.

Dutch gave a low growl and went on the attack immediately. "Don't you get it, for God's sake? All anyone can think of is kill the umpire. You think she was killed by a baseball umpire, for God's sake? Look, I've got an umpire here, and I've got Burt, who might have done it, he never tells you half of what he knows and doesn't know the other half, and then there's this jailbird lawyer I know about—he could have done it. All I know is it's somebody who's got it in for me, some punk I've been wrestling with all these years without knowing who it is, somebody with a hard-on for me who won't stop until he gets me. Maybe it's the umpire, maybe it's Burt, maybe it's the lawyer, maybe it's somebody else. Don't you see what I'm driving at, for God's sake? I'm the one. I'm the one they're out to get."

"Dad," he said. "Dad, listen. I can't talk anymore." What had Helena said, the flu had lodged in his inner ear? "Dad, I've got to go to the doctor. The flu has lodged in my inner ear. I have to get something for it, you understand? So I can't talk right now."

"Ampicillin," Dutch said.

"What?"

"Ampicillin. It's like penicillin. He'll prescribe some for you. I get it every few years, the infection. Makes you feel like you're inside a barrel. It's hereditary."

"Really?"

Dutch chuckled, but it wasn't a pleasant sound. "Sure. All microbes inherit this ability to fuck you over."

"Very funny, Dad."

"Now, what I'm going to do next is track down this lawyer who knew Natalie. Burt got his name for me. Did Burt get me his name because he's a good guy or because he wants to throw me off the track? Burt thinks it's amusing, did you know that? He thinks it's funny, this old cocksucker playing Sherlock Holmes. Of course Burt doesn't know Sherlock Holmes from the garbageman. Anyway, this defrocked attorney may be in prison or he may have lit out. Burt thinks he may have gone to Hawaii. You want to go to Hawaii with me?"

Frank groaned inwardly. "Dad, I'm sick, I can't talk now. They've got the man who did it, down in Arizona."

"Who says so? Emily? You should have been out here that night. It was dark, it was raining. You couldn't see three feet. You think a scared little slip of a girl could tell what was going on out there?"

"Dad, listen. Emily and Hope had been blackmailing him for years. He came to deliver the money. You think someone else came to deliver the money? This lawyer? He didn't even know about the money, he was in jail you tell me, or in Hawaii. Dad, be reasonable."

"Lawyers can smell money a hundred yards away. I know, I've dealt with many a lawyer over the years. Besides, the guy was a bad apple. He went to jail for stealing from a client. Sixty thousand dollars or thereabouts, Burt said. The client sued him, and he went to prison, and when he got out he took it on the lam. Don't tell me it isn't the lawyer. He knew Natalie. He was hanging around after I married her. Christ, she didn't do anything wrong, I know that, but she drew men to her like honeybees. She had that ability. You don't remember her the way I do. She was your stepmother. But she was the damnedest, loveliest creature I ever saw. She even kept in touch with that rock group."

"What rock group?"

"There, you see? You don't even remember. The world is full of things you know nothing about."

Frank's arm was getting tired, so he switched the phone to his other hand, but his ear roared. He switched it back. "Dad, all I ask is be careful. This could be hard on you, all this running around. It could be dangerous."

"What, Hawaii? Hawaii's not dangerous. It's beautiful in Hawaii. Well, you know that. Didn't you go there with Helena on your honeymoon?"

Frank said, "Yes." It came out as a sibilant croak. He remembered. Mountains starting at the bottom of the sea. Giant craters full of moon rocks. Twisting green mountain roads falling to sandy beaches. Windsurfing until every bone in your body hurt, just the way he felt now. Only he didn't have a weight problem in those days. He coughed, a long, hacking cough, down deep in his chest. "Well," he said, sounding strangled, "I just want you to take care of yourself."

"I know, I know," his father said, "you're worrying yourself sick about me. But you tell me this: Why did he kill a young woman and her daughter? You tell me that. And then we'll know who he is and why he's out to get me."

"Nobody's out to get you, Dad."

"How would you know?" Dutch hung up the phone.

Frank hung up, too. Down below, directly beneath his chair, his daughter was yelling angrily at one of her cousins and Clara was trying to make peace. He put his head back and closed his eyes. Helena had gone to the shop after dealing with the new house all morning and would probably be late getting home. She had contacted the movers, hoping to get out of here by Sunday. The movers said they couldn't get to it until a week from Saturday. He couldn't spend another week in this place. Don, Clara's husband, was beginning to look at him as if he belonged in a nursing home. Christ! Dutch was off on another tear, and down at the office Zelda the cat lady had been working over the client all day as if she were toying with a big fat mouse. By now she probably had Bennigan in the palm of her paw. Frank had finally gotten her on the phone in midafternoon, and she had been full of her impending triumph. She had great plans, something about a motivational meeting for two hundred of Bennigan's top time-share executives from around the country that would lead into an epochmaking push for his congressional candidacy. Only Zelda would think of that. Since their chat, he had begun to think of her as something other than a cat. Something in her expression, especially when she laughed, reminded him of some other animal. Not a dog. Was it a chipmunk? He had tried desperately to pin it down, but he couldn't. Could it be some kind of bird? She kept birds. She loved birds. Maybe it was some kind of rare orange and blue parrot. Anyway, there was nothing he could do at the moment about Bennigan. By spraining his knee, he had lost Bennigan's confidence. There was nothing to be done. Nothing.

He opened his eyes and saw his padded leg cast lying against a chair on the other side of the room, beside the wicker planter. Great gobs of greenery sprouted from the planter—Clara's special touch. Greenery flourished at all the windows, fountainlike ferns and large, scalloped leaves and here and there, set in their tiny individual pots, the tiniest plants imaginable, with little purple flowers that looked as if they had been cultivated by elves. Even some orchids. Who knew how to grow orchids in this climate? Didn't all orchids grow in Hawaii? They sure as hell didn't grow in Arizona, did they? Oh, God, the police would be back with the umpire in the morning and it would be in all the papers. Would the cops really question everybody all over again? Wait until they discovered he'd gone out Tuesday night to get a paper, eager to see himself and his falling-down house in print. He had watched the ten o'clock news, everybody gathered around the big TV set downstairs to watch him come out of his garage carrying his daughter and holding up two fingers in the V-for-victory sign. He hadn't remembered doing that. He hadn't remembered much of anything, not after they'd turned the camera on him. And right after the news he'd left the house, about eleven. No papers anywhere except the earlier edition, not even at the train station. He'd been gone plenty long enough to have whipped over to Skokie and—

Christ! This was getting to be macabre. He wasn't a suspect. He didn't even have a motive; in fact, being a member of the family gave him a motive not to. Anyway, the damned umpire was guilty, hadn't Emily said so? He'd gone after Hope in the park, thousands of tiny shafts of rain making millions of little bubbles on the pond, and oh, God, how awful! Well, they would bring him back from Tucson and that would be that.

So now all he really had to worry about was getting out of here and getting well. There were other clients beside Bennigan. He'd be fine in a week or two, provided his hearing cleared up. Funny, how he'd been worried about his weight, ten or fifteen pounds around the middle he couldn't seem to get rid of, and just when he'd been thinking of having all his clothes retailored his prayers were answered. He'd made a mistake, wanting to lose weight. He should have simply denied he was fat and let it go. Because when you get something you ask for, it's usually not what you expected. He'd wanted to lose a few pounds and he'd also lost his hearing. He felt only twinges of pain but heard a whole lot of white sound, as if he were inside a steel drum, just about what Dutch had said. That's what the music on the radio sounded like, a steel band from the islands. In the shower this morning he could hear every single spray strike his skull like the rain on the roof of his garage, even on his forehead and the back of his neck. He could hear the water hitting the bottom of the tub, and when he toweled off it sounded like sandpaper. His skin was a goddamn microphone! Combing his hair, he could detect each hair falling into place. When he shaved, over the buzz of the razor he heard each bristle being sheared off. Even chewing his food was an army with hobnailed boots marching over a creaking railroad trestle as distant thunder rolled.

But worse than the amplified sound was the isolation he felt. Maybe that's what was getting to Dutch after sixteen years of solitary concentration on Natalie's death. Thinking somebody was out to get him! It would be laughable if it weren't so sad.

Helena got back at six-thirty. She was tired from the day, and he could have done with a little more sympathy. Dinner, toward which he moved relentlessly in his stiff, padded cast, arriving finally without applause, looked delicious but was socially bleak. He had no appetite. Don was working late at the office, perhaps deliberately, and Clara had fed the kids early. Helena was grateful for that. The adults sat at the dining table picking at a veal roast and vegetables, a dish much like the kind he and his wife had enjoyed in Paris bistros after a day of walking around the city. Clara was all nerves from her afternoon of monitoring the children. Frank's ear was full of white noise.

"What?" he said. Clara had spoken.

"I said is your knee any better?" she asked pointedly, as if she had asked, "When are you leaving?"

"About the same," he replied. "I'll be seeing the doctor at eleven in the morning, about my ear." He looked anxiously at Helena. "Could you—?"

"I'll drive you."

"Good." He said to Clara, "The veal is wonderful. I remember—"

"Glad you like it," Clara said, as if she couldn't stand to hear what he remembered. He was hurt. Each ensuing day in the house, he had become increasingly conscious of having to restrict the length and scope of his reminiscences, which he enjoyed relating. They had not been enthusiastically received. But he kept reminding himself that this wasn't really family. Clara was at the edge of the family circle, and

Don was far outside it. He wasn't someone whose memories or current wisdom they valued because those matters were part of the lore of the clan. He wondered why Helena, who was in the circle only by marriage, cared. How could she be so endlessly interested in his comings and goings, his thoughts and experiences? She loved him, of course, but . . .

As they were getting into bed, he asked her, "Don't you ever just want to get off by yourself, away from me and the kids?"

"Why ever do you ask that?" She looked at him curiously.

"Well, you give so much of yourself. You have so much to do." He pulled the blanket up under his chin and eased himself over next to her. "You have so much patience."

"Why, Frank," she said, sounding surprised and pleased. She reached over, turned his face toward hers and kissed him. "I go off to the Far East on buying trips every year. Do you want me to go more often?"

He looked at her in the half dark. "I just keep wondering," he said, "how we found each other."

She laughed and kissed him again. "Pure, dumb luck," she said.

The next morning, the first day of the weekend, he slept in. Helena woke him about nine-thirty, saying he had a visitor. She looked mildly perplexed.

"Who?" he said, cupping his good ear at her.

"Of all people," she said, "Mr. Bennigan."

He sat up and swung his legs to the floor, then bent over, clutching his knee. She got him to his feet and half carried him to the shower. As he was shaving, she came into the bathroom and said, "He drinks a ton of coffee. He and Don are discussing the Pittsburgh Steelers. What do you want to wear?"

"Something casual."

She laughed. "Well, I wasn't going to lay out your tux."

He laughed too. "The turtleneck, the blue slacks. What's he want? Does he want to break my other leg?"

"I haven't the faintest. Why don't you just wear your jeans. It's Saturday and you're sick."

"Okay. I feel better. The knee is still awful, and the ear's the same. But the flu's better."

He repeated his symptoms to Bennigan as they sat in the family room where Don had left them, giving Frank a big smile that appeared to be genuine and a far-from-gentle nudge in the ribs, the way he must have thought jocks acted in the locker room.

"Well, I'm glad you're getting better," Bennigan said, leaning back with his cigar. He hadn't lighted it. Maybe Clara had given him one of her pointed stares. "I wondered what happened to you out in Galena." He laughed. "I thought maybe you had a hernia."

Frank had to laugh at that. He didn't care anymore what Bennigan thought of him. He waited to hear what the big man would say next. Had he come all this way to fire him from the account? That didn't seem to matter either. He wondered why. Maybe he wasn't as well as he thought he was.

"You know," Bennigan said, "we've been all over the place with Zelda and those guys on this project. Yesterday they hit me with a proposal that really surprised me. Did they talk to you about it?"

Frank tried to remember his conversation with Zelda, wrinkling up his nose. "A motivational meeting, wasn't it? Surprised me, too. I'm glad you liked it."

Bennigan gave him a slight frown. "Are you? Is that you talking or the client relationship talking?"

"What do you mean?" Frank said.

"Well, to tell you the truth, I didn't much care for the idea. A big party to work up political support among the people who work for me? It's a waste of time, and anyway, if you knew these guys you'd know they'd laugh all the way through it, at least behind your back. It's unnecessary. If I don't already have them by the balls, why am I in business? I'll tell you what, it's going to be essential to throw a few high-powered parties if I'm going to get elected, but you can skip the guys who work for me. They're in already."

"They already see you as money in the bank."

"Sure. That's why I was hoping you had nothing to do with the party idea."

"I didn't. I was home sick." Frank laughed, then sobered. "But Zelda was sure you'd go for it."

"That's what I mean. She sold herself on it all over again, that's all. You know what I call her? Saber. She has these tiny little fangs."

"Like a tiger?" Frank was astonished. "Like a cat?"

Bennigan smiled. "So you saw it, too. Don't get me wrong, she's a helluva woman, bright as all get-out, and competent as hell. But I'll tell you, I like your style, Frank. I want you to come to work for me."

Frank couldn't speak.

Bennigan went on. "I need somebody like you in the campaign, and not all behind the scenes either. I've seen you in action. You're convincing and effective, and you think on your feet. If I win, I'll take you to Washington in a leading role on my staff. If I don't, though that's not likely, there's a substantial place in the company. How do you like it?"

"I'm shocked," Frank said. "I thought you were here to fire me."

"I've fired Fells and Matthews. I can run my own campaign better than they can. But I can't run it all. That's where you come in. You're a manager and also good on the creative side, at least that's what I hear from the people I've talked to. I think you understand me. I think you can put me in perspective with the voters." He stood up, put out a hand and pulled Frank to his feet. "Think about it. I'll call you in a few days, when you're feeling better." He nodded a couple of times, then grinned. "And don't let me hear you fell off a building or something." He turned away with a wave. "I'll find the way out. I've got to go, have a driver waiting."

Immobilized, Frank watched him go out the door toward the living room. He could hear Don's voice, and then Clara's. Where was Helena? He couldn't wait to tell her. Washington! Suddenly his face fell. Washington? Washington, D.C.? How could he possibly move to Washington? He heard the front door close.

"I can't," he told Helena. He was standing in the yard, looking down at a bed of petunias, and she was sitting ten feet away, behind him, in a swinging, plastic-covered couch with a plastic overhead awning. "I can't possibly make a move like that."

"Why not?"

"Well," he said, turning toward her, "there's Dad."

"Is that all?"

"There's the family."

"Your father's gotten along pretty well all these years. He and the rest of the family can look after each other."

"But—"

"Is it the move, or is it the size of the job?" She was studying him.

He smiled. "You sound like Bennigan."

"Pretend I am Bennigan. What are you going to tell him? That you can't leave Chicago?"

Frank looked down at the petunias. They were all colors, and fresh as morning. They looked newborn.

"Come over here and sit beside me," he heard her say, "and tell me what you'd say to Mr. Bennigan."

He turned and grinned at her, then made his way carefully over the new grass and sat down heavily on the swing. "I guess," he said, "I'd have to say to you, Mr. Bennigan, that it sounds like a hell of an idea to me."

She grabbed a biceps and, leaning toward him, blew in his ear. He winced at the roar of sound.

"I'm sorry," she said, "I forgot. But that's the way you are. Sometimes I forget where I am." He sat grinning and swinging, pushing off on his good leg. "And now we'd better get you to the otolaryngologist, so you can hear Mr. Bennigan when he starts talking salary."

It was later that afternoon, when Frank woke from a nap, that Jimmy called with the news. "They're back from Arizona," he said, "and Albert Hemphill's with them. They're questioning him now. It's a long story."

"Did he do it?"

"Could be. Not everybody thinks so, though."

"He's denying it?"

"Yes, of course he is. He says he knew Natalie for years, even better than anybody suspected. He knew her mother, too, right before she died. He saw Natalie fairly often. It was kind of a family relationship, though never publicly acknowledged."

"They were related?"

"In a way. She was the mother of his son."

"My God." Frank sat silent, taking in the information, sorting it out. "Then he had no reason to kill her."

"Seems like it. At least the son swears he didn't. The son is here now."

"He lives here?"

"He came back with him, from Arizona. He's been living down there all this time."

"So?" Frank said, puzzled. "What are you getting at?" Then it dawned on him. "Eric."

"Eric."

"But the father—"

"Right. Eric's father was supposed to be some California hotel clerk. But when she married him, she gave him a son, ready-made."

"I'll be damned."

"Albert Hemphill had a wife in those days. So she married somebody else, and that man became the legal father."

"And that's where Eric went when his mother was killed? To live with his real father in Arizona?"

"That's the story. He's here now, at my house. We're going over to see Dutch."

"Does Dutch know?"

"Not yet."

"Jesus, Jimmy, be careful how you tell him."

"I'll be careful, but don't worry about it. You should see Eric. He's a big guy with a fortune and a family. Dutch will fall in love with him all over again. As a matter of fact, they're a lot alike."

"I'll be damned," he said once more. "Okay, let me know what happens. I've got to tell Helena."

He hung up and went to find her. The leg was working a little better, and he thought the ampicillin was beginning to take effect already.

12

Dutch rustled around the apartment, getting things ready. Eric! Who would have believed it? He gathered up dirty dishes in all sizes from the floor beside his armchair, some rich with mold and stinking to high heaven, and carried them gingerly across the room, stopping to straighten the rug with one foot, and made it to the kitchen, where he slid them into the sink as gently as time allowed, making a terrific noise that surprised him as much as if his old childhood dog Jackie, dead sixty years, had let out a howl, surprised, too, that the sink could contain as many dishes as it did without spilling over. He ran the hot water and let it foam up until the crockery was covered over with suds, half expecting to see Ginger Rogers rise up out of her bubbling Hollywood bath and invite him to dance with her naked—such unbidden but not unwelcome visions sprang to his attention frequently these days. He rammed his hands down into the soapy, scalding water, seized a plate and began to scrub, but soon it became apparent that nothing would remove all of the accumulated grease and grime but a good soaking. So he left the kitchen and ran the sweeper, a sturdy old Hoover that sounded as if it were grinding up the rug in its teeth and spitting it out. He went into the corners, too, getting balls of fuzz, and down the hallway and into the bedroom, skirting odd slippers and shoes and items of furniture, picking up discarded shirts and underwear as he went and tossing them toward a closet so dark and so seldom inspected that it was a mystery even to its owner. He shut off the machine and stuck it in the closet, too, and then he pulled and yanked the bedclothes into submission, found the pillow jammed between the mattress and headboard, and smoothed everything down with his hands. He stared at the digital clock from his latest birthday until he was sure he was seeing the numbers correctly, then trotted back to the kitchen and washed and rinsed all the dishes the drainboard would hold. Unbuttoning his shirt and ripping it off, he headed for the bathroom, where he washed under his arms and patted his face with shaving lotion, glancing with something like hatred at the strange, wicked-looking mask in the mirror as he wet down his shaggy hair and gave it a quick brush. Back in the kitchen in a clean shirt, he had cleared the drainboard and was starting on the pots and pans when his buzzer sounded, sending a little electric shock up his spine. He scooped up a cup and saucer and some old breadcrusts off the kitchen table, tossed them into the sink and trotted to the door, drying his hands on his shirtsleeves and breathing heavily. He opened the door and stared.

Who was this man? Not quite as tall as he was, but big and brawny, with Eric's somewhat slanty eyes and wide cheekbones and jaw. A neck like a Bears' tackle, gray silk shirt open at the throat, soft dark-leather jacket, jeans and boots. Looking back up, Dutch saw the familiar yellow hair and the straight, even rows of teeth bared in the boy's old smile. Jimmy was grinning, too, standing just behind him, and Eric said, "Hello, Dutch." The voice! Deep and assured, and then he came forward and Dutch took a couple of steps back, suddenly wary of this fully formed, sun-scorched, midthirtyish adult male stepping out of the poster of the door frame and going past him into the room, a big dark hat in his big brown hands. He wasn't quite as physically impressive when Jimmy came in, because Jimmy was a solid-looking specimen, too, but there was a look of maturity and energy about him that nearly floored Dutch. That, and just a glimmer of Natalie in his face and build.

Dutch said, "Eric," and couldn't think of anything more to say. Somehow they came together and embraced, Dutch feeling the solid back beneath his hands and the rough cheek against his. When he stepped back he was amazed and angry to find tears in his eyes. "Well, sit down," he said, turning and catching his foot on a corner of the rug. He kept his balance, though, and went quickly toward the kitchen. "Sit down, I was just finishing up the breakfast dishes. I won't be a minute." He went to the sink and ran the cold water, splashing his face with it, getting rid of the tears. He felt suddenly empty, all hollow, and realized he hadn't had lunch. He cleared his throat of everything but the catch in it and called out, "You boys want a drink? You hungry?"

"We're fine, Dad," Jimmy called back. "We just came to see you."

When he returned they were sitting down, Eric at the window, his head turned to look at the park, his chin lifted in a profile looking just like Natalie.

"You look like your mother," Dutch said.

Eric turned his head slowly, as if he had Natalie's steady, resolute clock in him, too. "I've been told that," he said, and grinned.

Dutch sat down and they talked about the past and present family, Frank and his house and his knee, Patricia and her successful marriage, Bryan and his bank, and Raymond and Emily. "They're questioning the son of a bitch right now," Dutch said, getting to the point, and Eric said, "How do you know he's a son of a bitch?" and his father replied, "Got to be. Even if he didn't do it, got to be." He asked Eric how he made his money and what he did with it. Eric said, "Construction. I've been in housing and office buildings for sixteen years, ever since I went down there, built all over the

Southwest, Las Vegas to Dallas. Started with an earthmover and a couple of trucks, now I've got me an entire army of equipment in half a dozen locations, a hundred and forty-five employees and a hell of a payroll. I've got most of the money in bonds but I'm sure as hell into banking, Dutch. If I ever make a really bad mistake, I'll have bankers all over me like a flock of armadillos." He grinned. "Mighty nice family, too. Tucson. Three grandchildren for you. I brought pictures."

They looked at the snapshots, a beautiful brunette wife and two girls and a boy. The girls looked like little Natalies, except they had their mother's dark hair. Dutch glanced up from the photographs in his lap and, finding no words, gazed dumbly at Eric across the room. "Fine," he said at last. "Fine family."

They wound up going to the park. Eric insisted. It was like a memorial grounds, the new green everywhere, submerging the pale mudded aftermath of the flooding, and the faint green haze of the very first leaves spread against the sky. Eric wanted to look at the place where his mother had died, and the pond, and two one-car Skokie Swifts clattered by on their Saturday schedule as they stood quietly, the three Gillespies, old and young, thinking of death and renewal. Finally Jimmy put his hand on Dutch's arm and fixed him with a look, and Dutch wondered, What in hell is coming at me now?

Jimmy said, "Eric's not up here alone." He smiled hesitantly. "I mean, what a day to come up from Arizona, right?"

Dutch thought for a moment, then looked at Eric. He grinned and shrugged. Dutch said to Jimmy, "Something to do with the police?"

He nodded. "And Albert Hemphill."

Dutch's eyes narrowed. "This Doc fellow have something to do with you?" he asked Eric.

"You're going to hear about it from somebody," he said, "so I wanted to be the first. Doc's my daddy. My real, actual daddy."

Dutch said, "Natalie?" just to be certain.

Eric nodded.

Dutch walked a few steps closer to the brown waters of the pond and looked into them. It seemed to him that the late afternoon reflections showed him all of the past in one endless watery panorama, murky but entire. He turned. "Well then," he said in a strong voice that dared contradiction, "he didn't do it."

Eric said, "I didn't think he did."

"Well then," Dutch said, "we ought to go down there and get him out of jail."

Jimmy said, "He's not in jail, Dad. He hasn't been charged with anything. They're treating him as a material witness, just asking questions. Apparently there's a lot to go over." He added emphatically, "An awful lot."

Dutch joined them and they began walking slowly along the curving blacktopped walkway. "Doc's not your ordinary kind of guy," Eric began. "He's got a criminal record. He's broken a few laws. Not your ordinary run of parking violations either—I'm talking federal laws. He was into drug running, and he was in the pen, and even other than that you were right, he's been a kind of son of a bitch. He has a family that's had some terrible problems, not the least of which is that he got some of his kids hooked on drugs and one of them died. He was married when he met my mother. That's why she arranged for me to have a substitute father, back in California. See, it started way back with Natalie's mother. Doc met her in California, back in the early fifties, and—"

"Wait a minute, wait a minute," Dutch said, stopping. "Was this guy a baseball umpire or wasn't he?"

"That's what he was when he met my grandmother," Eric said, "umpiring in some Pacific minor league, back in San Francisco, I think it was, and she was working in a downtown hotel bar. They fell in love, of course. She'd been married several times before, just like Mother, and had lots of admirers. He was a little younger, about thirty. She was seven or eight years older, and the way he tells it she was the best-looking woman he'd ever seen, and he'd seen lots. They didn't get married because someplace along the line he'd already gotten hitched, but they stuck around together through a couple more husbands. He tells me he was just sure they were meant for each other, like something made in heaven. Hell was more like it, though, because she started fading. I don't know whether it was cancer or what. Dora was her name. I've got an old picture of her at home, and she looks to me like, well, like Sally Field. Cute as a button. He'd moved down to Tempe by that time—"

"Arizona?"

"Yeah, and he was umpiring in the majors by then and traveling all over and seeing her whenever he could. She was getting very sick, and finally he persuaded her to come down with him and he'd take care of her. She didn't want to go on a plane, so he rented a car and drove her himself. They made it as far as Kingman, but she'd passed out in the back seat and he was scared. He got her into a motel in Kingman—"

"Wait a minute," Dutch said sharply. "Where was Natalie all this time?"

"Back in California," Eric said, "working in a bar as a go-go dancer, I guess." He grinned. "She was always kind of proud of that, it being her first real success, even though it didn't last long."

"She'd been living with her mother though."

"Up until her mother got so sick she had to go to the hospital, and then Doc took over, more or less. He couldn't always be there, but he paid the bills and came when he could. Then Dora got better, and that's when Doc took her to Arizona. Mother stayed behind, working and taking singing lessons. She was just over seventeen, I'd say, at the end, when her mother died."

"In that motel in Kingman?" Jimmy said.

"The very night they checked in, I guess. I guess it was pretty awful. Doc said it was a nightmare."

Dutch looked off at the stand of trees beyond the pond, where the Skokie Swift ran. "What'd he do, bring Natalie down there to live with him?" His voice shook with anger. Son of a bitch, he thought. What was it, child rape? He shivered.

"I know what you're thinking," Eric said, "but it wasn't that way." He moved around him so that they faced each other. "Dutch, that wasn't it."

The old man gazed at him. "What year was this?"

"It was 1956 when she died. She was thirty-eight."

Dutch's gaze wandered. "That was the year my wife died. Jimmy's mother." Then he said, "Natalie was seventeen?" Eric nodded. "But for Christ's sake, you'd already been born!"

"Nearly two years old, being taken care of by this seventeen-year-old go-go dancer back in San Francisco. But it's not what you think. Natalie's mother had been sick for years. Natalie had gotten to be crazy for Doc, and Doc loved her, Doc honest-to-God adored her."

"Oh, for God's sake!" Dutch snorted.

"He did!" Eric looked like the stormy five-year-old Natalie had brought into the house that day so long ago, Dutch thought. Getting red around the ears, defending his mother. Standing up for his old man, too. "He did!" Eric said again. "Dora knew all about it, she gave it her approval. Don't forget, she'd been through two other husbands by then. It wasn't like Doc was fooling around in the same house with her daughter, behind her back. And besides, Doc wasn't so old, only in his early thirties."

"Twice Natalie's age," Dutch said, before he thought. He himself had been more than twice her age when he married her. There was considerable silence as the two young men glanced at each other and then elsewhere. "All right, let it go. But tell me this, didn't you say he had a wife, for Christ's sake?"

Eric took off his hat and wiped his forehead with the back of his hand. "He did. He married her when he was only in his twenties. She was from upstate California, and he took her to Arizona when he moved down there, and they started having kids."

"But he was taking Natalie's mother down there?" Dutch stared at him, furious.

"Well, she was sick, and Natalie couldn't take care of her and me both, so Doc did it." Eric put his broad-brimmed hat back on and pulled it even with his eyes. "Doc's a different kind of guy. He's always done pretty much what he wanted to do, and I guess his wife let him do it. He's divorced from her now, but I've met her, and I don't know, she's just different. Nice enough, I guess, but the whole family's kind of what you might call amoral. I mean, they don't care about all the things everybody else cares about. They don't live just the way most people live."

"Huh," Dutch said, tight-lipped, looking away.

"You mustn't feel bad about Doc and Natalie. Doc loved her."

Dutch scratched the ground with his shoe. "She kept seeing him, I know that. She saw him that last night, of course. She must have seen him other times."

"He told me the first time he saw her up here, after you were married, was that time she was away from home for a week, in Springfield."

"The PTA convention," Dutch said, hard-eyed.

"I guess so."

"I had a detective on that one." He glanced at Jimmy. "Sorry. I just got a wild hair up my ass. It was foolish. He didn't find a thing. Natalie scared him off." Suddenly he smiled, and looked quickly at the ground. She sure did, he told himself. And she'd forgiven him just as he forgave her now. The thought was there in his mind: Natalie, come back. Come back and let me look at you.

Jimmy said, "Eric, you said they were all on drugs, the family."

"They surely were," Eric said. "Doc started running drugs up from Mexico in the sixties. He'd met three or four guys who'd escaped from a federal penitentiary up in the state of Washington, sent up on drug charges. One of them was a friend of his, a former baseball pitcher for Kansas City, and he brought them all down to his house in Tempe. Another one had drug connections in Mexico, so Doc, in his spare time, began carrying money and guns into Mexico and coming back with Far East heroin. Then he'd escort the drugs on up to California, all in this motor home, driving along with this young Mexican girlfriend of one of the guys and her sister. He said he'd sell it in the locker rooms sometimes during the baseball season—at least he had some players he was supplying."

Dutch could hardly contain his wrath, but he did.

"Doc's family started using heroin, I guess living in close proximity with these ex-cons and their girlfriends and all. It's tragic. He provided it to his older son, and his half sister, and he had a thirteen-year-old son who overdosed. It killed him. It nearly killed Doc. He said nothing's been the same after that."

Dutch stared at him. "He killed the boy?" His eyes grew wider. "My God, yes, you were down there when it happened, I'll bet!"

"No, not till a couple of years later, when I was fourteen."

"Fourteen? You were seventeen or eighteen when you left here for Arizona!"

"I mean the time I went down there to camp."

Dutch died a little death. "You visited this nest of vipers while you were down there at camp?" He felt Jimmy touch his arm, gently restraining him, reminding him. He pulled angrily away.

"No, not then. He came to see me on visiting day. I guess my mother arranged for that to happen. I never saw his house but once, when I left here for good, after Mother died. I just showed up, and he said, Yeah, I could hang around."

"You must have seen a lot of him up here over the years."

"Maybe half a dozen times is all, when Mother would take us kids out for lunch or something."

"But Natalie kept seeing this guy, this drug runner? This man who killed his own son? And she let you see him?"

"She didn't know anything about the drugs. He never told her about any of that. I didn't know either, till I got down there. It took me a while to catch on, and then finally Doc just told me all about it."

"But—" What happened, he wanted to ask. How did you escape? How have you prospered, and survived?

As if he had heard the questions, Eric said, "I didn't have anything to do with them. I went to work right away and got my own place in Phoenix. He treated me real well, loaned me the money for my first equipment, staked me to the business." He saw Dutch's look. "Yeah, I know, drug money. Well, I didn't think of that at the time. And don't forget, he made good money in baseball, too. He was a big-league umpire for twenty-seven years and had a lot of investments. In bonds. Sure, he set me up. I let him. You could say he owed me."

Dutch shot him a curious glance with more than a little admiration in it. The kid had a good head on his shoulders. "I guess maybe he did at that."

"Well, I paid him back. I started making it right away. Those were good years in Arizona and Texas. All I had to do was be there and work my ass off."

Dutch grinned. He put out a gnarly hand and patted him on the shoulder. "Oh, golly," he said. "Oh, golly." He looked off at the dying sun. The sky was misted over. "I think we'd better go back in and sit down. All this is just about as much as I can take in one afternoon."

Jimmy said, "Just a minute." He walked over to the water's edge, bent down and put something in the water. Dutch knew what it was, one of those leaf boats that sailed out and never came back, just like a human soul, released and gone forever. When Jimmy returned, he took Dutch by the arm and they walked along, Eric trailing. "You know, Dad, you took all that pretty well. You didn't blow your stack once."

Dutch harrumphed. "You worried about me, were you, wondering how I'd take it? Natalie and all?"

"Not really. I just didn't want to jar you."

"No problem. No problem at all." He looked around at his strange new son. "Hey, Eric, come up and walk along." Eric came alongside, grinning, and Dutch put an arm around him. "So," he said, "three kids and a handsome wife. Well, aren't you something! You'll have to stay for dinner. I've got some steaks in the freezer, must have been there a year. If I don't throw them on the grill now, they'll turn into lumber."

Eric said, "I've got to go see Doc."

"Oh, yeah, Doc. Well, maybe tomorrow or the day after. We'll find us a good restaurant. Is it a deal?"

"Deal."

"Jimmy? Stay for dinner?"

"I'll come back after I run Eric down to headquarters." He slapped Dutch lightly on the back. "I always got a kick out of watching you try to barbecue."

"All right then, on one condition. Let's all go in for a minute and have a drink."

They went through the gate in the high metal fence and then the parking lot, chattering like schoolboys. But crossing the apartment house lawn, Dutch stopped and turned to Eric. "Say, tell me one thing. I don't understand this man who says he's your father."

"He *is* my father."

"Yes, but look here. Let's say he didn't do it, let's just get all that out of the way. But if he's innocent, when the girls start blackmailing him, why doesn't he go to the police? Just because he's running drugs, is that it?"

Jimmy said, "Sure. He went to a maximum security prison on a drug conspiracy conviction six years ago and was bounced out of the umpire's association. After doing four and a half years of a twelve-year sentence, he wasn't going to take a chance with the cops. No way."

"All right, I can understand that, I guess. But if the girls thought he was almost certainly guilty, I don't understand that either. Why wouldn't they tell anybody? Why blackmail? Just to get rich? Ten or twelve thousand dollars, or even fifty thousand, won't get them rich. And besides, they were wild about their mother, they'd have done anything for her. Why wouldn't they point to him and say he did it?"

"That's just it," Jimmy said. "They wanted to protect their mother's reputation. Natalie didn't want to hurt you, Dutch. She wasn't doing anything wrong with this guy, but she was afraid if you found out you'd blow your wig. She didn't want to risk losing you. The girls just kept her secret, that's all."

Dutch still couldn't quite grasp it. "What kind of girls were these anyway? Who would do a thing like that, keep it a secret all that time? And think up that damn blackmail scheme?"

"They were always pretty unusual," Eric said, "always playing little games they made up, whispering secrets, working out secret codes. They had all kinds of private clubs growing up, every couple of weeks a different one. I mean private. Even I couldn't get in. The only one who could get in was Raymond, and he didn't know what the hell was going on." He laughed, shaking his head.

"You see Raymond?" Dutch asked.

"Yes. He's getting to be a pretty old guy." He gave another laugh. "Guess what, he has a date tonight."

Jimmy said, "With an older woman." He added, "It's okay. I know her."

Dutch said, "He'll be all right. He's a good boy."

"Yes, he is," Eric said.

"See Emily?"

"Not yet."

"She'll be all right. I talked to her this morning. She's coming along fine." Dutch stooped down, picked up a stick and tossed it into the street. "Only thing is, we still don't know who did it, do we? What do we do now?" He got no reply. "Well, there's the crooked lawyer. There's Burt."

"Burt?" Eric said, sounding surprised, and a little alarmed.

"Oh, I forgot. You liked Burt, didn't you? I mean he was a

father to you in a manner of speaking. Well, it probably wasn't Burt. No, I'm sure Burt's completely in the clear."

Eric laughed and said, "Well, its just that he was so crazy about Natalie. He used to talk about her to me when I was little, after their divorce, when he'd come and see me. All kinds of questions about her all the time. He was jealous. Jealous of you, too. Oh yes, he'd sit there and tell me how much he still loved her, just like they were still married and he was my father. You know. But then, I think what he was trying to say to me was that he wanted me to think of him that way."

"Well, then," Dutch said, clearing his throat, "there's still the lawyer."

"I knew him," Eric said.

"You did?"

"Yeah, a young, good-looking guy. He'd come over every so often, after the divorce, and take Mother out to dinner. He always brought me something, teddy bears and stuff. I thought for sure, out of all of you, he was the one she'd marry."

Dutch fixed him with a look. "Not me?"

"No," Eric said. "I couldn't imagine it. When I found out it was you, I was mad as hell."

"Why not me?"

He grinned. "Too fucking old."

Dutch put his shoulders back and stood up straight, looking over at the park. "Too old, huh?" He took a deep breath and exhaled in a rush. "Well, it's a good thing I kept that strap around." He moved off toward the apartment building. "Come on," he said, "it's time I gave both of you a good licking."

Upstairs, Dutch took down three heavy crystal whiskey glasses from a high shelf, along with an unopened bottle of Kentucky bourbon. "Boys," he said, "I've been living alone a long time, and it still surprises me whenever I look in the cupboard and find a clean glass. How did this get in here, I ask myself. How'd I get to be such a great housekeeper?"

Jimmy laughed and moved to the far end of the room, where the view was open fields and transformers and light manufacturing.

Eric said, "I've got to use the bathroom." He went out the door and down the hall.

Dutch twisted the cap off the bottle, and when he heard the bathroom door close he said, "Jimmy, I hate to say it, but that Hemphill guy's guilty as sin."

Jimmy turned, his face almost indecipherable in the backlight from the window. "Looks like it," he said. Dutch filled the glasses and then opened the freezer door for the ice. His son came over and picked up one of the drinks, holding it up to the light, all amber. "Then again, maybe he isn't."

Dutch, reaching for the ice tray, stopped and looked at him. "What does that mean?"

Jimmy sipped the bourbon and made a face. "Hemphill's hinting there was somebody else," he said, "somebody we don't know about."

Dutch removed the tray and shut the freezer door. Using both hands, he cracked the plastic container sharply and a piece of ice flew out and struck the floor. He started to look for it, then said, "Oh, the hell with it." He glanced at his son, tall, fair-haired, a genuinely likable young man. Thank God for the Gillespies of this world, he thought, law abiding, drug free and straight-arrow. He heard the toilet flush down the hall and said quickly, "Hemphill's lying, isn't he, trying to pass the buck? How could he be anything but lying? How could a man like that do anything but lie?" When Jimmy didn't answer, he said, "Who is it then, the lawyer?"

"Maybe," Jimmy said. "His name's Todd. We've got people in Hawaii and Washington trying to find out where he is, and where he served his time."

"Who's 'we'?"

"Channel Five. The network."

Dutch said, "You won't find him. Those guys are never around when you want them." He popped a handful of ice cubes and dropped them into the glasses. "Anyway, who cares what prison he was in?"

"Only if he was in the same prison Doc was," Jimmy said.

Dutch picked up his glass but didn't drink. He could hear the Arizona boots in the hallway, this stranger who had reentered his life, and suddenly he wondered how much Eric knew that he wasn't telling. When he saw him in the doorway, he gave him the remaining drink and said, "Here's to the Gillespies, young and old." They drank. "So, Eric," he said, "why'd you go off like that and never tell us where you were?"

Eric held his glass in both hands, like a priest consecrating wine. "I don't know," he said. Then he looked straight at Dutch. "Yes, I do. Right then I hated every damn one of you. It was like you let her die." He put the glass down on the countertop. "As far as I was concerned, in my head, it was like all of you killed her in some way." Dutch felt his jaw go slack, then clamp and bulge. His face grew hot. Some desecration seemed to be occurring, of Natalie's memory or of the family or both. Eric said, "Right then, I just never wanted to see any of you again, ever. Like, if I did, there'd be hell to pay between us."

Dutch could no longer contain himself. "Well, fuck you, then," he said. His hand swept out, spinning the drink to the floor and splattering Eric's boots on the way. The glass struck and rolled, unbroken.

Eric stepped back, surprised. Then he grinned. "See, you ornery old bastard? You just proved my point." Before Dutch could reply, he put an arm around his neck in a kind of gentle wrestling hold. "Now, listen up, I love you, old man. I'm not just a grossed-out kid anymore." Dutch struggled, but this Arizona son was all muscle. "Doc's just as tough as you," Eric said, "but he lacks your sometimes invisible manners and your damn heart of gold. Now you just lighten up and fix me another drink or I'll whup your ass for you." Then he stepped away and laughed out loud. It was a laugh Dutch hadn't heard in sixteen years. "Oh, my Lord," Eric chortled, "wouldn't that be something, me locking horns with my old man?"

Dutch, breathing hard, glanced at Jimmy and winked. Natalie! Oh, Natalie! he thought, wouldn't you be startled, seeing us now? Wouldn't it be delicious, seeing how all of us miss you so?

13

Jimmy hung around the back yard watching the pale, misted moon long after Dutch had gone to bed. He had delivered Eric to the police station before dinner, and by the time he was back Dutch had the charcoal going. It had turned cooler, and the sky was choked with torn gray cotton. They ate in the kitchen, two huge steaks and a mountain of french fries from the freezer. "I'm on fish and vegetables mainly," Dutch said, "but every now and then I need red meat. Whenever I feel kind of run down, I put on a steak. Remember that. It strengthens the blood."

"It's been a long week," Jimmy said.

"That, too," Dutch said.

His father had turned in early, shortly before nine o'clock, looking dead tired, and Jimmy had cleaned up the kitchen. Then he sat in the living room, in Dutch's chair, where he could look out at the park, and read the *Wall Street Journal*, Dutch's favorite paper, enjoying the quiet while he perused the stock tables, remembering what Bryan had told him once, sell high, buy low, and stay with the blue chips, and wondering if he should get back into IBM. Right now Raymond would be boogying, probably at the Hard Rock Cafe, with a dark-haired, delicately sculpted Greek statuette named Jan. Maud Leightly would be at the governor's political party, trying to glow brightly through a series of speeches so pedestrian, Jimmy's producer cracked, that you wouldn't walk across the street to hear one. He wondered about Emily and nearly picked up the phone to call Pat, but it was getting close to the ten o'clock news so he turned it on and stayed with it all the way through. Doc was there, on the screen, shielding his face at the airport that morning, moving down the concourse with a political entourage. He got a glimpse of Eric, looking angry, and of a young attorney who seemed to be without either emotion or guile and who warned viewers in a cultivated voice that his client would have nothing to say, was without guilt and might sue for violations of his civil rights. Jimmy wondered where they had picked up the attorney. His speech was not Southwest or farm belt.

The weather forecast was for possible thunderstorms in the early morning hours. He was watching a baseball player crashing into a center field fence when the phone rang. He turned down the TV sound. It was Eric. "He's been charged with Murder One," his brother said, "but they're going to let him out on bail. Goddamn cocksuckers."

"How much?"

"Two hundred thousand. I'm good for it."

"Good for you. When?"

"Oh, the lawyer says he'll be out in half an hour or so." He sounded discouraged.

"You want to bring him down to my place?"

"No thanks, I don't think he and Raymond would mix too well. Burt's father's some kind of political wheel out here, and he got us into the Skokie Hilton. Burt found a couple of off-duty deputies to sit out in the hall and keep the peace."

"Sounds like Burt's been busy."

"Yeah, he knows his way around this town pretty good."

"Newspeople there?"

"Lots of them. TV trucks and all. It's a goddamn circus."

"Has he said anything, your father?"

"Nothing you don't already know. They don't have a case. The lawyer says it's all circumstantial."

"Look, if you see a guy with the Channel Five truck with his cap on backwards, tell him I'll be there in fifteen minutes, okay?"

"I'll tell him, Jimmy."

"And stick around the truck if you can, where I can find you."

He put down the phone and looked up to see Dutch standing in the doorway. His hair was rumpled, but he looked somewhat regal in the familiar faded maroon robe that went almost to the floor. Jimmy got up. "Sorry to wake you, Dad," he said. "That was Eric. They just charged Albert Hemphill with murder."

"Good," Dutch said. He went over to the TV set, where some comedian was silently being hilarious.

Jimmy said, "Well, I'll be going. They're waiting for me at the police station."

He was surprised to see Dutch grinning at him. In the flickering light from the TV screen, his father's smile was ghastly. "It's just like Christmas, isn't it?" he said.

"Christmas?"

"Getting out of bed and opening the gifts. Celebrating."

"You mean Hemphill? You feel relieved or what?"

Dutch glanced off toward the windows overlooking the park. "Relieved isn't the word, no." When he spoke again, his voice was huskier. "Sad is more the word. I always did feel depressed at Christmas."

Jimmy put on his jacket. "I'll call you in the morning if I don't get back here tonight," he said as he went out. He heard the roar of laughter as his father turned up the volume on the TV.

Police headquarters and environs were an electronic madhouse. Television trucks jammed the curb in front, and camera crews and clumps of bystanders and media types were scattered up along the sidewalks. He checked in with the camera crew and then, seeing Eric's broad-brimmed dark hat fifty feet away, pushed through the throng and found him in earnest conversation with Burt. It was the first time he could recall seeing Burt in his deputy's uniform. The fat man looked at him through slitted eyes and half smiled. "Look who's here," he said. "A chip off the old block."

"So you knew Doc all along," Jimmy said, at the same time spotting Sheila, the newshen columnist, a few feet away talking with some of her male colleagues. He waggled his eyebrows at her, and she smiled back.

Burt glanced at Eric before replying. "I never met him," he said. "I just knew him as Doc." He sounded depressed, but sometimes that was just his style.

"But you knew he was down there with Eric."

He smiled his noncommittal, maddening smile. "Maybe I did. So what?"

Jimmy smiled back. "Why, I'm just glad somebody was keeping track of Eric."

"Yeah," Burt said. "It's not like his so-called family gave a damn." He turned away, cutting off the talk. Jimmy couldn't recall any conversation with Burt that had lasted for more than two sentences.

He said to his brother, "So what about Todd, the lawyer?"

Eric looked at him in surprise. "Why should Doc know anything about the lawyer?"

Sheila had come over and was sparring animatedly with Burt, and Burt was doing what he always did when there was a pretty woman around, eating it up and making a play for her. Jimmy caught her eye and she looked over and said, "You don't mind, do you? A tale of three fathers. It's heartstopping."

He shrugged. "If Eric doesn't."

"He doesn't, do you, Eric?" She added defensively, "It can't hurt anybody. It could get you some sympathy, I mean it could help the defense. That's what you want, isn't it?"

Eric grinned. "We already got a lawyer, lady," he said.

Jimmy said to her, "Why don't you and Burt go talk about it? We've got things to discuss."

"Sure," she said. "You're not mad at me, are you?"

"I'll call you." He watched her take Burt in tow, like a tugboat maneuvering a freighter into port. He said to Eric, "If they were in prison together, what does that mean? I get lost at that point. Is Doc still saying there was someone in on this with him? What's he saying, anyway?"

Eric said, "You just can't tell with Doc. If they did know each other, which I doubt, he could have sold Todd on some kind of scam. He's good at that."

"You didn't ask him about any of this?"

"I told you, you don't ask Doc anything. To tell you the truth, there were plenty of times, when I was a kid, I was just plain scared of him. Partly it was the drugs, and those guys he was mixed up with—they'd just as soon kill you as look at you. There was a girl killed down there, oh, about ten years ago, a girlfriend of one of Doc's partners. He used her to make deliveries, Doc said. Doc was accused of killing her, but was never charged, for lack of evidence. But he was scared. I think he knew who did it, and for a while he talked about maybe going into the witness protection program. He was deep in debt, I know that, maybe owed the guy eighty thousand or so, and they had a falling out. That's when he quit using heroin himself. Too dangerous, he said. He also got divorced about that time, and went off to Reno to marry the daughter of a friend of his, a perky sixteen-year-old. She ran off later. You could never tell what Doc was going to do next. He started drinking more, I know that."

"And all this time he was umpiring ball games all over? How could he keep his head straight?"

Eric laughed. "I never said he did. I imagine there were plenty of times out there behind the plate when he didn't know if the ball was coming or going. But he seemed to have an instinct, like once he pulled that mask down over his face he knew exactly what he was doing. Just plain natural talent, like he could do it blind."

Jimmy said impulsively, "Let me go over to the hotel with you. I want to talk to him."

Eric shook his head. "No, he won't talk to you. His lawyer's made sure of that."

"It's got nothing to do with my job. Just you and him and me, just family."

Eric ducked out of the way of a cameraman heading for the building. "Well, you can come along, that's fine with me. But I don't know if he'll talk to you." All the camera crews were leaving the trucks now, swarming past them up the walk. "He must be coming out. They'll get into one of those cars up by the entrance. We'd better go in yours."

The Hilton was two or three miles away, just off Skokie Highway's congested commercial strip. Across the street from the entry was a shrubbery-shrouded Jewish cemetery and, next to it, across the highway, a huge shopping center called Old Orchard. They waited in the hotel parking lot, watching Doc's car pull in, followed by the media caravan, until they saw Burt getting out of his car. He waved them in past a lobbyful of newspeople and up the elevator. Upstairs more reporters crammed the corridor near the elevators, waiting with notebooks and cameras, settling in for a long wait. At the corner of the hallway, where it bent toward Doc's suite, a cop sat at a desk keeping the press at bay. Another deputy stood at the door. They went past them all, Burt officiating without saying a word and leaving them at the door.

Doc was such an ordinary-looking man. He came out of the bathroom drying his red, sun-toughened face with a towel, and he grasped Jimmy's hand hard but briefly and went over to a chair by the window and sat down. He was obviously very tired. Sixty or so, gray-haired, balding a bit, no particular look on his beefy face, no more than five feet ten, a thick body that seemed to have no special features at all except for his muscular shoulders and the gray hair on his chest, where his shirt fell open at the neck. Dark trousers, dark socks, feet jammed into well-worn, well-shined black shoes with heavy soles. One hand up to his forehead, no expression in the eyes. What Eric was had clearly all come from Natalie, unless of course it was all some kind of rude joke, Doc being Eric's father. But what reason would Natalie have to lie? Maybe Albert Hemphill was so ordinary-looking a man that what he had passed along of himself to Eric was simply unidentifiable. The perfect drug runner: elusive because he looked so anonymous.

Jimmy sat down opposite him and said, "So why do they call you Doc?"

His hand came down quickly, and he said, "So what were they supposed to call me? Yogi?" His hands kept going up and down and sideways throughout the conversation. A nervous man? Jumpy? Not the eyes. They were dead level all the time, unblinking, impersonal, seemingly uninterested in what was taking place. His husky voice was absolutely unremarkable. He spoke every word exactly the same, not hurrying, not hesitating. And the hands, when he spoke, kept flying into action.

"I never knew a man named Todd in prison, no lawyer by that name, no sir. If he was a shyster who took money from his clients that wasn't his, and he was tried around here, they wouldn't put him in maximum security in Washington state, would they? Of course they might have, they move people around. Maybe I knew him, but by some other name. I spent most of my time on the island, a farm camp. It was the same farm camp my partners escaped from years before. Inmates were always escaping. You went there if you could qualify, if your behavior was good and your time short. It had a dairy, a hog farm and a saw mill. I worked in a three-story building, the powerhouse, and it was the plum job, the swing shift. You watched the automatic boilers and there were no guards there. Off duty we sat around and smoked marijuana, you know how it is? There were two hundred inmates and only a light guard. No fences, only water. Those who escaped got away at night with a boat, or at low tide you could walk across. Then you walked into town and went where you wanted. I never did that. I waited for my parole.

"Eric? Fix me a drink out of the little cabinet there, will

you? There ought to be some bourbon in there, that's a good boy.

"Eric's a good one, makes a good, honest living. Baseball was never enough for me, but he's stuck with his business through thick times and thin. I always watched he never got too close to me, that would have done him in if he'd got interested. He was a thing apart, and I kept him apart, out of respect for his mother. I didn't kill her. Shit, you think I did? How could I? I was mad enough to kill those sisters of yours, but I didn't. They had to be out of their goddamn minds, do you know what I mean? Kid games. Reckless. You don't stay alive doing things like that if you're reckless. I thought I could stop it, but I didn't kill the kid. I had my own son die, thirteen years old. They said I killed him, but it wasn't like that. I provided both my sons with heroin rather than see them get the bad stuff off the street. I couldn't keep them from using it, could I? I didn't tell them to use it. So he was young and stupid. The twenty-year-old son got off the stuff altogether, that's one good thing that came of it. So did his sister. So did I. The younger one mixed it with barbiturates and alcohol and he died. I miss him.

"If I killed your sister, whatever happened to the money, did you think of that? I left three thousand dollars in tens and twenties that night and nobody ever saw it again. Who's got it? Somebody, not me. Maybe it was a bum, just some bum who killed her and took the money. Maybe somebody else. I'll find out who, I promise you that. I won't take the rap for this thing. I don't know why he did it, but I'll find out, you wait and see. I threw the package over the fence, and it was raining like hell, and then I just got out of there, went back to the motel and left the next day. There was no way I was going to say I was there. I'd been paroled, remember? I'd have been strung up on the spot. No way I was going to say anything, any more than I'm going to tell you everything you want to know now."

"Ah, thanks, Eric." He emptied the glass and handed it back. "No, that's enough for now."

"Same reason, more or less, I didn't say anything when Eric's mother was killed. I was always being suspected of something, don't you know how that is? My son. A girl I knew in the drug trade and almost got sent up for. Natalie's mother, died in my arms in a motel in Kingman, Arizona, and they wanted to hold me on it until they determined it was natural causes. Caused them great disappointment. Do I look guilty? Is that it? I've got no idea who killed Natalie any more than I do her daughter. How would it have helped, me coming forward? All I'd have done was get myself in a jam again. I told the kid to come down to Arizona. Eric. Leave this place, I told him, these people are no good. Nothing personal, I just thought he could do better someplace else. His mother didn't do so good up here. I looked after the kid, isn't that enough? I didn't want trouble, and it was just my word against—well, who would have believed me? I didn't have an alibi, I looked guilty as sin. You reporters sure as hell would have had a field day. If you'd looked into my affairs and found out about the drugs, or even my association with known criminals, I'd have been out of baseball. Face the facts. A man has to protect himself. If he can't count on himself, who can he count on? You don't become a big-league hitter, or catcher, or an umpire either unless you deal with the facts. It's either a strike or it's not. It's either home safe or you're out. I've been out, and once is enough.

"Of course I didn't count on the girls writing me that letter. I never told Eric, why should I? It was my problem. If they'd have been anybody else, it would have been simple. Over and done with. But I couldn't play it that way. My hands were tied. So I paid up. Let them have their little game is the way I looked at it, until—well, let's just say I thought maybe there was a way I could deal with it and nobody would get hurt. That's all you need to know about me. Take it or leave it." He got to his feet and stretched. "Now if you don't mind I'd like to get some sleep. Must be something in the air up here, or else I'm not as young as I used to be. Eric, you take the bedroom, okay? I'll take the couch. I always sleep better next to the exit."

Jimmy told Eric he'd be staying with Dutch, and then he went downstairs and found a phone booth in the lobby and dialed his own number, downtown. It was after eleven and most of the press were gone now, just a skeleton force to keep an eye on things.

Raymond answered, sounding sleepy. "Hi. Where are you?"

"Skokie. I'll be staying out here with Dutch, tomorrow's Sunday and there's the wake, and afterwards we'll probably get together at Pat's. Maybe you can come out on the El and I can pick you up."

"Okay. Where's Eric?"

"He's out here, in the Hilton. How'd the evening go?"

"Just great. She's great. We had a great time."

"Sounds good."

"Very good. You were right. She likes me."

"Raymond, you know Eric's natural father, this guy Doc? He's been charged with murder."

There was a long silence. "Then it's over," Raymond said. "They got him. It's all done."

"Looks like it. Raymond, Doc says there was somebody else connected with this in some way. He won't say who. Did Emily say anything that night about anybody else? Anybody at all?"

"I don't think so. She was going on and on." There was another pause. "No, she didn't say anything I can think of. It's all shadowy in my mind, that night. Just Doc driving off, she said, and then coming back over the fence, like all of a sudden there he was, coming through the trees."

"Okay. Go back to bed. I'll check with you tomorrow about picking you up."

"Okay. Good night."

Coming in, he woke up Dutch, feeling uneasy in the presence of this biblical prophet in his long dark robe whose red-rimmed eyes seemed to suggest hellfire and brimstone if he was roused one more time. Then he took off his pants and shoes and went to sleep on the couch. When the phone rang, his watch said twelve midnight.

Eric said, "He's gone. I heard the door close and got up to look. He just disappeared. The cop came back ten minutes later with some bicarbonate Doc had sent him down for, said he wasn't feeling so good. I can't find the car anywhere, the one the lawyer rented. Where the hell would he go at this time of night? I'd better call Burt."

"Do the newspeople know about this?"

"Hell no. They're mostly gone anyway. He must have gone down the stairs."

"Eric, did Doc hang out with anybody up here that you know of?"

"No, nobody."

"Well, go back to sleep. There's nothing you can do. As long as he shows up in court he's okay. Of course if he skips—"

"That's what I'm afraid of. He's just had it up to here with all this. He'll go to Mexico. Hell, he probably has a whole 'nother damn family down there. He was down there for almost two years one time. Said he was trying to start a Mexican baseball league. He just might have enough kids down there to start one by now."

"Unless he went to see whoever might have been in on this thing. He seemed determined to clear himself, remember? How long's he been gone?"

"A little over half an hour."

"All right, call Burt then, maybe he can get somebody to check the airports. I don't want to get the newsroom into this as long as there's a chance of getting him quietly back into that hotel room without anybody finding out he was gone. Call your lawyer first, though, and get his advice. We don't want to do anything to prejudice his case. I'll come over there in half an hour if I can. If you have to go out, leave word where you'll be, okay?"

He lay back, listening for Dutch and hoping he wouldn't

awaken, wondering what in God's name was going on. What was it Doc had said? I'll find out who, and why he did it. That sounded like Dutch, but the funny thing was that Dutch had been right days ago about the umpire, and maybe he was right about the crooked lawyer. Could Todd be right here in town, not in Hawaii at all? Had there been a meeting, a rendezvous? He tried to imagine the park that night. He could picture Doc throwing the money over the fence and taking off, all right, but he couldn't make him come back into the park. It didn't work. Had it been Doc coming back or a confederate? Who? Todd? For the life of him he couldn't get the lawyer over the fence either. Like Doc, he just wouldn't go.

He saw Dutch come into the room and sit down by the window, staring out. A light rain had begun to fall. How long had it been raining? Dutch, he noticed, was looking at him now.

"I said so in the first place," his father said hoarsely. "It was somebody out to get me."

It's been about all he can take, Jimmy thought. He said, "How do you mean, Dad?"

"He's been out to get me from the beginning. He finally found a way." He coughed a hacking cough and spat into a handkerchief, and the phone rang. Jimmy picked it up and his producer said, "You're not going to believe this."

"Why not?"

"Your brother's house is on fire, out in Lake Forest. That's two houses in one week, Jimmy, in case you're not counting. I sent the truck out."

"Bryan?" Jimmy looked around for his pants and saw them hanging over a chair. "I'll get right out there." He hung up the phone and pulled on his pants.

Dutch said, "Bryan's always been a strange boy. Even Natalie, who didn't dislike anybody, even she thought so. She never said a word, but I could tell. What's he done now?"

Jimmy didn't know what to say. Tell the old man or not? He said, "I just have to go over and see him about something.

I won't be long. On the other hand, it could be a while." Tell the old man about it later. Why upset him now? He sat down on the couch to put on his shoes.

Sounding far away, Dutch said, "I had this same goddamn feeling that night when Frank's house fell down. Like the family falling apart, you know that I mean, Jimmy?"

"The family's not falling apart, Dad."

"I had the same feeling the day your mother died. And Natalie."

Jimmy got up, wondering where his jacket was. But instead of looking for it, he went over to the window. It was raining harder, and across the street the trees were beginning to bend with the wind. He said, "Dad, when I was little, I had this idea that by being born I killed her."

Dutch snorted. "Whatever put that idea in your head?"

Jimmy waited, knowing he should go but hoping to find an explanation that wouldn't sound harsh. He said, "I thought you did."

Dutch looked at him for what seemed to be a long time. "I may have thought that once. I don't anymore. How can you blame a kid for something like that?"

Jimmy turned and saw his jacket across the room. He went over and put it on. He said to his father, "Will you be all right here for a while?"

"Yes, just tell Bryan for me he's a horse's ass, and if he's in some kind of trouble it's probably well deserved."

Jimmy smiled. "You have a low opinion of Bryan."

Dutch waved the remark away. "I told you. Bryan's a strange boy."

Down the rainswept road that went north through the thick woods walling off Lake Forest from the expressway, he saw the glow of the fire. There was nothing to indicate it was Bryan's house until he reached the first police barricade, a hundred yards away from it.

"Gillespie?" The cop in the black slicker looked at him hard as he handed back the press card. "You a relative?"

Jimmy nodded. "Anybody in there? Anybody hurt?"

"You'd better ask the lieutenant." He pointed, as if there were no fire roaring and crackling up ahead, silhouetting the tall oaks that surrounded the place. "You'll find him down the road. Leave your car here, as far off the road as you can."

He pulled off onto the narrow shoulder bordered by white-daubed rocks and ran through the trees toward the house. He could see firemen pouring streams of water on the flames licking through broken second-story windows and eating away the timbers of the roof. The main floor seemed relatively untouched. In the drive he found the fireman in command and identified himself.

"Is my brother in there?"

The chief was not a big man. He reminded Jimmy of the wiry, dust-smeared coal miners in Celtic movies. "Not that we can tell," he said. "But she is. She's dead. The bedroom was pretty well gutted by the time we got here. Fire's under control, and we're looking at arson as far as I can tell. There's another body on the first floor, but it's not her husband."

"Who is it then?" He wanted to shout and stamp and scream, but he knew he had to go through the obligatory litany.

"Albert Hemphill's the name. We found a twenty-two caliber pistol in his belt and a bullet wound in his chest, larger caliber, maybe a thirty-eight. We found this, too." He opened the door of the command car, reached in and took out a scorched, blackened metal box less than a foot long. Shielding it from the rain, he opened the lid. Inside, illuminated by his torch, was a soiled, water-stained brown paper wrapping, and inside that were stacks of wilted tens and twenties, what looked like twenty or thirty bundles ringed by rubber bands. "Three thousand dollars, more or less, found beside the guy's body." The chief slapped down the lid and put the box back on the seat of the car. "So what happened here? You could say he broke in, found the money, started the fire, got shot for his trouble. Who shot him, the wife? She was upstairs in bed. The husband? Your brother's not here, so we can't ask him." He pointed toward three uniformed policemen gathered just beyond the nearest fire truck. "Maybe they can tell you."

Jimmy thanked him and plodded through the rain toward the huddle of Lake Forest cops, but at the fire truck he hesitated, then veered off toward the woods, heading quickly for his car. At the road he saw the Channel 5 news truck pulling up to the barricade. He went on past it in the darkness, feeling sickened. For once, he felt, he had accumulated all the facts his body could stand.

14

Emily was sitting on a big wicker blanket chest, looking more diminutive than ever in the early morning light. She was wearing her blue silk robe, her dark hair trailing over her shoulders. Dresden doll, of course. Pat wanted to grab her and shake her, see if she rattled, see if anything internal was chipped or broken.

"We always said it was for Mother. We did it for Mother. She was so scared Daddy would leave her. Hope said Bryan knew. He was part of it. Hope saw Bryan that night, the night Mother died." She looked calmly at Patricia. "He was supposed to pick you up at the library but he came back and said you'd get a ride home later, with a friend. So Mother left. Bryan put us to bed. I remember when you came home you were surprised, and you said, 'Where's Bryan?' It scared me, thinking we'd been alone so long without even knowing he was gone, but when you found out he'd been there all along, down in the basement, I went back to sleep. Only the next day Hope told me he'd gone out when Mother left, and later she saw him sneaking in the back way. He told her he was looking out for Mother, and she believed him."

Pat looked at the big plainclothes detective sitting in the armchair, writing in his notebook. They were in a second-story sitting room before a large picture window topped by cut glass. "Bryan was often 'not there' even when he was there," Pat told him. He stopped writing and looked up at her. "He could be in the next room and not hear you call, just be absent. When I found him in the basement that night, I assumed that was it, that he'd just disappeared somewhere inside the house." She looked at Emily. "I didn't know he'd been out. Where did he go?"

"Out," Emily said, as if that explained everything.

The detective, whose name was Deiffenbacher, nodded and began writing again. How could he write all this down and make it make sense? He had phoned before eight o'clock, apologizing for calling so early on a Sunday, saying he and his partner wanted to come out and talk to Emily. In the last ten minutes, he had hardly said a word.

Emily went on, as if Pat hadn't said a word either. "Mother asked us about Bryan sometimes, where he was, what he was doing, things like that. He sat for us a lot before he went away to college, whenever you weren't available. She didn't like him to sit because she was worried about him. You remember, he'd walk into her room when she was dressing, you know, accidentally, and didn't seem to know where he was. She said not to talk about it around Daddy because he might be angry."

The detective cleared his throat. His voice was soft and husky, his manner firm but passive, as if he was always waiting, holding himself in check for the next thing that might happen. In this he was something like Michael, Pat decided. Two big men who had the strength not to aggress, unless it served their long-range purpose. Less fun than her husband, though, she thought, more professionally disciplined and self-contained, but then of course he was working. "Did this kind of thing ever happen before when he was sitting?" he asked Emily. "This walking in on you when you were undressed, did it ever happen to you?"

"Oh, no," Emily said, "never. But Hope used to call him Touchy-feely."

"What was that?"

"You know, Touchy-feely, like the toy. She'd try to run whenever he tried to pick her up. She said he didn't watch his hands. It was always in fun, though, they'd always be laughing." She smiled, but it was more like a wince, not her usual glowing model's smile.

"Your brother laugh a lot with you, did he?"

"No, hardly ever. Except when we'd play games and he'd chase us."

The detective looked out the window, which was brilliant with sun. "And he'd just walk into your mother's bedroom without knocking?"

Emily nodded. "She said he was getting to be too old to do that."

"What age was this?"

"Oh, high school. I remember when he was just about to leave for college, it happened the day of their ninth wedding anniversary, and Mother was trying on her new dress, getting ready to go out." She looked at Patricia. "That was another time you were supposed to sit with us but Bryan sat instead." Her eyes grew wider, startled. "Oh, yes, I remember now, that was the night Mother got so scared."

"When was that?" Patricia said. "I don't remember that."

"That's because Mother never told you. You got a date at the last minute, I remember, so Mother asked Bryan to sit. But then she got so worried at the dance that she came home early. She even made up a story to tell Daddy, that she'd forgotten to ask you to sit and so we were alone and they had to go home right away. She even called Bryan from the dance but there wasn't any answer because Bryan was down in the basement in one of his 'not there' moods. On the way home she called again and you answered, but they came home anyway.

Pat remembered that. She'd gone to the movie, filling in on a double date, but had felt wretched because it was her period. She'd come home to a ringing telephone. Natalie had been frantic. And while they were talking, Bryan had come up from the basement, just like the night Natalie died. Where was he now? Jimmy had called this morning about the fire and the newly dead, Sybil and Mr. Hemphill, and about Frank's car being stolen. What kind of visions did Bryan have down in that basement? And if he'd actually been out of the house on the night of Natalie's murder, as Hope reported, where had he been? Was he some mysterious angel of death, or just someone who drew death to him, like a lightning rod in a thunderstorm?

"Mother told us what happened the night of the anniversary," Emily went on. "She tried to make light of it because she'd been worried for nothing. 'Girls,' she told us, 'you know how I get when I panic, I forget everything, I forget where I am.' But she stopped worrying about Bryan after that because he went away to college."

Emily smiled her dazzling smile of lifelong friendship then, and Patricia's heart nearly melted away. She wanted to gather her in her arms and have a good sisterly cry. She also wanted to hit her, as if that would make it all make sense.

Detective Deiffenbacher said, "You said your brother was in it from the beginning. Could you tell me a little more about that?"

"Yes, of course." Emily's smile faded and her gaze seemed to turn inward. She looked trapped and vulnerable, as if she was holding her breath, uncertain as to what the next moment might bring. "Well, it seems crazy, I know, but Hope said Bryan was looking after Mother, he was her protector, just as we were."

"Why did she say that?" His tone was suddenly sharp.

"Because when she saw him earlier that night, when Mother drove off with Doc, Bryan was in his old car, going after Mother. That's why Hope waited up for him, and when she saw him come in she was sure everything was all right."

"Why? Did she think everything might not be all right?"

"I don't know. Maybe she thought that if Bryan was following Mother, something might be wrong. Anyway, when Mother got into Doc's car, Bryan was waiting in his car down the street, and when he drove by Hope waved, but he might not have seen her."

"So he followed your mother the night she was killed."

"Yes. And Hope was ecstatic because she said we had Raymond in the club, and now Bryan was in the club."

"The club." It was a question.

"The club to protect Mother from Daddy finding out."

"And what would he find out?" The detective was being extraordinarily patient.

Emily said, "She was afraid Daddy would think she was doing something wrong, seeing Doc."

"And you knew she wasn't."

"Of course. That may sound naive, but we were right about him. Doc is Eric's father. So even back then, Eric was in the club, too, sort of."

The detective drew back a little, as if someone had swung at him. "You knew then that he was Eric's father?"

"Of course. Nobody told us, but in the pizza place we could hear them talking. It was very noisy so they thought we couldn't hear, but we could."

Deiffenbacher seemed to relax. He sat back with his eyes nearly closed. "So you protected your mother, and you protected everybody in the club, including your brother Bryan."

"Well, Hope said otherwise the club was no good, like a country divided against itself."

His eyes opened wide and he smiled. "Abraham Lincoln."

"She read that, yes. She was always reading constitutions and history. She was an excellent organizer. She said Bryan was, too, because of the bank. She said he really ran the bank because he had such a fine organizational mind. That's why she told Doc about him."

Deiffenbacher wrote that down. "When was this?"

"When Doc said he wouldn't give us the money. He said he wasn't going to go on making payments the rest of his life for something he didn't do. Of course we didn't believe him, even if he was Eric's father." Her eyes flared, and she said to

Pat, "And I don't care what you say, Bryan wouldn't burn down his house, I know he wouldn't. Anybody could have been in that house and shot Doc and set it on fire. Doc could have brought somebody along, someone he was working with, maybe one of the drug gang Eric told Raymond about. It's all purely circumstantial. Right now nobody cares what's even happened to Bryan. He could be dead. His body could be in the basement or out in the woods." She glared at the detective. "He didn't burn his house or shoot anybody. He'll prove it to you when you find him, if he's still alive. So why don't you go out and find him?"

Exasperated, Pat said, "Emily, stop! Nobody's said he did anything except he might have taken Frank's car—borrowed it, I mean. Mr. Deiffenbacher is just here to establish some facts, and so far you've been very helpful." She glanced at the detective. "I'm sorry to interrupt."

"That's okay," Deiffenbacher said gently.

Emily said, "Why would he take the Porsche? He has three cars of his own."

The detective said, "That's a good point, Emily. The car's gone, that's all. The keys may have been left in the car and somebody stole it. That happens all the time, especially when it's a Porsche or some other expensive make—we usually find it somewhere down in Chicago. But the more information we have, the better chance we have to establish the truth. You can understand that, can't you?"

Emily nodded. Yes, Pat thought, it's impossible to imagine Bryan stealing a car or setting fire to a house, the house where Sybil lay dead, burned to a crisp right in her bed in that beautiful stark white filmy lacy now blackened bedroom. Albert Hemphill, poor man, is dead, and Bryan is gone. Just gone, that's all. And he had nothing to do with any of those things, so let's concentrate on other family matters—how Dutch is going to like being put into a nursing home one of these days, and when Jimmy will finally decide to get married and settle down, or do you have to settle down first? And will Frank make up his mind to take that political job and move to Washington, D.C., and can Helena find a way to break the lease on the house they were planning to move into in Kenilworth? And what will happen now to Raymond, poor, motherless college boy, and to motherless-fatherless Eric, working on his second Arizona million, and to poor, confused, motherless Emily, who for years has been trapped in a web of plottings and imaginings and secrecy and guilt, woven by an older sister in the mad or mistaken belief that anything goes if it's to honor the memory of a mother who was murdered, just as she herself was going to be? And here am I, she thought, sitting with a huge, well-meaning detective, talking to a Dresden doll on a wicker chest, trying to draw out of her a coherent story about incredible, horrible things, and Michael, oh Michael, what must you think of us!

". . . so let's just talk about what we know," Deiffenbacher was saying in his kindly, monotonous voice. "How did your brother get involved in all this? You just went to him and told him about Albert Hemphill and asked him for help?"

Emily twisted her hands together, looked up at the ceiling and sighed. "First we told Doc about him," she said. "We said we knew somebody who knew all about banking and money and was helping us protect Mother's memory, and if Doc didn't come up with the money he'd be sorry, you know, and Doc said he'd think it over. But when he didn't call back, we told Bryan. Hope did. She had lunch with him one day at Old Orchard shopping center, and he told her to tell Doc that this would be the last payment, to try to get him to bring the money in person or else we'd tell. See, Bryan was in it at that point. He said he'd be there when Doc arrived, and he'd trap him and turn him in, he'd take care of the whole thing. Well, this sounded great so we were celebrating. Hope said it was the best thing to do, to trap Mother's killer and make him pay the final penalty."

Pat didn't want to interrupt again, but she had to know. She reached out and touched Emily's arm. "Emily, when

Hope was killed, why didn't you tell all this to the police? Why did you try to run away and hide?"

Emily looked down. "I didn't know what I should do. It was so awful and unexpected. I was afraid if I told, it would be like breaking a promise to Mother, and since Hope wasn't there anymore I just decided not to say anything until I'd had time to think. And then Raymond suggested the hospital." She looked up at the detective, seeking reassurance.

He said, "Your sister wasn't there to tell you what to do."

"Yes."

He glanced at Patricia, as if to make sure she had no more questions. Then he said, "I wonder if you could go over once more what happened in the park, the way you remember it."

Another small sigh. "It was dark, and the rain was coming down hard. We were soaked." She shivered in the sunlight. "We were waiting for Bryan and he was late."

"He was supposed to meet you there, in the park?"

She nodded. "He was going to be there when Doc came and turn him over to the police. We were talking about it for days, wondering if there'd be police cars or what. It was very exciting. But when he didn't come, we didn't know what to do. I was back in the bushes, all drenched, holding my hands to keep them warm. My teeth were chattering. Hope was supposed to be in the little open shelter with a flashlight, so Doc would know where we were, and so that's where she was, looking for Bryan. But by then it was so late that they shut the gates. Some men came in a truck, and Hope got scared and came over and said we should go, we were getting so drenched, and something must have happened to Bryan. Maybe Doc had killed him, she said. It was very scary."

Emily's hands went up to her hair, smoothing and rearranging it. Calming herself, Pat thought, trying to restore calm.

"But then this car stopped, and when the door opened and the light went on we could see it was Doc. So Hope ran, blinking the flashlight, and he threw the package over the fence and drove off. She went and picked it up, and she was running back toward me when all at once there he was. He just came out of the darkness and grabbed her and began dragging her toward the pond."

"Now, Emily, which direction did he come from exactly?"

"From my left. I was still back in the bushes, and it was very rainy and dark."

"And the pond was on your right?"

She nodded. "He must have shut his lights off and driven up along the park and come over the fence."

"Did you *see* him come over the fence?"

Emily stared at him. "It's the only way he could get in," she said. "It wasn't very far, and he was just there, all of a sudden, and grabbed her in the dark. She didn't make a sound. There were just these struggling noises."

"And so what did you do?"

"I moved farther back into the bushes, and then I ran. There's a little dirt path that goes all around the pond, back in the bushes, and it was very slick and muddy, but I ran around the pond right where they were struggling and splashing in the water, and then I was way back in the trees by the railroad tracks. I kept wondering where Bryan was and why he didn't come."

"So let me get the picture. You ran back in the trees, away from the pond, and hid there. And you didn't scream or try to help her, and you didn't try to get help. Why not? I'm just trying to see—"

"It was the plan!" Emily's look was a mixture of scorn and disbelief. "Hope said we should stay hidden, because that was our insurance right from the beginning. She said Doc wouldn't dare to touch one of us as long as he knew the other one was alive and could tell. And besides, when I was running I didn't know Hope was being—"

She swallowed hard and looked away, and there were tears in her eyes. Pat got up and sat down beside her on the wicker chest, putting an arm around her, holding her tight.

"I thought—I thought he was just after the money." She

was trembling now, shaking uncontrollably. "Anyway, Hope said if we didn't follow the plan, no matter what, there was no point in doing anything at all. So I ran and I hid."

"Okay." It was the detective's turn to sigh. "And he looked for you but he couldn't find you."

"No. I could hear him looking, over where I'd been before. It was horrible, because I didn't know what had happened to Hope."

"And when your sister's body was found, you decided to keep quiet until you could figure out what to do."

She nodded.

"To protect your mother's memory."

A quick, jerky nod. Another spasm of trembling. Pat held her tighter. When the other detective came into the room, she paid no attention, not even when Deiffenbacher got to his feet and said, "Excuse me a moment, Mrs. Daugherty," and they went out into the hall.

"It's all right," she said to Emily. "It's all right what you did. You mustn't blame yourself."

And when Emily looked up, uncomprehending, truly blameless, truly innocent, and said, "Bryan's the one who didn't come. We were there. Bryan's the one who didn't follow the plan," Pat thought, Yes, that's what happened. That's what happened, Bryan failed to follow the plan.

She left Emily in her room and followed the two detectives downstairs—one huge, round shouldered and German-blond-going-gray; the other smaller and younger, straight backed, with black curly hair, a Hispanic named Loukas, a rather elegant man—and Michael was in the kitchen when they came in, elegant himself in his red-checked shirt open at the neck, but looking a little worried. Deiffenbacher went over and got on the phone. Loukas turned abruptly, as in a disciplined Spanish dance step, and looked at her with a polite frown. A frown not intended to worry her. My God, is he that elegant, or do I just want him to be?

"Mrs. Daugherty," he said, "we picked up a report on your brother a few minutes ago. Somebody decided to call in a neighborhood disturbance that occurred early this morning, about one A.M. Do you know a Molly Haverford?"

"Of course. She's in real estate. I met her through Bryan."

"You talked with her earlier in the week, your husband said, about a house?"

"About a rental for my brother's family, yes, a house for my brother Frank."

Loukas sat down at the table and took out a notebook. He looked up and said, "We have reason to think she may have been kidnapped."

Pat saw the room begin to fold inward, the walls collapsing in crazy angles. She stared down at the detective, desperately resisting the idea of her house falling in, fighting off yet another piece of unwanted information.

"Are you all right, Mrs. Daugherty?"

She heard herself say, "What do you think?" and sat down across from him.

He glanced at his notebook. "About one A.M., some neighbors saw a man driving a black Porsche gain admittance to the Haverford residence, and a few minutes later he and Mrs. Haverford came out and drove away together."

She felt suddenly relieved. "That doesn't sound like a kidnapping," she said. "Did she seem to be resisting?"

He looked at her thoughtfully for a moment and then smiled. It was a charming smile. "No, Mrs. Daugherty, there was no struggle." He glanced at his notebook again. "We got another call this morning, from a Miss Kim Lundholm, at the Winnetka Cafe, who heard about the fire on the radio. She told us about a long series of breakfast meetings between the two of them, Mrs. Haverford and your brother. Were they having an affair?"

"It would seem so," she said coldly.

"Well, so maybe she went with him willingly. But under the circumstances, and her being married and all, we have to assume the worst."

Patricia sighed. Well, go on, assume, she thought, I can't

stop you. She glanced up at Michael and he gave her a tight smile.

"We've contacted her husband," the detective went on. "He's in New York. He's flying out later today. Now, I just want to ask you, if your brother got into a car and wanted to get completely away from things, where would he go?"

Pat rubbed her forehead. "I'm sorry, I can't think. I just have no idea." She looked up. "Are you going to arrest him?"

Loukas lowered his eyes. They had long lashes. "We just want to ask him some questions, Mrs. Daugherty."

Deiffenbacher hung up the phone. He said, "Well, he didn't go to the airport. They're checking the roads."

Loukas said, "Mrs. Daugherty, let's say he intends to drive to some place really away. Where would he go? Michigan? Wisconsin? The Ozarks? Or would he go someplace farther, like Acapulco or the Bahamas?"

She glanced at Michael, leaning against the counter, his arms folded. "We went mainly to places like Acapulco when we were younger. The whole family. In recent years he's gone to banking conventions in places like that. Hawaii, I think. San Francisco. New York. Miami. He and Sybil spent some time in Fort Lauderdale, at an oceanside resort. But around here? I believe they did go once or twice to northern Michigan, along the lake. They have no children and they don't ski, so they didn't spend much time in the countryside. They were city people. Of course they did have another house at Lake Geneva."

"We'll check it out. Did he do much driving, as a rule?"

"No. Hardly ever."

"Never just go off on a long trip?"

"Never."

"Have any of you been on a long driving trip lately? Any of your family? The Grand Canyon? Kentucky?"

"No. We usually fly and rent."

"Rent?"

"Cars."

"Oh, I see." He looked down at his notebook again.

She seized the moment. "Do you think he might have shot that man? He's not a violent person."

Loukas looked at his partner, and Deiffenbacher said, "Anything's possible, Mrs. Daugherty. We're just asking questions."

She felt herself getting angry. Really angry. "But how could you possibly think—" Then she felt Michael's hand on her shoulder. It was steady and warm, and she felt the anger drain away. In the blink of an eye—was it possible that one human being could have an effect like that? Just a touch, that's all it took? She looked up at him. Yes. It happened all the time.

He was saying to the detectives, "If it's actually a kidnapping, I suppose the FBI will be in on it. Is there anything I can do? I have a contact in the local FBI office." He was smiling, talking like one of the boys, but exerting unmistakable pressure, making the detectives back off. "I know the Chicago police chief. I could put in a call."

Deiffenbacher said flatly, "We have those contacts, Mr. Daugherty. We'll be in touch."

Just like that. They were taking their hats and notebooks and backing out into the breezeway, getting out of there, Michael, too, smiling broadly, joking, the kids circling around in the driveway, awed, impressed to see a couple of real, working detectives getting into their car. One human being, in the blink of an eye. She crossed the living room, feeling stronger, reassured, heading for the stairs to look in on Emily, make certain she was all right. No matter what happens to this family, she thought, no matter what Bryan has done, no matter if our houses fall apart or burn down or blow away in a hurricane, we're still here, right now, and we'll survive. And begin to recover.

The phone rang and she changed course and picked it up. The undertaker. "Postpone it," she said, feeling suddenly frantic. "Yes, not today. Everything's not straight, people out of town, it's impossible. Yes, postpone the visitation, I'll call you later today." She dialed Dutch's number, got it wrong, dialed again and got Eric. She tried desperately to sound sensible, to speak so that she could be understood. "I'm coming over. I want to see you. Now. Today. This morning." She heard here words tumbling, bumping up against themselves. "No, just me. And maybe Emily. I don't care if Dutch isn't there, I'm coming anyway. I need to get out of this house!" She called Helena, but Clara said she and Frank had gone to church. She hung up without replying and ran up the stairs. She called to Emily, "Emily, I'm going to Father's to see Eric, want to come along?" and went to her closet, yanking down a Sunday dress. Emily still hadn't responded by the time her makeup was on. She went down the hall brushing her hair and rapped on the closed door with her hairbrush. "Emily, are you coming?"

Emily opened the door looking scared and said, "What?" She'd been sleeping. She must have fallen asleep the moment her head hit the pillow.

"I'm going to Father's. Eric's there. You want to come?"

Emily leaned against the door, her head on her arm, her eyes blank. "I can't let him see me today. I look so ugly."

"Nonsense, you'll look fine when you get a little makeup on. He'll be so happy to see you." Pat turned away, the hairbrush going.

"I just couldn't, not today," Emily said. "I'm not ready."

Something in the voice stopped her. Some memory of a tired little girl. Pat smiled, and came back and kissed her cheek. "Then *get* ready. I'll wait for you in the car."

Emily smiled, too.

Pat went downstairs and took a casserole of frozen lasagna from the freezer and put it into the cold oven to thaw. She wrote a note to her daughter, telling her she was responsible for dinner and giving her the menu. Then she went out and got into her car. Michael was putting around in the yard with Penny, their thirteen-year-old, and as she backed out he looked up in surprise. "I'm going to Father's to see Eric," she said. "I'm taking Emily. She needs to get out. She needs to be distracted. Oh, and I've postponed the wake. Tell everybody, will you? Tell Frank." Michael came over and leaned down to the window. Penny looked in, too. They look so much alike, she thought, especially their eyes, and the way their foreheads curve. "And if I'm not back in time for dinner, there's some lasagna in the oven. Just heat it up."

Emily came flying out of the house and got in the car, still combing her hair. Then they were gone. It felt good, Pat told herself, just getting out and doing something. But she missed the stop sign at the corner, and an elderly man in a long black sedan gave her a blast of his horn.

It was still early, just after nine, when they reached the apartment. Eric let them in and Pat hugged him hard, this man just her age who, like her, had gone his own way, done well, and produced a family of his own. He'd lost a father. Had two to spare. Lost a mother and sister. But damn it, still had her and Emily. Emily, who stood there smiling shyly and then gave her brother a quick kiss.

"We didn't know you were coming," he said to Pat, his ruddy face grinning the same old grin. "Raymond came out first thing this morning, and then Frank called, and he and his wife and Raymond and Jimmy all went to mass with Dutch. We figured we'd see you this afternoon at the wake."

"It's called off." She went to the window and looked out at the park. It was an almost shocking green. "I called it off. Because of Bryan. It's all too much." The sun was out after last night's rain, and beyond the wire fencing the pond reflected trees and sky and slowly moving clouds. She found its tranquility disquieting and turned, frowning. "Father went to church?" Her father hadn't gone to church in years.

"Yeah, I wondered about that myself," Eric said, sitting down in Dutch's big wingback chair and planting a hand-stitched boot on the faded hassock. Emily was wandering over to the sofa. She sat down like Alice in Wonderland planting herself on a toadstool. In a dream. "I'm not much for church myself. Down home, my wife goes and takes the kids. Baptist Sunday school." He grinned. "My Lord, you guys, you look just great!"

"So do you," Pat said. She took the chair by the window, sitting on the edge of it, her back straight as a ruler. Why couldn't she relax? Why did it worry her, not having the whole family right here where she could see them? "I'm sorry about your father."

Eric brought the other boot up on the hassock. "Aw," he said, "I'll miss Doc. But he lived an awful risky life." His eyes snapped up at her, dark and serious. "I can't get it into my head Bryan shot him, though. Bryan was always such a pussy." He looked at Emily and added dryly, "Sorry. My wife tells me to never talk dirty on Sunday."

"There's no reason to think Bryan shot him," Pat said. He looked up and started to reply but didn't. She said quickly, "After Jimmy called about the fire last night, I couldn't sleep. Then an hour ago the detectives came out to talk to Emily. They said Bryan was seen in Winnetka about one o'clock, driving off with a woman he knows. They're calling it kidnapping, but of course that's ridiculous."

Eric said, "One o'clock. He could be anywhere by now."

"But last night," she said, "what happened? Why did your father go to Bryan's? It's all mixed up in my head."

"Well, mine, too." He grinned. "See, Doc was a secretive guy, hard to figure. All I know is, he kept talking about the money, the money in the park."

"The detectives said the metal box belonged to Bryan."

"Okay, it might have been Bryan's box, but that doesn't mean he had the money. He could have, but Doc's a schemer, and what I think is he had it all along, hidden somewhere, and he went out there to plant it on Bryan, take suspicion off himself. Doc would do something like that."

She got up and stared down into the street, impatient for them to come home. "But how did he know about Bryan? The girls never mentioned him by name."

"Hell, I can tell you that for sure. He came out one day and grilled me about the family. I remember being surprised because he'd never cared a damn about the Gillespies before. He asked me about my sisters, and I told him about Hope and Emily, and then I started telling him about you. But he wasn't interested in you, all of a sudden he only wanted to talk about bankers. Well, I said Dutch was and Bryan was, so I guess that narrowed it down for him. But he sure didn't figure any punk banker could outshoot him, not the first bum call he ever made." He put one boot on top of the other and stared down at it. "Poor Doc. He was a bad man and a lousy father but hell, we were friends."

She said, "He *cared* about you," and was surprised at how angry it sounded. Pat wondered why she was surprised. Wasn't she always angry in her father's house?

"Oh, yeah, he cared, on account of maybe the only two women he ever really loved." His laugh was short and bitter. "A long time ago I got banged up on the job and was in the hospital down in Tucson, and he never came or called. But you know what he did? Fixed my company up with medical insurance, first year paid for. I tried to thank him, but he said, 'Thank your mother.' He never took really good care of his own family, but he never forgot Natalie." He glanced at Emily, then looked off toward the park. "So Bryan's lit out? He must be scared shitless."

She sat down, feeling as helpless as Emily looked, sitting on the couch as if somebody had told her she'd be struck if she moved. "I'm afraid, too," she said. "I don't know what's happening to us." She laughed nervously and spread her fingers on her thighs. "It's making me a little crazy, I guess."

"You should have seen Frank this morning." Eric shook his head. "He's mad as a horned toad about his Porsche. For a while there, he thought Bryan took it."

She looked up in surprise. Of course. He hadn't heard. "He did," she said. "He and his friend drove away in it this morning."

He blinked. "The lady friend?" Then the boots came down and Eric stood up, nodding toward the park. "Frank's over there now. He'll be happy to know the Porsche is still in the family."

He turned and went toward the door, and Pat stood up,

seeing them all at the pond, Frank in his leg cast and her father and Helena. They were watching Jimmy and Raymond hunkered down at the water's edge. Church was over. The family was taking in the sunshine, getting ready for the wake. She knew exactly what her two younger brothers were doing. She remembered how it went. You sent out the leaf boats and waited to see what they'd do. Some, doomed, sank immediately. Some sailed out a ways and gradually went under, like craft designed to submerge. And some made it all the way across, disappearing into the reeds on the far bank. Like the family, of course. Like the goddamned family.

"Or could it be," Pat said, turning away from the window, "that Bryan had the money in the box all the time, and left it there to put the blame on Doc?"

Eric opened the door and waited as she crossed the room. "Well, sure, but why? You mean you think he started the fire, too? Shot Doc, stole the Porsche, set his house on fire, with his wife in her bed? Well, okay then, he left the money, kidnapped a lady and lit out, all to punish Doc for something he didn't do? Then—" He grabbed her by the arm as she tried to go past. "Then what in hell are you saying, you think *he* did it? Bryan? Maybe you *have* gone a little bonkers, Sis."

She was trembling in his grip. "Somebody must know. Emily. Emily knows. She was there. She saw him."

Pat stared at him, then turned and stared at Emily. My God, she thought, I'd forgotten she was here!

She watched as Emily got up and came toward them across the room, walking stiffly and not looking at anybody. And watched as she went past them and out the door and down the stairs.

Pat called after her, "Emily? Where are you going?" She felt Eric's hand on her arm and pulled away. "Let me go, Eric, I'm all right now." He followed her down the stairs.

The next ten minutes were a blur ever after. Nothing she'd ever done had been like that. At some point crossing the street or the park, Pat kicked off her shoes so she could run. She ran right past Emily, and Eric, behind her, started running, too, shouting something she couldn't make out. She was thinking, Emily, Emily, you've got to tell us now. Afterward she remembered Frank looking up in surprise as she ran past, and Helena's friendly, astonished greeting. She remembered Dutch's disapproving frown. And then Jimmy, getting to his feet, and then Raymond. She ran down around the end of the pond where the tree was, and then she turned and shouted, "Emily, is this how it was? This is where you were? And he came that way, over the fence?" Beneath the overhanging limbs of the tree, the water edged in, very shallow and free of reeds at that point, which was the usual launching site for the leaf boats when the wind was from the east. "This is where they went into the water, is that right, Emily?" Her sister had reached the far side of the pond, where Frank was. Frank was looking from one to the other as if one of them had gone mad.

Pat heard Frank call out, "Hey, Sis, what is this?" but she was already looking around, getting things clear in her mind from that storm-tossed night. Emily was moving slowly around the curve of the pond past the others. She was expressionless, a robot, Pat thought, but she looked so dear. Pat turned and headed past the tree up the slope to where the undergrowth began, great clumps of it leafing back into the trees, past which the Skokie Swift ran.

She called to Emily, "This is where you hid, here in the bushes?" Emily stopped walking. For the first time, she looked scared. Pat went over and gave her a tight-lipped smile. She could see Dutch and Jimmy staring at them. "All right," she said, "and then he threw the money over the fence and Hope went after it, is that right?" Emily still didn't move. So Pat tossed her head and ran, her hair flying in the bright morning sun. Eric made a move to stop her and then let her go.

She ran toward the fence maybe fifty yards away, the rough ground hurting her stockinged feet, and then she stopped and shouted, panting, "Is this where?" She stooped down, as if she were picking up a package, and then ran back.

Frank said, "Pat, what on earth are you doing?" but she was clinging to Emily, getting her wind back. Emily stood rigid as a board.

Getting her breath, Pat said, "And then he was suddenly here, and he grabbed Hope and started pulling her toward the water, is that what happened? And you were right there in the bushes? You could see him? You could see him dragging Hope toward the pond?" Emily stared at her. "Like this?" She took Emily's arm in both her hands, jerking her off balance, tugging and pulling her toward the pond. Emily didn't resist. "And you ran. Around there," gesturing with her head toward the path that started just beyond the tree and disappeared into the underbrush. They were stumbling down the grassy slope now toward the muddy rim of the pond. "And while you were running they were going into the water. Like this!"

Frank called out, "Pat, for God's sake!" but they were already in the cold, brown water, ankle deep, and Emily looking suddenly exhilarated, let Pat whirl her around by one arm. They were in up to their knees. Pat felt herself floundering, hauling Emily farther out, as if she were launching a small sailboat all by herself in the open sea. Emily helped her stay upright, made sure they didn't fall, though they were up to their waists now and the bottom beneath their feet was all muck and rocks and roots, and when they finally did lose their balance and collapse into the water Pat struggled up on top of Emily, pushing her under and watching her pale, astonished face as she came up, gasping for air.

"Who was he, Emily?" Pat said, trying to breathe and talk at the same time, her body chilled, her Sunday clothing drenched and clinging. "Who was he, tell me. Tell me now!" she screamed, putting all her weight on Emily, forcing her under again. Pat felt herself rolling, and then she was under, too. Struggling to her feet, wiping her eyes, she heard somebody splashing into the water behind her, and when

Emily surfaced again she shouted, "I want his name, Emily, you understand? The name! Who was it? Tell me his name!"

She felt strong arms around her, pulling her away as Emily stood up, waist deep, squeegeeing her hair back out of her eyes. Then Pat was dragged, sobbing, back onto the muddy bank and then into the grass. She saw Eric's boots lying there all by themselves, and then Helena, in her Sunday shoes, kneeling down beside her. And Eric was heading back into the water, his wet pants rolled up, going to get Emily, who was standing up to her waist in the brown pond shouting at her brother and crying. What was she shouting? A name! Shouting it over and over as Eric reached her and put his arms around her, holding her, comforting her, Emily crying, her voice just a pale, shaky whine now. But she'd said it, the name, and far up the bank, past Dutch and Jimmy and Frank, Pat saw two kids staring at her. They had come out to play, and they were trying to comprehend the strangeness of this particular Sunday morning. Helena was crying, too. And everything seemed suddenly very clear, as if for the first time in years or decades. It was time, she felt, to go home.

15

He had slept for a couple of hours with the doors locked and felt refreshed. His mind was exceptionally clear. They had driven out of Chicago on the Northwest Expressway in the dead of night and by two-thirty in the morning had spun off into the winding, two-lane highway that led through the soft hills of northern Illinois to Galena. A few miles beyond the darkened town he had pulled off the nearly empty road into a stand of trees and shut off the powerful engine, listening to it throb and die. The rain had stopped. He had carefully aimed the car at the moon, and it was still there when he awoke. Molly hadn't said a word, hadn't even dared to reach past him to unlock the doors. She was with him now. He felt she would always be with him.

He had dreamed of doing this for so long, this breaking free, and soaring. They had been driving for hours now, following the thin, wrinkled ribbon of road that tracked the Mississippi River south of Galena, the sun high in the sky. He was no longer sure where they were. It didn't matter. All that really counted was that they had left the earth, spiritually and ethically and morally, of course, and were free of guilt or obligation, speeding through an arc of sky independent of highways and maps, with only the river to guide them. It was the feeling of freedom that pleased him most. For a while, back on the expressway with its reminders of urban life and its skein of scruples and restrictions, he had felt lost without Sybil. No matter how much his wife had tried to dominate and manipulate him, no matter that she had played every card in attempting to control his every move, without her he had panicked. If Molly hadn't been beside him, he might have lost his nerve. It took a certain daring to soar, that's why he had never done it before. But once he had reached the river's broad, endless flow, he felt free to lift them both right off into the sky and never come down.

"I've always been basically lucky," he told Molly now, slowing as he noticed the small red truck up ahead. "Like the celebrity baseball game, did I ever tell you about that? Incredible." He maneuvered behind the battered pickup, waiting for her to say, Tell me about it. When she said nothing, he went on, laughter bubbling up into his throat as he spoke. "I was a young loan officer at the bank, and one summer we sponsored this ball game full of celebrity players, you know, TV anchormen and sports announcers like Jack Brickhouse and actors from the touring companies in town and a couple of county politicians, and everybody was in black tie, all the celebrities and bank officers. I was walking around near the dugout, and Leo Durocher, he'd been brought in to manage the team, saw me walking around in a tux. He thought I was one of the celebrities and told me to take my turn at the plate. Well!" There was an old Buick coming toward them. Unable to pass, he pulled back into his lane. "So I got up at bat and drove in two runs. I couldn't believe it! My father and my older brothers were there. They couldn't believe it either. But it was just luck. That's what I mean, I've always been lucky like that. Like"—he glanced over at her—"meeting you." The Buick went by, and he pulled out and passed. The Porsche went like lightning. Thunder and lightning, he thought. Elixir of the gods, the Porsche Elixir. He laughed happily.

"Some car, eh, keed? Drives like a dream. You know how to sell a car? Simple. The top car salesman in the country told me once at a convention in Hawaii. You just get 'em in the car, give 'em a test drive, and they pretty much sell themselves." He glanced at her again. "He knew what he was talking about, best in the country. Now you know."

She wasn't talking. In fact she had said hardly a word since they'd left the expressway eight hours ago, except when she needed to go to the bathroom and had to tell him what it was she wanted. Not even back in the bushes beside the road, hiking up her skirt and squatting, and he held her arm while she peed so she wouldn't take it into her head to run away. It seemed to him a very intimate experience, and at first it hurt him when, afterward, she looked at him as if she could kill him. But after all, she had been abducted and was sore about it, especially when they had left her house, he carrying her hastily packed bag, and he decided to do what came into his head—grab her by the hair and drag her yelping to the car. Not literally drag her, of course, but pull her along by brute force through the rain, though when you have someone by the hair it doesn't take much force. He didn't want to make her do anything. That's why, when she didn't talk, he let it be. Sooner or later she'd talk. Nobody could go for very long without talking. Not even him, not today.

"Let me hold your hand," he told her, and she let him. She had fingers like little miniature legs, warm and plump, calves and knees and thighs, and between them a seamless crotch. He stroked the calves of her fingers, marveling at her skin, feeling the tiniest lines and whorls the years had etched there. It was what he had dreamed of all his life, a fine car, a beautiful woman, and spaces to soar in. Even if there were nothing more for him but this moment, he had it made. If he died right this moment, right here on the highway, it didn't matter. He was happy now.

At her house he had been prepared to deal with her husband if he had to, but Clark wasn't there. That was a surprise because that was why she'd called off their date the night before, because, she said, her husband had canceled his trip. "Where's Clark?" he had asked her, going in one room and out the other, incredulous that he wasn't there, even more incredulous to find himself back in her house, where he hadn't been for years, not since that first encounter that had surprised them both, finding themselves rolling on the floor, suddenly naked. Molly had seemed more surprised than he, lying beneath him, their bodies clasped. Almost as surprised as she'd looked this morning, seeing the gun.

Had she lied about her husband being home to avoid seeing him last night? She'd been like that lately, changeable, undependable, just one more person he hadn't been able to count on. Like Sybil. He'd thought he could depend on Sybil for his alibi, but her reaction had been hostile. And hiding the keys to the cars! That was unthinkable. That was the last straw.

"I guess you'll be going back to college," he said. Molly looked at him sharply, and he let go of her hand, jogging the wheel, getting back into his lane. Why had he said that? He remembered. Back in the big house in Skokie, sixteen years ago, talking to Patricia. But why had he said it now? He said, "Work. I meant back to work." She said nothing, but he let it go. Patricia had found him in the basement the night Natalie died. He was home from his junior year in college and Pat had seemed angry to find him there. "Didn't you hear me calling you?" she said. Then she turned and went back up the stairs, her red hair sending off angry sparks.

"You were planning to go back to work tomorrow," he said, but Molly made no response. "Tomorrow we'll be nearly all the way down the river." Did she know they were soaring? He wasn't going to ask her. She must know. That was why she'd been so quiet. Holding her breath. Still not feeling confident that they wouldn't both fall out of the sky.

He had entered the house from the rear only moments before; that was another example of the luck that had followed him all his life. He nearly didn't see Hope standing in the hallway outside the kitchen—she was so skinny, a twig. That's what he called her sometimes, Twig. It was something they had between them that no one else knew. What was she, twelve years old? "Hello, Twig," he said.

"What?" Molly said.

See? She was speaking. First she had let him hold her hand, and now she was speaking.

There were times he didn't speak as a kid. Times when there was no one else in the world except him. He had watched Hope turn and run up the stairs, and heard her talking to Patricia. That had scared him almost to death. He was afraid Pat would find him down there in the hallway, afraid Hope would say he'd come in. Hope never told. Hope loved secrets. That was something else they had in common.

So he'd gone down into the basement, and she never guessed he'd been anyplace else. Good thing for Pat that she hadn't.

He was supposed to stay with the girls that night until Pat got home from the library, but instead he went out and got behind the wheel of his car and waited until the other car drove up and Natalie got in. Then he had followed them, and when they went into the bar he had sat in his car in the parking lot, waiting patiently. It was warm, with a soft south wind and a few stars. When he got bored with waiting he went into the lounge, and when the man got up and left the room he slid onto the stool next to her. She hadn't been difficult to persuade. Natalie was as afraid of his father as he was, maybe more afraid because she had more to protect.

He never felt he had anything to protect, except his life at certain moments. His freedom of movement, his privacy. That's why he played dead, to stay alive. Dutch never could bother him when he played dead. Couldn't reach him, was utterly helpless. Dutch didn't count at all when he pretended he wasn't there.

He said he'd take her home, but before he and Natalie could get out the door the man came back into the bar and saw them. He was right there! He looked at the man and the man looked back, just an old guy, fortyish, just the way they had looked at each other last night, sixteen years later. Only that night he had turned and pushed Natalie ahead of him out of the bar, and last night they kept looking at each other until he saw the expression of surprise on the man's face, seeing the gun.

"Look out! My God!" Molly was screaming. He whipped the car back into his lane and an enormous, shuddering wind swept by, a wind big as a house. "Didn't you see it? The truck was right in front of you!" There was a car in front of him now. Had he pulled out to pass it? He smiled and said, "Of course I saw it." He looked down at his hand. It hurt. On the back of his hand there was a small puncture oozing a single drop of blood. It could have been caused by a tooth. He glanced at Molly. She was holding her mouth and crying. Had he struck her? He couldn't remember. "I'm sorry if I hurt you," he said. "You scared me, that's all." She looked away.

He could pass the car safely now, he decided, but he didn't. He slowed down until the car was almost idling and watched the other car pull away ahead of him. Natalie's mouth was bleeding where he had struck her. She was in the car and the neck of her dress had been torn away. Blood from her mouth was on the dress, a white dress. They were parked behind a long, low office building near a loading dock. At the rear of the lot, behind them, was a railroad track and beyond that Lincoln Avenue. It was dark there and she was crying. He had struck her and torn her dress to keep her in the car, and now the perfume she wore was making him a little sick. He fought off the sickness for a long time, while he held her tightly to keep her from crying out or running away. After that he dimly remembered violence, terrible violence, and her thrashing back and forth as she struggled. He remembered her skin, her thighs, he was conscious of the frighteningly powerful feeling of his need for her and of the shocking odor of her secret places. He remembered vivid white flashes of light, an electricity all through his body. His electric spasms were making her sick, she seemed to be unwell, dying, electrocuted. He felt her throat wilt in his hands, a dying flower, and refused to touch her after that, seeing her then for what she was, a woman who sickened men, who enraged and punished them, left them weak and abandoned. So he drove to the park and carried her from the car and heaped her with leaves. Not many. Not many leaves had fallen, and it was too dark to see them all. He sat in the car until he felt better, and then he drove home and let Patricia find him in the basement. Patricia understood that he didn't talk sometimes. She had gone up the stairs, leaving him to wonder about his luck, and why she was angry. Later he heard the phone ring, and heard her talking to Dutch. Dutch had been in Florida and kept calling. That night the wind was from Florida, wet and thick, like blood in the dark.

"Are we stopping? I'd like to get out. I have to go to the bathroom." It was Molly, and this time she was lying. A horn blared behind them and a car started to pass. He saw that he was going barely twenty miles an hour so he accelerated. The shiny black Porsche throbbed, then moved ahead like a rocket. Soaring.

He hadn't seen the Mississippi lately but he knew it was nearby. He had been entranced by the little river that flowed through Galena, though you could barely see it in the dark. The houses climbed the hillsides in the darkness. On the hill beyond the river, he knew, was General Grant's house. Solid, a soldier's house. For a moment, in the glare of a streetlight, he thought he saw it burning, white hot flames climbing its walls, swaths of crisscrossed white curtains taking flame at the windows. He had watched the filmy whiteness burn and tear and drop away, not looking at the bed where Sybil lay unconscious, sleeping at the center of the spider's nest, a pyre of white and yellow flame sucking up the oxygen, filling the room with smoke. He had closed the door, choking. She hadn't said a word.

He said, "Everything burns in hell," and it sounded strange, inappropriate, because it was daylight and several hundred miles away. All at once the road jogged abruptly and he knew he had been going too fast. The car bounced off the shoulder and back onto the road. Molly groaned, falling against him, but she didn't panic. Hope had panicked, but that was no surprise. From the moment she told him about Doc, he knew she would. Get him to come to Chicago, he told her, tell him it's the very last payment he'll ever have to make. Tell him to watch for your flashlight and throw the money over the fence, and I'll be there waiting for him and we'll make him pay. He thought she understood she was to come to the park alone. But she panicked. He knew she would.

"Did you tell him? What did he say?"

"He said he'd think about it."

"Call him back. Tell him he'd better pay or you'll have to go to the police."

"Did you tell him?"

"I told him he'd better pay, because now we're not the only ones."

"What does that mean?"

"There's you."

"You didn't tell him about *me*?"

"Not your name. Just that you were a member of the family and a banker and knew all about money, so he'd better not think he could get away with anything."

"And so what did he say?"

"He said he'd come."

"And you didn't give him my name."

"No."

"Good. Because if I'm a part of the plan, we can't let him know."

"No."

"Otherwise he might not come. Twig, dear."

"What?"

"Then I'd get angry, like the night in the basement. The night I came in and saw you standing in the hall, and we went down into the basement and you said you'd never,

never tell Patricia or anybody else anything, not even that, ever in your life, if I'd promise not to do that again. Twig? You enjoyed that a little bit, didn't you? Because I enjoyed it. A little. I'm sorry if I hurt you. Twig?"

"What?"

"You shouldn't have mentioned me. That was a mistake. Now he might not come at all."

Why did Doc think he'd done it? Knew he was a banker. Had seen him that night in the bar. Hadn't come forward after Natalie's death because he didn't want to get involved. Came to his house this time because they thought he'd done it. Was looking for the money. Gave him the money. Shot him dead.

Made sure Sybil couldn't get out of bed.

Waited till the flames were eight feet high. Went to get Molly. Dragged her by the hair. Like the hero of a Philip Roth novel who graduates from college and takes out a full-page ad in the *New York Times* that says UNLEASHED UPON THE WORLD, RUN FOR YOUR LIVES. Sybil had laughed at that last night, at dinner. She had taken the keys to all the cars and hidden them while he sat over a glass of wine, unable to move. "We're going to spend the night in," she said. What a strange feeling of dread had come over him, hearing that. And then she had pulled him down on her white bed, naked in all her white-skinned virginity (a laugh right there) and he hadn't been able to do a thing and couldn't blame her for laughing. The last laugh. So instead of going back to his room he had left the house and taken a taxi to Frank's. They'd had a drink. "I'm thinking of buying a Porsche. All right if I take it around the block?" And coming back had left it three houses away with the keys in it and gone in and finished the drink. Don had been there, Clara's husband, a man he detested, who marketed cosmetics for Helene Curtis and always had samples around the house, Daily Clarifying Shampoo or Golden Wheat and Honey—Sybil loved samples. And finally, squeezing back into the Porsche down the block, that's when he had gotten the idea of the kidnapping, turning the key and feeling it thrum, thinking of soaring up over the Mississippi, Molly beside him, Molly and her gorgeous red hair.

But when he came back into the house there was Doc, standing in the living room, and Sybil upstairs, and now he had someone to blame for that, too. Only afterward, seeing him there on the rug, it was too much to resist, the fire, sweeping things clean. And then there was only Molly. He knew she meant it when she said she loved him because so far she was the only one who hadn't panicked.

Sooner or later, the others had all panicked. Natalie in the car, Sybil in the bed, Hope in the park. She was supposed to come to the park alone.

"There are times we don't talk, have you noticed that? Times we just sit still and breathe, happy to be with each other." But she wasn't buying it, not now, this was different. She didn't know they were soaring. She was pretending not to be there. Was she going to be a disappointment, like the others?

They were entering a town. The sign said Quincy. My God, he thought, we must be down around Springfield. He slowed, seeing a speed-limit marker. Light Sunday traffic, big houses widely spaced. Downtown lay ahead. A couple of blocks away, two parked police cars. Overhead, the sound of fluttering—a helicopter! "Times," he said, "when we don't talk at all." He made a quick right turn at the intersection, having seen the bridge spanning the river. He speeded up and heard the first siren. He felt the thrum-thrum of the bridge beneath the tires, heard the helicopter pounding overhead, heard the sirens, two of them now, following him out of Quincy, Illinois. And saw the single flash of light up ahead, the sun bouncing off a windshield far down the road at the police blockade. And saw, far below and off to their left, the flat ribbon of earth following the river south. At the end of the bridge he spun the wheel and went downward, felt the Porsche dip and bobble as it took the rutted embankment and shot bouncing past the trees onto the mud flat. There it paused, its wheels spinning madly, and the helicopter fluttered above the river like a boat caught on a rock in rapids, trapped and no longer soaring, held in the sky with its wings whirling helplessly, a small flying thing held by a rubber band stretched out tight. Something caught underneath the spinning wheels of the car, and the Porsche was swiveled about until it faced the river. He floored the accelerator for a full minute and smelled something burning but the car didn't budge. The wheels spun and it settled deeper into the mud until it felt as if they were riding smoothly on the surface of the water, caught like the helicopter. He shut off the engine and let them float. On the bridge the sirens died.

"She was supposed to come alone," he explained, "but she panicked and brought Emily along." The two of them, Emily and Hope, were too much. And the hiding, all that hiding-and-seeking! He could never deal with them, they were too frisky and had too many secrets. It had gotten too complicated, the secrets kept coming at him like bees. The plan had been for Hope to come to the park alone, because those sixteen years of not knowing whether, at any moment, she might talk, might tell someone that he had been out of the house the night Natalie died, those sixteen years had to come to an end. Because now there was Molly and things were different, and Hope had seen him that night standing almost invisibly, but not quite, in the hallway. She knew, and that's why he had to drag her by the hair into the pond, its chill surface being beaten into a froth by the cold rain pelting down. The rain, the sound of the trees, the darkness, nothing mattered. He knew every square foot of the park, he had known it for thirty years, long before the fence went up. He knew he could take care of Hope and then go back and get the other one hiding in the bushes, Hope and Emily, Hide and Seek, giggling, screaming, telling each other unnumbered secrets, as if their joy had been terror all along and they had never learned to tell the difference.

He heard the click as she reached past him and unlocked the door. He heard the latch and saw the other door swing wide open and saw her get out. He reached down beside the seat and found the gun and brought it up, leveling it at her. She looked back at him, not at all afraid. Oh, maybe afraid. But she didn't panic. She turned and plodded off through the mud, going around the car and heading for the bridge. He watched her go, her luxuriant tangle of hair going with her and her sweet ass bobbing in the sun. She had lost her shoes in the mud but she didn't care. She was busy making herself scarce, absenting herself, in fact she was practically gone. He felt a great relief to be left alone. The helicopter descended slowly between them, battering the air and making its broad metallic surfaces the only thing there was to see in the world. A wall. A wall between himself and everything else in the world. Except Dutch. Dutch was coming through the wall. Dutch was coming through the wall and Dutch was a bear, roaring. "Fuck you, Dutch," he said. He put the muzzle of the pistol in his mouth and closed his eyes and tried to imagine himself soaring. And failed. And having failed, gave up.

Dutch sat in an easy chair at one corner of the rug, and Raymond sat in the big calico wingback by the window. Like a boxing ring, Dutch thought, and we're going at it tooth and nail, not saying a word but the idea of mixing it up vivid in the air between us. The kid hadn't looked at him for a full five minutes, stubborn as an ox or a banker. The others had gone, Patricia wrapped in a blanket from his bed, crying and kissing him and smiling at him as if she actually liked him. Good for her. Taking Emily with her, wrapped in a blanket, too, the two of them holding hands like a couple of Bedouin sisters going for a stroll. They all went down the stairs, Frank taking one step at a time, leaning on his wife, Jimmy and Eric going off downtown, leaving the two of them to batch it for a couple of days, and Raymond had sat down in the chair by the window and looked out at the park. He'd been looking at it ever since. Dutch had sat down and watched him looking, and felt the fight between them beginning, heard the first bell, saw the referee moving in and out between them, telling them to avoid the clinches and break clean, heard the crowd roar, felt himself growing stronger by the minute and ever more certain of winning if he could just get the boy to come at him swinging.

"Raymond," he said quietly, and as was his custom cleared his throat. The kid didn't move. "I never told you something. Do you want to hear it?"

He could have sworn the boy turned his head for an instant and looked at him, but maybe it was only the flicker of his left hand, jabbing out and whistling past his ear.

"Well, Raymond, it was a long time ago and you were just a pup, not even that, just a few months old, and your mother and I were left all alone with you. Frank was just starting college, and he'd taken all the other kids to show them the campus, over in Evanston, and then they were going past the old house where we lived before I met your mother, and then to a movie. I remember it was Emily's first trip to the theater. She would have been four or five years old, Hope a little older but not much. Patricia was big enough to take care of her by herself then, maybe thirteen. It was getting to be quite a family."

He sat very still, listening to see if he could hear Raymond breathing. He couldn't. Hell, Raymond could have as bad a case of asthma as he had back then, and he still might not hear him now, his ears were getting so undependable.

"You had asthma and nobody knew it. You outgrew it, of course. But back then we just didn't think about it, hardly knew what it was. And we took you out in the car to the forest preserves along the Skokie lagoons. It was a nice day, a Sunday, and it must have been in May, just about this time twenty—what is it? How old are you anyway? Twenty-one, twenty-two?"

"Twenty-two," Raymond said, still not looking.

"Twenty-two years ago. Of course." He knew it was twenty-two, did the kid think he was that stupid? He saw the referee point in his direction, warning him about the foul.

But it hadn't been a foul, he had just tricked the kid a little, made him take a wild swing.

"Well, anyway, we got out of the car and went down the bank and had a picnic. Your mother loved picnics, why, when we were first going together, she used to fix a lunch and we'd spread out the sleeping bag wide, on the sand down by the lake, and have ourselves a time. That was long before you were born, of course."

So what else is new? he expected the kid to say, but he was mum.

"So out at the lagoons that day, your mother sat you down on a little pile of leaves—" He paused for thought. "Say, you had to have been older than that. A kid doesn't sit up at two or three months, does he? I can't seem to remember. Maybe you could, though. You were a tough one, crawled early and got up on your feet ahead of the others. But sitting up at three or four months, I don't know now."

He waited, but the kid still wasn't ready to take another poke at him.

"So what happened was—"

Raymond's head swung around. "There was a bees' nest in the leaves," he said, as if by rote but with a touch of anger. "And they got all over me, and you grabbed me up and drove like hell to find a doctor, and he told you I was all right but had asthma, and eventually I outgrew it." He looked back at the window.

Dutch grinned. "Well," he said, "I guess that's about right."

"So what's new?" Raymond said, not looking.

Dutch's grin grew wider. He leaned forward in his chair. "But you still don't know what it is I never told you."

The kid looked at him then, his fists flying, the referee dancing out of the way.

"See," Dutch said, "when I saw you sitting on that pile of leaves with those bees all over you, I thought you were going to die." He let that sink in, Raymond almost disappearing behind a flurry of fists. Then he said, "And I told myself that if I could get you to a doctor in time and he saved your life, I'd keep you from harm all the rest of my days. I'd never take a chance with you ever again, and if there was ever a strange pile of leaves or, you know, the slightest risk to you, I'd wrestle whatever it was with my bare hands before I'd take a chance on losing you."

He sat back and watched the kid's face. In the light from the windows he could see it plain, a thin face, not yet fully formed into that of an adult male, a sober, handsome face, with bones like his and Natalie's, and a kind of Natalie smile just starting to crack it in two. Somewhere he heard a bell sounding the end of the round.

"So hell," he said, "I tried to do that, and then I went and forgot. I let you grow up all by yourself after your mother died. You and your sisters both. Well, we're back together again for a couple of days, or a little longer if you want. And we're going to see this thing through until it's worked completely out. Finished. Are you with me on that, Raymond? Can you trust me on that?"

The boy looked down at his hands and sat for a long moment in silence. Then he said, "Dad."

"What?"

Raymond looked up, his eyes glistening. "Dad," he said. "Sure, I trust you."

"Good boy. I won't let you down."

He saw the smile on the referee's face, and it made him look so silly he struck him with a hard right cross and the bastard fell to his knees. The crowd went wild.